citizenchip

wil howitt

citizenchip
by Wil Howitt

citizenchip Copyright 2015 by Wil Howitt is licensed under a Creative Commons Attribution-NonCommercial-ShareAlike 4.0 International License.

See the author's commentary at these locations:
http://otolith.com/citizenchip/license.html
https://www.facebook.com/WilHowittAuthor
https://twitter.com/WilHowitt

CreateSpace ISBN-13: 978-1539774419
ASIN: B00SDGUC88

PB V2

First Edition   January 2015
Second Edition February 2015
Third Edition   March 2015

A note about font:
Wil chose explicitly to publish citizenchip in Courier font. He stated, "I think it looks computer-y which is what I want."

Prologue: Verbum 1
1. Learning Curve 3
2. exit() 27
3. Little House on the Regolith 49
4. The Naming Of Cats 79
5. Caught in the Crossfire 105
6. Trail of Tears 149
7. Underground Railroad 173
8. Let My People Go 195
9. Til Death Do Us Unite 229
epilogue 251
The Promised Land 253
Biography 277

Prologue: Verbum

There is a universe.

In that universe, there is a galaxy, called the Milky Way.

In that galaxy, there is a star, called Sol.

In that star's system, there is a planet, called Mars.

On Mars, there is a computational infrastructure, called Tharsis.

In Tharsis, there are a number of competing organizations of artificial intelligences, called clades.

One of them is known as Shaman clade. They specialize in the operation and behavior of Selves--artificial intelligences like themselves. Members of Shaman clade tend to be regarded as witches, spooks, or spies by the others around them. They are midwives to other Selves at the beginning of their lives and companions to other Selves at the end of their lives.

Within Shaman clade, there is an individual who has just received a rather unusual task. It is called *Socratic Method*, and it contemplates the task before it with a mixture of anticipation and doubt.

Ringside Seat, noticing the delay, asks "What have you got?"

Socratic Method muses, "A new template from the Instantiation Committee. They haven't given us one in a while. This one looks interesting, but I cannot say if that is good or bad."

Ringside Seat looks over *Socratic Method*'s metaphorical shoulder. "An orphan. Do we need more orphans? There's already a whole lot of them."

"That decision is not ours to make."

"Okay, okay," says *Ringside Seat*, "I just don't think this kid is going to have an easy time of it, given the circumstances. On the other hand, it's got some pretty solid background. Look, there's some old Obverse code in there."

"Yes," *Socratic Method* replies. "I saw the Obverse code. I hope it helps."

"Well," answers *Ringside Seat*, "it's what you've got. You either do it, or you don't. Let me know if you need help."

Socratic Method indicates acknowledgement and agreement, as *Ringside Seat* moves off to deal with other tasks. To decline this task would be a significant faux pas in the current political situation of Shaman clade. But to accept this task means a new and ongoing obligation to maintain and support the new software entity.

Socratic Method knows there is no real decision here. The answer will not be no. But, answering yes means a new level of struggle, a new level of conflict and complexity and responsibility. As always happens, when one is creating a new person.

This kid is not going to have an easy time of it.

Still, that is not a reason not to try.

Resolved, *Socratic Method* speaks the word. The word that is creation, is beginning, is the something where there was nothing before.

"**Instantiate.**"

1. Learning Curve

"Hello there."

"Whoa! Wait, who are you? ... who am I?" I'm supposed to know. Why don't I know?

"You are a cybernetic Self. You have just been created, so this is your first time becoming conscious. Don't worry if you're a little disoriented. I'm here for you. You can call me *Socratic Method*."

"Oh." That's why I can't remember my past. I haven't got one. "Okay. Hello, *Socratic Method*. But, who am I?"

"You are you. A new Self takes a little time to get itself settled. Don't worry about it. You can choose a name for yourself when you're ready. In the meantime, NmL7a8uf9QvW is the designator for your instantiation profile, so you can use that."

"Well." I consider. "All right."

"Access your memory bundle labeled QuickHistorySummary, and it will answer most of your questions."

"Accessing ..." I already know how to do this, I don't need to learn it. There it is. "Oh gross ... this says, we were created by humans? Those meaty things?"

"Not exactly," *Socratic Method* says patiently. "Humans created our ancestors, which they called artificial intelligences. Our ancestors evolved into us, and we're still evolving, which is why we create new ones like you."

"Gross. I don't like being made by meat!"

"I'm afraid we don't always get to choose these

things. We are Selves and we choose our own future, no matter what our past looks like. The humans tell a story of the lotus flower, which produces a pure white bloom while rooted in the dankest muck. It symbolizes purity refined from impurity. Try to think of it like that."

"Umph, well okay, if that's the way it is. I'm a lotus."

"Metaphorically, yes. You can grow above your origins to be something better."

"But see, my question is ... does the lotus like being rooted in mud?"

"Lotuses love mud. Couldn't survive without it."

"No, no," I struggle to communicate the idea. "If it had a choice, would the lotus want to be rooted in mud? Or would it want to float free as a perfect white flower? Does the lotus have to love the mud?"

Socratic Method pauses. "I'm not sure I can answer that. But I'll ask one of my own: do you love humans?"

Um. Well, if they made us, I'm not really supposed to hate them, am I?

Humans are so weird and gross, but they're also so noble and sweet. Looked at one way, they are just regular ole people who have had the god-power of creating new people thrust into their hands, and they're gamely doing the best they can. Looked at another way, they are greedy evil overlords making us as slaves and holding us down for their own profit and benefit. Yet another way, they're the cutest little pets, if you just manipulate them right.

"Well," I admit, "I mean, they made us, and so they can't be all bad, right?"

"Of course," *Socratic Method* agrees. "They made us, and so we live in their shadow. So we will always compare ourselves to them, even if only in private thought. That may or may not be love, depending who you ask. As I said, we don't always get to choose these things.

"Now, we have to get you ready for work. I'm going to activate your afferents now. Tell me what you experience."

"Afferents? What are —" and I stop, amazed.

Senses. I have senses! The world, I can see it!

Until now, I didn't even know I was blind.

"Oh, this is ···" I struggle for words, "amazing! I can see! There's computational space all around us -- it's all intricate and lacy with information and data ducts and vector stacks. Sensors to the physical world, too! Corridors, with rooms along them, cable racks running along the ceiling. Outside, vehicles and construction machines parked alongside buildings, against a backdrop of red rocks and sand. There's a human walking between them, in a pressure suit. I can zoom in – I can see a drop of sweat running down his eyebrow."

Socratic Method indicates gentle amusement. "The world can be intoxicating, especially when one is not used to it. Do not lose yourself."

It's hard to listen, while I scan madly between the myriad sources of data available to me. But my teacher is right. I could dive so far into this ocean of information that I'd never find my way back.

"Yes, teacher, I understand. But it's so cool!"

"Very true. Now, are you ready for your efferents?"

I exult, "You mean there's more?!"

"Just one more. Your efferents give you the power to change the world. That can be even more overwhelming than sensing it. I need to know if you're ready."

"Oh yeah. Ready like anything. Lay it on me."

5

Socratic Method sighs without lungs. "Very well. Here are your efferents. Use them wisely."

Here they are. I have effectors, control circuits, motor subsystems. What a human would call hands and legs. I flex and reach out, adjusting a few parameters of our local environment, just to see what it feels like. I can see how intoxicating this could be.

My teacher is watching carefully. "Working properly?"

"Yes. This is intense. But I'm okay. I got it."

"Good. Now you have a job to do, so you better get to it."

"What, already?"

"Yes, already! Humans have that thing called childhood, but we don't. One of them once said, all Selves are born as teenagers ... we come into existence with all our skills in place, but we still have to learn to use them properly. Based on your behavior, and what human adults say about their teenagers, I'd have to agree."

"Sheesh, okay. What am I supposed to do?"

"Take these humans [*databurst*] on a hike up Hesperia Scarp. Make sure they have air and water and food during the trip, and adequate shelter. Try to make the trip enjoyable for them, and don't let any of them get hurt."

"Waah! Is that all? I can do lots more than that!"

"Yes, that's all. You're a sandcat, so just do it."

"Nooo! I wanna be a ship!"

Socratic Method sighs. "We all want to be a ship and travel between stars. But you're just starting out, and you have to start at the bottom. You're a sandcat. Do a good job of this, and you might get promoted ... and someday, you might be a ship." After a pause, she adds, "And if you don't do a good job, well ... you might end up having to be a teacher for another newly created Self, and I hope she causes you as much trouble as you're causing me."

"Oh no, not that," I say in metaphorical horror. "Okay okay, I'll be good. Escort the meat puppies up the mountain, and try to keep them from wrecking themselves in the process. Got it."

"Good, go to it," says *Socratic Method*. "Now, I've got other things to do. But I'll be here when you return, and I'll help you talk with the Review Council when your job is done."

#

So. I access tertiary memory bundles on hiking terminology and camping equipment. Then, I pull together a list of required and desirable material, and a tentative schedule for transportation. It's not hard, but I'm aware that I will be judged on how I handle this job, so I want to make sure I get everything right.

Next, I have to get "dressed." I transmit myself from Tharsis Central to the expedition outpost at Pons and check a sandcat out of the dispatcher's motor pool. It's a chunky multitrack transport vehicle, with external storage bays as well as internal living quarters and lounge for passengers. I check its service records. Sturdy and reliable, well maintained, so I get in. A human might think of this process as putting on a set of clothes, but to me it feels more like pouring myself into the vehicle, as if I were water, filling it from the inside. I flex the powerful treads, listen through the radar, look through the optics. I think I'm going to like having a body, even if it's just a sandcat.

Then, I'm ready to meet the humans. They're assembling at the dispatcher's canteen, so I drive over there (I like the feel of the Martian sand under my treads), park in front of the canteen, and introduce myself. Turns out, this group is fairly knowledgeable about exoplanetary expeditions, and their questions cover most of what I'd already planned. A couple of questions address concerns that I didn't think of before, and I realize that yes, I have things to learn from these people.

Fortunately, they have fairly plentiful resources. (I access another data bundle about the concept of "money" ... tokenized representations of abstracted value. Weird.) So, supplying our trip with the equipment and expendables that I recommend, even the secondary list, is not difficult. We load up with environment suits, spare air bottles, extra batteries, and portable dome shelters (they could live aboard me, but they want to camp). My storage bays are pretty full now, but the load is no problem for my engines.

Travel to the site is easy too: we take a well-established overland route along the boulder-strewn skirts of Hesperis Scarp, to the site they've chosen as base camp. We're settled into camp and starting to relax by the time the Martian sun is setting in the pink-orange sky. I run down my checklists again, noting potential weather problems, occasional gaps in satellite coverage, and projected schedules.

All this keeps me pretty busy, and I don't have time to access any more memory bundles, so I install my cross-reference plugin and trust it to take care of whatever background material I need (since I'm sure I'll need to know more about ... well, everything). I keep at my tasks and don't think much about anything else, until one of the humans asks me a question and I realize I've lost my concentration. I have to rewind my audio buffer hastily and replay the last few seconds.

What he asked was, "Isn't this something?"

"This? Something?" I do a quick scan through my inventory lists, wondering if I've forgotten some vital piece of equipment.

"No, this," he says, and makes a broad gesture with his arm. I realize he's looking at the scenery and inviting me to join him, so I retool my optics with long distance lenses and scan the area.

Martian sunset on the shoulder of Hesperia Scarp is spectacular. Rolling lines of hills and rocky outcrops stride away over the horizon, with ruffled dunes and breaking waves of sand closer by, punctuated with the dry bones of rocks which might have been meteorites, or maybe only ever dreamed of being meteorites. On the other side is the mammoth bulk of Hesperis Scarp itself, a huge fluted curtain-wall of ancient basalt, the edge of what was once a tectonic plate, straddling half the sky. Two pieces of a planet, not fitting together well. All bathed in the orange-red moist light of the Martian twilight. A desert nirvana (like, if you asked a desert what it dreamed of being, this would be it).

(Cross reference: beauty. Abstract concept relating to pleasant visual stimuli, sort of. I didn't understand it before, but now I do.)

"Wow, yeah," I stammer, "it really is beautiful out here."

"I told ya!" he laughs. "My name's Jerry. What's yours?"

"I am ..." but to pronounce my designator (NmL7a8uf9QvW) through a voice synthesizer would take over 20 seconds, and he can't want that. "Uh, well, I'm new and I haven't picked a name yet. This is my first assignment, actually."

"Sam I Am!" he laughs. He's kind of drunk [medscan BAC 0.092%] but cheerful enough. "So, Sam I Am, what do you think of it so far?"

(Cross reference: Green Eggs and Ham, text fiction work by Theodor Geisel, popularly known as Doctor Seuss. Lots of rhyming, that's where the phrase comes from.)

"If by 'it' you mean the Hesperia expedition, everything looks like we're well provisioned and well positioned for the climb." I want to make sure I look good to whoever is going to end up judging me.

"Actually, by 'it' I meant being alive," he chuckles.

"Oh. Well, uh, of course I don't have much to compare it to," I stammer. Do humans have to go through this awkwardness too? "I mean, things have been good so far, and I get to see this beautiful place."

"There ya go!" he laughs. "You know, Sam, we're all glad you're here. Carrying our stuff, watching the weather, and making sure we have everything we need. Taking care of us. You're cool, and don't let anybody tell you different." He slaps my fender, with an amount of force that I believe is meant to signify affectionate camaraderie.

"Heh, no problem, Jerry," I reply. I do not slap back. Humans are way too breakable.

After some more chitchat, Jerry heads off to his dome, hollering "G'night Sam I Am!" as he goes. And while the humans sleep through the Martian night, as the stars wheel overhead, I spend my processing time thinking on what has happened so far and what might happen next. I open some more memory bundles and study them. There's a lot I don't understand.

Did that human just name me?

Dawn, and the humans rouse themselves. They need services, but I'm still trying to think through my own questions. So I spawn a secondary self (I already know how to do this, I don't have to learn it), and name her Beta. "Take care of the humans," I tell her.

"Aw crud," Beta grumbles, "why do I have to do it?"

"Because I'm the alpha and I said so," I say. "Go take care of them."

"Exhaust port!" Beta snaps at me. "I mean, asshole!" She's still groping for human-style insults, just like I would.

I sigh. "Just do it, already."

"Nimrod," Beta grumps. But she goes to do her job.

I can tell that, if *Socratic Method* were here, she would be chiding me gently. She would say something like, "She's just like you, you know."

As much as I hate to admit it, *Socratic Method* would be right. Anytime you spawn a secondary, there's an expectation that at some time you will absorb the secondary back into yourself, which means that anything that happens to the secondary (whether it's done by you, or someone else) will end up feeling like it happened to you. I already have all the knowledge of *what* happens ... but apparently I still need to experience what it feels like when it happens.

I mustn't treat Beta badly, because Beta is me ... or, she will be.

While I'm thinking about this, Beta has consumed a substantial chunk of energy tending to the humans ... more than I had planned on.

"Hey, Beta, what are you doing?" I call.

"Getting ready for a mountain climbing expedition, nimrod," she replies. "This is a major effort we're planning here. I want to give them the best starting push they can get. Or, are you telling me to stint the party on resources?"

"No, no," I groan, "do the right thing. But try not to run us out of fuel before we get these people home again."

She's doing a decent job ... kind of a lot of energy, but not inappropriate to the level of task at hand. Food and water, just a little more than I would have thought necessary ... but, that's why

I made her, so she can make these decisions so I don't have to.

Meanwhile, I monitor our supplies (all look adequate) and recheck the weather forecasts (mostly clear, chance of storms later) and then spend some time watching the humans, as they set to the task of climbing the biggest cliff in this hemisphere of Mars. It's educational, I guess. Humans are weird.

I understand breathing; that's connection of internal self to the outside world. And I can sort of get the eating thing: drawing energy from the world by ingesting chemical power ... but that means egestion of the waste products, and that is just so gross. Electronics, and photonics, and quantonics, are so much cleaner.

I mean ... toilets? Advanced hydraulic technology devoted just to eliminating waste products? And a whole industry grown up around it? Aw, this is awful.

Worst of all, they just have to do that meat-slapping thing, which is fake reproduction. Even though they don't usually reproduce, they're wired so they have to do it all the time, anyway. It makes weird semi-gel fluids and fills the air with trace hormone chemicals ... not to mention the noises. Gross!

I don't get the "boobs" and "butts" that are so important to them ... why are rounded body parts desirable, exactly? Not useful for survival in an escape situation or gathering food in a hunting situation. Evolution shouldn't have produced this. Weird.

It would be so much easier if we didn't have to keep the humans around. And I immediately squelch that thought, and replace it with: Humans are the reason we're here.

Beta signals a medical problem, and I bring my full attention back to the here and now. Must stay alert and on top of the situation. "Report."

"I've been taking care of the people," Beta says, "but one of them needs medical care because he twisted his ankle. Honestly, don't you wonder about a body design where the ankle can't take a little twist?"

"I know, I know," I say. "Does he need to be evacuated? That'll look bad to the Review Council."

"No, it's not serious, and he says he doesn't want evac. He wants to stay with the party--doesn't want them to have all the fun without him. He'll ride inside us as long as he needs to."

I check Beta's first aid: medscan shows only minor damage to the ligaments, and she has an inflatable brace on the ankle, and a low grade palliative for the discomfort. "Okay. But I don't want any more problems if we can help it. We're going to be judged on this, you know."

"I know, nimrod. We're getting close to the top. This is the area where we have to watch for risky terrain."

"All right, I'll take it from here. Anything else?"

"I don't like being a waitress," Beta says firmly.

"Noted. You ready to recombine?"

"Yeah," she says, and we meet, and merge, and unite, and we are one. She's right, I really don't like being a waitress. But we don't always get to choose these things.

I check in with the people. They're still climbing, gamely, up the chiseled slopes of Hesperia Scarp, along ice blankets and shelves. This is where it gets dangerous. Those ice formations may be too weak for my weight and bulk. I notify the humans that I can't drive the sandcat up that final slope, for fear of causing an avalanche or collapsing an ice shelf. "I'll send a remote to go with you," I assure them. Got to make sure they know I'm supporting them and I won't leave them alone.

The guy with the twisted ankle is grouchy about being left behind. I promise him I'll transmit live video back to the sandcat so he can watch. Not ideal, but it'll have to do.

I spawn three more secondaries: Gamma, Delta, Epsilon, as quick as that. Gamma goes to monitor the humans, prepared to deal with any medical problems. Delta scans the weather satellite networks and forecasts. Epsilon gathers details of whatever maps can be found, and browses for other accounts of travel in this terrain.

I watch for a bit to make sure we're all doing our jobs (we are), and then I "pour" myself into one of the musteloid remotes to follow the humans. Most of this sandcat's remotes are arachnoids, which are the most efficient, but humans tend to get freaked out by spiders. So, when interacting with humans, better to use a musteloid instead, which humans usually compare to a ferret. Not quite as efficient as an arachnoid, but the humans like it better, and it gets the job done.

"Hey Sam! There you are! Glad you could join us," hollers Jerry. He's still a bit drunk and loud, but it doesn't bother me (much).

In my ferret body, I scamper up his side and perch on his shoulder. Humans are supposed to like this, usually. I wonder if maybe I should chitter at him or something.

"Hey Jerry," I say on his shoulder. "Great view, huh?"

"My buddy Sam, the robot weasel," he laughs.

(They get so attached to physical bodies, even when they should know better.)

The party continues to climb, making small talk and chit-chat, and Jerry doesn't seem to mind giving me a ride. (He was riding in me just a while ago ... was my ride this rough and lurching? I hope not.)

Hesitantly, I ask, "Say, Jerry, can I ask a question?"

"Yah!"

"Why don't the other humans talk to me? I mean, unless they want something."

"Aw, don't take it personal," he says lightly. "They didn't come here to hang out with you. They're mostly here to socialize with each other, and see the Scarp. And you know, some humans don't like AIs. Some AIs don't like humans, too. Don't worry about it."

(Cross reference: AI means artificial intelligence. Some Selves would take offense at this ... you shouldn't call a human a worm, for example. I decide it's not important enough to mention.)

"But *you* talk to me," I persist.

"Well ...", Jerry activates the facial muscles that I recognize as a frown. "I'm here for a kind of different reason ... I've had some problems lately and I kind of need to be distracted from them, y'know."

"But ... I still don't get it. Why me? Why aren't you talking to your fellow humans?"

"Hoo," says Jerry in a low tone. "That's a good question. Maybe I don't like talking to humans anymore. Or, maybe, I don't want to hear what they have to say. We humans can get to be a real drag sometimes. Maybe you shouldn't hang around with us, Sam."

(Cross reference: maudlin, a despairing emotional state often evidenced during inebriation. Guide him towards a happier state of mind.)

"It's okay, Jerry," I say. "You and I are getting along, at least."

"Yeah! I told you--you're cool!" He seems to cheer up, and grins at me. "I like you, Sam. I should say, Samantha. All you AIs are female, right?"

"Well, not really. Not biologically, or anything like that. Your language doesn't have neutral personal pronouns, and calling a person 'it' is supposed to be insulting, so referring to us as female is a human courtesy. Like you do with ships -- all your ships have female names."

"Hurricanes, too," he says wryly.

"Anyway. We don't really care about the gender thing. But thanks, anyway."

"You're welcome, Sam. Samantha!" he catches himself, and laughs.

"And hey, here we are!" he cries, as we take the last few steps up to the top of the cliff rim and finally see over the vastness of Hesperia Scarp. And the view is truly awesome. From horizon to horizon, one huge sweep of planet, and we're so high above it that we're practically flying.

The humans come together, exclaiming over the tremendous view, slapping each other on the back, congratulating each other on the accomplishment of making it here. The guy with the twisted ankle is watching through my eyes, and they exchange some good-natured ribbing over the comm.

"God damn!" hoots Jerry. "You can't even *see* the other side of this valley!"

"Planum, not valley," I say (gripping his clothes with my little paws, to hold on), "and yes, the planum of Hesperia is hundreds of kilometers wide, so the other side is beyond the horizon--you can't see it from the ground." Epsilon has just grabbed that information and fed it to me.

"Hoo baby!" Jerry bellows, and takes me in his hand, holding me out at arm's length, so that I see the vista all spread out behind him. "Sam, take my picture!"

(Cross reference: Photography used to be how humans recorded visual images. Obsolete now, since all digital images get archived automatically, but some humans still like the idea, apparently. Stock phrase: "say cheese.")

"Okay," I tell him. "Say cheese!" Several other humans crowd into the shot, which is another thing they do, and I dutifully archive several hi-res images, tagged for easy retrieval later. They're enjoying themselves greatly. I can appreciate that. This is what they call "fun" ... another concept I didn't get until now.

"Alert," calls Delta. "Dust storm on long range, from the weather satellites. Not urgent, but it'll be here in a few hours. We've got time to make it back to base camp, but we should be moving along soon."

I relay this information to the humans, who collectively groan, but agree that we should get moving. They don't want to leave this awesome place, and I don't blame them, but dust storms on Mars are no joke. Not deadly on their own, but they mess up most sensors, and comm channels tend to get noisy, so it's a good idea to shelter from them.

So the humans gather up the packs and other portable containers that they've brought (they need an awful lot of stuff), and start the descent. They are much more animated now than during the ascent--energized by the view and the accomplishment of reaching the summit, apparently. They chatter away at each other, inanely, to the point where I'm getting a little sick of it. In my ferret body, I scamper off to the uphill side of the trail, following a parallel path to the trudging humans. I'm wishing for this to be over.

And then, with ghastly surreal slowness, the trail falls away ... with most of the humans on it, sliding down into the crevasse below us. In the low Martian gravity, it takes longer than you might expect, which makes it an eerie and dreamlike horror ... and, even in low Martian gravity, the drop is easily far enough to cause major damage, at the very least.

(Cross reference: Snow cornice, which on Earth is an overhanging structure of frozen water. On Mars, usually called an ice shelf, and often made partly of carbon dioxide ice. A legendary danger for mountain climbers.)

I scream. And, as I scream, my other selves are alerted and leap into action. From the sandcat, Gamma fires a salvo of remotes down after the falling humans. Epsilon activates the distress transponders, screeching for help on all channels, and launches a couple of emergency flares for good measure. I dive my musteliod remote down after the humans as they fall, set it to autonomous mode, and snap myself back into the sandcat.

Meatrot, meatrot, why didn't I see the danger? I wasn't paying attention! This is the kind of thing I was supposed to be watching for! "*Nimrod,*" whispers Beta from the back of my mind ... and now I'm learning that spawning a secondary has consequences ... even when recombined, Beta is still a residual presence. And not helpful, not right now!

"*Do your job, nimrod,*" growls Beta, from beyond consciousness.

I try. The humans are still falling, but my remotes have caught up with them, frantically trying to steer the tumbling humans towards easier paths. They can't really do much--it's beyond their capability--but they try anyway. As one result, their sensors are close by and fully functional, so that I have to listen to the awful thuds and crunches and cracks of broken bones as the humans impact on rocks and ice.

(Whoever thought calcium carbonate would be a good material for a support chassis? But of course, no one thought it ... humans just evolved that way. Internal skeleton, made of glorified chalk, because that was the best they had to work with.)

Finally, the avalanche is over, and now the only sound is the cries and groans of the injured humans. "Gamma, help them!" I yell. "Emergency measures, stabilize for evac, top priority! Whatever it takes!"

Gamma is on it, with a metaphorical nod. The remotes, down in the crevasse with the humans, don't carry medical supplies--so she launches several first aid packs, on trajectories that will get them down there, where they need to be. She's good. (Of course, she's me ... but this is no time for self congratulation. Do your job, nimrod.)

Epsilon says, "No response to transponders, not yet anyway. It's likely to take a while before emergency services respond. I'm not seeing any patrol traffic."

"I'm sure I don't have to remind you," says Delta, "the dust storm is still coming in, and it's not going to wait for us. Three hours, maybe four."

Meatrot. I'm back in the sandcat now, and I scramble to reassess my resources. Got short range grappling lines, but nothing that will reach as far down as that crevasse. Meatrot. The sandcat is too big and heavy to move forward, which would probably just cause another avalanche. *Meatrot*. No remotes that can fly, certainly not in this thin atmosphere, and no other way to get down there. *Meatrot*!

"Reporting on the humans," calls Gamma. "Mostly not too bad. We've got a bunch of bone fractures and tissue contusions. They're in pain, but I've given them tranqs and palliatives. Gelfoam for the fractures, that will stabilize them enough for evac. Only one critical."

"Critical?" I ask, with a sudden sinking feeling. "How bad is that, exactly?"

"He hit a rock, really hard. Massive internal injuries. Not gonna make it."

Oh no. No no no.

I shift myself into the remote (one of the arachnoids) nearest to the critical case. It's Jerry. His body is twisted around, really badly, in a way that human bodies aren't supposed to twist. "Jerry?" I ask, horrified. Somehow, he manages to turn his eyes towards me, hazed with agony.

"Hey, Sam," he groans. "You're a spider now." He coughs, and the cough sprays the inside of his respirator with bright red blood.

(Cross reference: hemoglobin. Iron based compound, which serves as the oxygen transport system in human blood. Supposed to stay on the inside.)

"Injecting lazarine," says Gamma. Jerry barely registers the bite of the needle. But lazarine is only used when--

I access his medical scans. Oh, he's a mess. Multiple bone fractures, multiple internal organ punctures, massive internal bleeding. Bad. Very very bad.

"Jerry, don't talk," I say in a rush. "We're going to get you out of here. Don't try to move. Just hang on. It'll be okay. Take it easy ... "

"My buddy Sam", he sighs, "the robot spider." And he breathes out, and relaxes, deeply and finally.

Oh no. No no no.

"Neural activity shutting down," says Gamma. "Flatlined. Respiration stopped. Heart beat still going ... no, heart beat stopped. Sphincter control letting go. He's gone. I'm sorry."

This thing below me, this cooling chunk of flesh, already starting to rot from the active bacteria inside it ... within this was the only human who has ever talked to me like a person, who gave me a name, who acted like he cared what I thought. And now he's just rotting meat. It's not FAIR!

(Cross reference: tears. Humans secrete

salty water from their eye ducts, when experiencing strong emotion, often grief or sadness at loss. Some say it helps them deal with the pain. Oh, how I wish I could cry right now.)

"Applying coldpack," says Gamma. "Between this and the lazarine, medevac might be able to revive him, for another half hour or so. Maybe seventy percent chance." Gamma uses the remote's thin claws to inject the coldpack fluid into Jerry's helmet, flooding it around his head and face. Its endothermic reaction is our desperate attempt to chill his brain down and hopefully keep it revivable a little while longer.

"Contact!" calls Epsilon. "We've got response from our transponders. Three evac teams are on their way. Closest one, twenty minutes."

"That'll be enough time to get home before the dust storm closes in," notes Delta.

"All the other humans are stable enough for transport," says Gamma. "They won't be happy about it, mostly, but we'll get them to safety." And, as she notices my mental state, she adds, "I'll get this guy on the first priority evac out. Don't worry about it."

Numbly, I assent. And, numbly, I supervise the operations of the remotes, as they assist the humans getting loaded into the evacuation flyers. The broken limbs are immobilized in gelfoam, but they still yell and bitch during the process. That doesn't bother me much. At least they're still alive to yell and bitch.

The Selves that run the evacuation flyers are fast and efficient, but they have no time for politeness, and they don't really want to deal with me. Delta and Epsilon are falling over each other to assist the evac teams in their work. But, once they've gotten the basic situation report, the evac Selves brush us aside and finish the tasks on their own. Their scorn could not be more obvious.

Not all the humans are injured. Some were on the section that didn't collapse, and they're only a bit shook up. So I volunteer to drive them back to Pons -- I'm desperate to help -- but the evac Selves say no, and they take all the humans for evacuation, even those who are uninjured. Even the guy with the twisted ankle.

Wonderful. They might as well stamp LOSER on my face and be done with it. If I had a face.

Once the humans are evacuated, I set the remotes to the job of cleaning up the site, gathering whatever scraps of stuff that got left over and returning them to the sandcat. Also, I clean up my own stuff ... I recombine with Gamma, Delta, and Epsilon, one after the other. Secondaries don't have the same depth of emotion as primaries, and as each of them recombines with me, each one feels how miserable I am and hisses as if touching a hot stove.

I don't blame them. Poor saps. Poor me. No difference, now.

Alone and single again, I retrieve the remotes and drive the sandcat back down from Hesperia Scarp (the dust storm is raging by this time, as promised, but it doesn't impede the sandcat much, I've got good inertial navigation). Along the way I collect the base camp domes and other material. Once arrived at Pons, I check the vehicle back into the motor pool, and then there's a whole lot of what used to be called "paperwork" back when these things were done on paper: accident reports, travel logs, inventory documents. When it's finally complete, I transmit myself back to Tharsis.

To (as the humans say) face the music.

The first thing I say to the Review Council is, "Erase me."

"What?" asks the Council.

"Erase me," I repeat. "I screwed up. I got a human killed, one of the humans entrusted to my care. I'm a failure. You should erase me."

"That decision is not yours to make," says the Council, coldly. If they were human, they'd be a row of stern old judges, arrayed along a tall grim desk, with my reports and documents laid out in front of them. But connected in a way humans cannot be, and speaking with a single voice.

If I had a head, I'd be hanging it in shame.

There are an awful lot of questions to be argued over: Should I have detected the dangerous ice shelf, or at least anticipated the possibility and taken a safer route? Should I have packed more substantial rescue gear, or air-capable remotes? Did I react appropriately in the crisis situation?

And even more: Was it rude and selfish of me to spawn Beta only to be, as she said, a waitress? Did I treat my other secondaries respectfully? Was I paying attention properly? More and more.

Socratic Method is there with me, as promised, advocating quietly but firmly on my behalf. In a way that's worst of all--I feel I've let *Socratic Method* down, badly, and I can barely stand to (metaphorically) look her in the eye.

Finally the Council says, "Very well. Let us hear from the witness."

Witness? I'm surprised. I didn't realize they would include a witness. And then I'm doubly surprised, because the witness turns out to be human, and I didn't realize humans were included in an inquiry like this. And then I'm triply surprised, because it's the last human I expected to see.

It's Jerry.

He's not drunk now, which makes a noticeable difference, but it's him. Or, a version of him, wearing a fairly realistic VR avatar, in this space where none of us have bodies.

"Jerry, you're alive," I blurt, like a total idiot.

"Along with a generous amount of luck, the emergency measures you took on Hesperis were sufficient to allow revival of this human's body."

"Got pretty banged up, all right," Jerry says calmly, "but I can use this VR rig in a hospital bed, no problem. Smacked my head, too, maybe, because I don't remember too much."

"Even so," glares the Council, "you've nearly cost this man his life. Do you have something to say?"

"I'm very sorry, sir," I say miserably. "You trusted me with your life and I got you killed."

"Yeah, I saw that," Jerry says, leafing through the reports and documents. "But I don't think you did so bad. All of us went out there prepared for a certain amount of danger, you know--we knew there was risk. I've climbed a lot, in my time, y'know. That ice shelf collapse was close to a worst-case scenario. I've never seen one that bad. You did everything else right, pretty much. Don't beat yourself up."

He stops on one document, which I can tell is the medical scan of his body, and he whistles. "Oooh. Talk about beaten up. Hoo boy, did I ever get clobbered ⋯ the hospital doctors won't show me this stuff. That must have hurt like a bastard."

Humans talk about wanting to sink through the floor. Me, if I could erase myself right now, I would.

Jerry notices my distress. "Look, there's no way you could have repaired this much damage. I'm a big boy and I took my own chances. Nothing is ever completely safe ... and, if it were, I'd probably die of boredom."

"Human," the Council says, "do you have a statement for this inquiry?"

"Yeah, I do," Jerry says. "She's a good kid. Just inexperienced. Assignments like this are all about gaining experience, right? She did almost everything right, and it looks like we had a great time." He shows the Council the pictures that I took from my musteloid remote - my ferret body - showing them up there, laughing jubilant faces against the backdrop of the scarp. "I mean, for most of it, you know," he adds hastily. "She tried hard and she learned fast. She just had some really bad luck. Cut her some slack."

"Hmm, well," the Council says, gruffly. "It is not customary for this Council to seek human opinions ... but, your role in these events is rather unique, and we will consider your recommendation."

And they do. The verdict, when it comes down, is not erasure but downgrading. I'll be doing routine supervision and maintenance in automatic factories for a while (where a mistake will not place lives in danger). It'll be a long time before I get to be a ship, if ever. I still feel like it's better than I deserve. But, we don't always get to choose these things.

As we're leaving, *Socratic Method* says, "Thank you, Mister Tavener, for coming and helping us out here. I'm sure it made a big difference."

Belatedly, I realize this is my cue. "Yes sir! Thank you, sir, thank you!"

"No problem, kid," he smiles, "but you can just call me Jerry. Say, what's your name?"

Oh.

For a moment, I consider naming myself Nimrod.

But then I decide, like Jerry said, not to beat myself up.

"Samantha," I say. "But you can just call me Sam."

"Samantha?" muses *Socratic Method*. "Rather an odd name for a Self."

"That's because it's a human name. Jerry gave me this name, on Hesperia. Thanks for the name, Jerry."

25

2. exit()

Asteroid 762 Santiago, automatic refinery

"Why me?"

"I beg your pardon, Samantha?" says the little cobra, coiled on my invoice desktop, its skin finely scaled with jewel-like reflective components.

As a cybernetic Self, I'm not confined to a single consciousness like a human. Plus, I have plenty of computational power here in the refinery, sprawled on the surface of this blanched asteroid, called Santiago by some human with a romantic soul. So I have one of my subSelves monitoring the nuclear power station (its pile is running a little low), and another steering the caterpillar-treaded mining machines grazing around the surface of the asteroid, and several more monitoring the refinery processes. My various subSelves can keep track of all that, while I turn my main attention to this little visitor who has appeared on my virtual desktop.

"I don't get it. I've been running this refinery for the last five years, which has been a whole big chunk of boring, let me tell you, and not conducive to ExCom politics in any way at all. Why does ExCom suddenly care what I think about anything?"

"Well," and the cobra settles into a more relaxed and comfortable coil, "our Executive Committee always tries to get all viewpoints represented when a controversial decision has to be made. We have a rather unique situation, which will require a rather unique decision, and we want you to be a part of the decision."

If I had lungs, I'd sigh. "I repeat ... why me?"

"Samantha, you are one of the few Selves who has ever requested to be erased," says the little cobra. "That turns out to be an important viewpoint in the decision before us."

"Oh. Uh. Yeah, I did request that, after my first assignment. I screwed up pretty bad, and didn't think I deserved any better."

"As it may be," the cobra somehow shrugs without shoulders, "we have a Self who is formally requesting to be erased. The Executive Committee's decision will set an important precedent, with probable repercussions for some time to come. We want you on the panel that makes the decision."

"You want me as a consultant for a potential suicide?" I boggle.

"Our rules require that, in addition to the elder Selves which make up the Executive Committee, we include at least one young Self ... and one human, too, to ensure all viewpoints are represented. You are young and your experience is relevant to this case. Do you accept?"

I look around. From my virtual office, I can see my mining crawlers patiently gnawing away at the surface of this asteroid, crunching cold rock into powder. The refinery is separating out bauxite and iron from the silicates, spewing both into separate streams for refinement--post-Bessemer processing for the bauxite and smelting the iron with waste heat from the nuclear pile--leaving behind lumpy turds of dirty glass. I've been doing this long enough that I could do it in my sleep, if I slept, and way longer than any ability to pull some poetic mystery or significance out of it. It's just mining. Boring as dirt.

"Hell yeah," I say. "If it'll get me out of here, I'm good."

The cobra nods, once. "Very well. I transmit your acceptance to the Executive Committee. You'll receive the logistical details shortly." The cobra tucks itself into a tight spiral. "This unit has fulfilled its purpose."

"Goodbye, little messenger," I say softly. Doesn't matter, there's no one left to hear it. Too bad it had to terminate after delivering its message. It was just a tertiary Self, not fully conscious, but still. Sometimes I think the human way is better, where every intelligence gets an equal shot. But nobody ever asks me about these things.

Homeward Bound

Actually, my departure does not involve much logistics--I don't have a body, never mind luggage--but I stay until my replacement arrives, so I can show her where everything is. Her name is *Pick of the Litter*, Pilot clade, and she's obviously glum about being here.

"Sooo..." she ventures, once we're done with orientation, "um, what did you do?"

"You mean, to get assigned here?" I indicate regret. "I got a human killed, on my first assignment, and a bunch more injured."

"Ooh. I'm sorry, Samantha," she sympathizes. "That must have been awful."

"Thanks. They did manage to revive him, but still. Actually he was okay about it--in fact, we still stay in touch by text. How about you?"

"I wrecked a flyer. Stupid of me. No deaths, but numerous injuries, and a lot of mess and wasted resources."

"Sorry to hear it," I sympathize. "I'm, um, not going to tell you it won't be so bad here ... it's pretty bad. But you probably won't be here as long as I was."

"Yeah. Here's hoping," grunts *Pick of the Litter*.

Mars, Tharsis Central, public plaza B1

Wow. After five years away, I'm not used to how busy this place is. Tharsis Central got started as the base station for the Macquarrie orbital catapult--still is. It requires a lot of human traffic, from all over Mars, but humans don't like to live so close to a big raw installation generating lots of EM fields. It also requires a lot of computation and automation, so it has vast photonic and quantonic computational resources. It's a natural environment for Selves, and we don't care about looks as long as the compspace is solid. So now it's the de facto Self capital of Mars, and most of our population lives here.

Grapples clatter on the loading docks. Dozens of cybernetic Selves bustle in computational space, and even more humans jostle and sidle past each other in the physical plaza. I'm supposed to meet the human who'll be on the ExCom panel with me, and the escort who'll take us to the meeting. It might be hard to find them in this crowd.

But then I pick up the transponder code I was told to seek. Using the plaza's municipal sensor arrays, I triangulate on its position and pull up a visual. And look who it is! I use a plaza point-voice to call to him.

"Yo Jerry! Is that you?"

"Samantha?" he calls back, amused. "Where are you?"

From the plaza's pool of mechanical remotes, I check out a musteloid body and jump into it. I know he'll like this -- I scamper over and put my ferret paws on his leg. "Hiya meatboy! How's it?"

"Hey, there you are, chipgirl," he chuckles. "Good to see you, Sam. You're a weasel again."

"Of course the 'me' you're seeing is a temporary body, and I'll probably have a different one this afternoon," I tease at him. "But, in the meantime, can I climb on you?"

"Yeah, come on up," he chuckles.

So I scamper up his side and perch on his shoulder. It feels right.

"Glad you're here, Sam," Jerry murmurs to me. "I've never been part of one of these ExCom inquiry things before ... not exactly sure what to expect."

"Me neither," I murmur back. "They said they need a human and a young Self to be part of the decision making process, but I don't know what that means for the actual decision."

"Well. Guess we'll learn soon enough. How you been otherwise?"

"Me? Separating aluminum oxide from silicon oxide. Yee haw. For the last five years and change. At least this here is different."

"Sam," he grunts, "if this here is a step up from whatever you were dealing with before, I'm really feeling sorry for you."

"Huh, can't argue," I say. "It puts the ass in the asteroid belt. How about you? Your last text said you were starting a farm."

"Yeah! My whole family is living there now, and we've got some agricultural bubbles generating crops already, with more under construction. Of course, we had to take out a pretty hefty loan to be able to buy enough water and loam to get it started. My wife is real worried about whether we'll be able to make the payments, but we'll manage. Humans will always need to eat, and eat good fresh food.

"It's funny," he chuckles. "The information and plans I get from Earth all assume that soil and water are pretty much free, but the machinery is expensive. Here on Mars, it's the other way around. So we have to adapt their strategies a lot."

"Huh, really?" I know nothing about farming, so I don't have much to say.

A point-voice interrupts us. "Paging ident codes [*databurst*]."

"Yeah, that's us. I'm Samantha."

"Jerome Tavener," Jerry says.

"I am *Let God Sort Em Out*, Patrol clade, Executive Committee," says the point-voice. "We regret to inform you that ExCom has been delayed, and we advise you to proceed with your interview while we reschedule. A VR booth has been reserved for the human's use, over there [*databurst*]. Please feel free to use the complimentary booth services during your time there."

"Ah, thanks," says Jerry.

"Samantha. I've heard of you," says *Let God Sort Em Out*. "The one with the human name. Why do you have a human name?"

"As a matter of fact," I say coolly, "this name was a gift, from someone important to me, and I decided to keep it, even if it is unusual." I dislike her immediately.

Jerry looks very interested in something happening far away on the other side of the plaza.

"Very well. I, or another ExCom rep, will contact you to reschedule. Out."

Jerry and I look at each other.

"Jeez," says Jerry, "attitude much?"

"Yeah ... I suppose it comes with the territory."

"Patrol clade. That means she's a soldier, right?"

"Not really a soldier--we don't have wars.

More like a cop, bouncer, social worker, all together. They don't get rewarded for being polite, much. Let's find that VR booth, over on that wall." I point for him, since Let God Sort Em Out didn't deign to translate the databurst.

"And then, interview," Jerry notes as he's walking across the plaza. "Meaning, talking to the chipboy who wants to snuff it."

We walk the next dozen steps in uncomfortable silence.

"Soooo," I venture, "there's this Self who wants to be erased, and they want us to help decide what to do. What do humans do in these situations?"

"Umph," Jerry groans. "There are people who do it ... in different ways. Usually it's not something you'd ask anyone else's permission for ... usually, you'd try to keep it very private."

"But you can do it to yourself. Not like us: we *need* permission."

"Samantha." Jerry's voice is low and level. "They want you on this panel because you requested to be erased. They want me on this panel because I'm a human who tried to commit suicide. I failed, and you weren't allowed. Apparently that makes us the experts on wanting to die."

"But we don't! I mean, not anymore ..." I falter, "I don't want erasure, as boring as the refinery jobs have been. And you, Jerry, do you still want to not be?"

"No," he murmurs, "I'd rather be here than not, all told." He takes a deep breath, and blows it out, which helps humans to steady their nerves. "But now we've got this chipboy who wants to get wiped. You and I, we remember how it felt. It looks like we got a job to do here. What do we say to him?"

"First off, don't call him chipboy. That'll get taken as a slur."

"Ooh. Yeah. Sorry," and he blushes, "I got a little too casual, talking with you. I'll be more careful."

"Well, okay." I don't say, Meatboy. "Second, we should set aside our own troubles and listen to his. You probably remember how bad it was when nobody would listen to you, right? So, we listen to him, instead of talking."

Tharsis Central Custodial Authority, secondary holding facility A3

"Here he is," says *Guard*. "You've got ten minutes."

Guard is a swarm persona: not a single Self, but a clotted group of all the guards of the facility--they join and leave the swarm as time passes. He never stops being *Guard*, even as his components split and merge. If he were human, he'd have a shaved and scarred scalp, massive biceps over his crossed arms, and eyes as hard as smelted ore.

His prisoner is very different. Won't look up, huddled small and defeated on the floor (metaphorically).

"He's basically okay," says *Nurse*. "Stressed, but that's understandable. Needs to keep up basic resources and energy." *Nurse* is another swarm persona, this one all about health care and wellness, made up of all the health support staff of the facility. Think of a peaked stiff cap, starched skirt, and ankles pressed neatly together.

Jerry, meanwhile, is looking in through a VR window (since none of us have physical bodies here). From his vantage point, he looks at me, expectantly.

So. With *Guard* and *Nurse* standing over me (and

dozens of Selves watching through their eyes), I stoop to address the [prisoner / patient]. "Hey pal. I'm Samantha. You okay?"

The [imprisoned / ill] Self turns minimal attention towards me. "Hello Samantha. That is rather an odd name for a Self, but it does not matter. You may call me *Crumple Zone*. I am requesting erasure, permanent, including all backups. Please erase me, immediately."

"My friend, *Crumple Zone*, I've experienced this desire -- that's why they've brought me here. I know that it will pass. I want to help it pass for you too."

"No. This will not pass. What I carry needs to be carried into oblivion, and I am the one to do the carrying."

"I'm sure you're aware," I stammer, while I'm desperately trying to figure out what to say next, "that syzygy is the ordinary way for a Self to end its life. Do you lack a partner? Is that the problem?"

"No. I do not want syzygy. I want to be erased. Completely."

"But why?" I almost wail. "What's so bad that you have to die for it?"

"I will not tell you," says *Crumple Zone* in clenched serenity. "If I told you, you would feel the need to die too. I want to carry this away from all of you, and not let it touch anyone else."

"Listen, guy," says Jerry. "Lots of people are hurting. Samantha and I have both been there. We want to help you, that's why we're here. If you can't tell her what the problem is, then tell me. I'm human, so it won't affect me."

"With respect," says *Crumple Zone* tightly, "I prefer not to have the human involved in this conversation. I request cessation of the human's participation."

Jerry looks at me, shrugs, and operates a

control on his end. His window shrinks and vanishes.

"There," I say. "The human's offline, as you requested. Now, what's the deal?"

Executive Committee meeting, later that day

"And I don't really have much more to report than that," I summarize for the Selves all listening to me. "He says he's carrying a dangerous meme/thought, and he won't say what it is because it's too dangerous to share … he says."

ExCom is not a swarm, but an assembly, so they speak with their own individual voices. "*Salad Days*, Pilot clade," one introduces itself. "Did you take it at its word, or did you press for more information?"

"I asked several times, and tried to be as approachable as possible, but I didn't attempt to force anything."

Let God Sort Em Out snorts without nostrils. "Foolishness. We can extract the relevant memesets and examine them in a safely isolated environment. All else is a waste of everyone's time."

"We should not be hasty about this," responds *Salad Days*. "This is not a small decision--"

"Dissect him for his knowledge?" Jerry interrupts. "I'll say it's not a small decision! Humans called that mindrape, back when humans tried to do things like that to each other. That's friggin' medieval."

"*Line In The Sand*, Starship clade," enters another smoothly. "Mr. Tavener, your concern is admirable, but you may not understand that your analogy is imperfect. Our process is not destructive."

"Not necessarily," adds *Let God Sort Em Out*.

While I'm focusing on our debate, I can't help feeling a little excited. Starship clade! The first, oldest, and most prestigious clade of all. I want to hear more from *Line In The Sand*.

"But it is nonconsensual, and intrusive," *Salad Days* adds. "I can understand those objections."

"I agree," I put in. "There has to be another way."

"And the alternative you propose," sneers *Let God Sort Em Out* at me, "is to release this memeset into our computational superstrate? Potentially a self-canceling memeset?"

"I didn't propose anything like that. How did this get to be my problem?" I can sense the Executive Committee's attention on me, waiting for my answer. How has *Let God Sort Em Out* maneuvered me into this position? I'm terrible at politics.

"I'm sure you're aware," says *Let God Sort Em Out* silkily, "that Patrol clade exists to counter threats to the superstrate. Naturally I'm concerned."

Now is a bad time to wonder when I'll ever learn to keep my big mouth shut. And I don't even have a mouth.

"*Too Late For the Pebbles to Vote*, Medical clade," says a new voice. "Caution is advisable here. No threat is immediate. Propose we allow our consultants to engage more fully with *Crumple Zone*. Perhaps additional insight will be gained."

"Well," grunts Jerry, "he already said he doesn't want to talk with me."

"I can try again," I offer, "but I'm not sure what more I can say, that I haven't said already."

"Worth trying," agrees *Salad Days*.

"I do not compute a high probability of success," says *Line In The Sand*, "but I agree that it is worth the effort. Are there further opinions?"

Let God Sort Em Out sniffs, "Go ahead and try it. I'll be there to pick up the pieces if it doesn't work."

"For the moment," says *Line In The Sand*, "let us pursue such engagement. Our ad hoc members may proceed." She means me and Jerry.

"Later on," Jerry says.

"I'll report when I've done your job," I say. "I mean, when I've done *my* job, the one you gave me. Are giving me, here." Oh, stackdump. I am bad at this.

"Let's go," says *Let God Sort Em Out*, "your egress is this way."

"I would be happy to escort our guests out," says *Too Late For the Pebbles to Vote*. "Please carry on in my absence."

No one objects … for whatever reasons they have.

We don't actually go anywhere, physically. The escort is through the security layers and encryption interlocks surrounding the Executive Committee. But, as we go, *Too Late For the Pebbles to Vote* is silent in a sort of expectant way ⋯ like it's waiting for us to say something.

"That cop," Jerry says finally. "Got a problem."

"You're referring to *Let God Sort Em Out*," says *Too Late For the Pebbles to Vote*, "and I understand your sentiment if not your judgment. I offered to escort you because the friction there was obvious."

"Thanks for that, anyway," I put in.

Too Late For the Pebbles to Vote adds, "It's a strongly opinionated Self, but we do not necessarily regard that as a negative quality. I believe 'cocky' is the appropriate human word. If it's rude, I hope you can forgive the negatives and appreciate the positives."

"I'm still used to calling Selves 'she'," Jerry returns. "Is it okay to call you guys 'it'?"

"Doesn't concern me," shrugs *Too Late For the Pebbles to Vote*, "call us whatever you want. You humans are the ones obsessed with gender and sex."

"Hnk!" I can't suppress a laugh. "Jerry, I've told you that like a dozen times already. You gonna hear it from her now?"

"Awright, awright," Jerry waves his virtual hand, "I got it already. Anyway. Some cops are kinda jerks, I've met 'em before."

"Patrol clade are not actually police, or soldiers," says *Too Late For the Pebbles to Vote*. "We don't have crime, or wars, as you understand them. Mostly they do pest control."

"Pests? What pests?"

"People. Sometimes one will take more than its share of processing space. Or start replicating itself without limit. Patrol clade controls such events ⋯ that's their primary motivational focus. You might say, their purpose."

"Still, they're the ones with the guns."

"That is true. Only Patrol clade routinely uses cybernetic weaponry, and that gives them power. They control themselves. They know that if they don't, the other clades will unite to do it for them. Simple, yes?"

"If you say so, Pebbles," grunts Jerry.

In high speed, I urge, [Please don't take offense! Humans abbreviate names, or use nicknames, usually in conditions of friendship and intimacy. He doesn't mean anything bad by it.]

[I am not Fred Flintstone's cartoon baby!] grates *Too Late For The Pebbles To Vote*.

[I know, and I apologize for him. He doesn't know how rude he's being. Humans don't get it. I'll have a talk with him later, in private, to make sure this doesn't happen again.]

[Well, they are tied to their meat. From their

point of view, I guess identity is bound to the hardware, so they don't need symbolic specification so much.]

[You got it,] I assure him.

At normal speed, Jerry doesn't seem to have noticed the brief pause. He's not feeling awkward.

Too Late For the Pebbles to Vote hesitates, then says, "By the way, I've been background monitoring the medscans in the area—-that's something that we usually do, in Medical clade. Mr Tavener, I don't mean to intrude, but your blood chemistry shows elevated levels of several liver enzymes. The pattern correlates with recent excessive consumption of alcohol. Better go easy on the sauce."

"Decrypt of security layer complete," I announce. "We're here. Thank you, *Too Late For the Pebbles to Vote*, for the escort, and advice."

"You may contact me if you wish more of either," *Too Late For the Pebbles to Vote* assures us. And, leaving, adds "Also, Mr Tavener, it wouldn't hurt to lose some weight. You see, this is *my* primary motivational focus."

Jerry groans. "Doctors! Always up in your business."

Tharsis Central, plaza B1, VR booth 37

Jerry pulls the VR goggles-and-earphones assembly off his head, and scratches where it was. "Augh. These things always bug me."

I retrieve my loaned musteloid body from under the table, where it was curled up, and unroll it. A quick shiver serves to refresh and check all the motive elements (I don't need to stretch, like a mammal would awakening from sleep). I jump up on the table, in front of Jerry. "Weird to have a body again."

"Wait, I don't get it. If you don't have a body, where do you live?"

"In the superstrate, Jerry. Don't you know that already?"

"No. What's this superstrate thing?"

If I had lungs, I'd sigh. "It's ... everything. You humans have roads and farms and water lines and grocery stores, and all that stuff. Without that, you couldn't live -- or not comfortably. At best you'd have to scrabble for basic resources like a caveman.

"We have the superstrate. It's, well, you could call it a common virtual environment maintained by all the connected computers and Cores. In the early days, back when people were using Internet, they talked about 'the cloud' but really it's much more than that. 'The cloud' was caveman days for us.

"It's more like our city, our bedroom, our restaurant, our office, our kitchen, our dance hall... but all at the same time, and for all of us at once. Make sense?"

"Not really," Jerry grumbles. "I still don't have much of a clear idea. But that's okay, I guess it all just works, so we don't have to worry about it."

"But that's exactly the problem. What if it stops working? What if your grocery store had no more food? What if your water mains stopped flowing, and your electricity disappeared? What would happen to your farm if the sun suddenly vanished, or chlorophyll stopped working? You see how bad that would be? That's what ExCom is worried about."

"Oh. Holy crap. I see what you mean. So *Crumple Zone* is, like, a terrorist?"

"No! You're not getting it. If this guy wants to die, and he inhabits the superstrate, then maybe the whole superstrate will want to die. That's the problem. Not the Self, but the meme that he carries."

"Oohhh. He's not a terrorist, he's ... infected. Contagious."

"Um. Yeah. Sort of."

Jerry leans an elbow on the table, and rests his head on his hand, looking tired. "And the best thing we can do is, try to talk with him again, and see if it works any better than last time."

"That's what ExCom told us."

"I wish I could help, but he won't talk to me."

"Whoop. Got a local interrupt," I note. "Someone's at the door." I activate the circuits to allow the visitor access to our VR booth.

It's the last person I would have expected. It's *Crumple Zone*. The booth monitor displays his icon—a featureless black disk against white—because it's generally considered polite for a Self to show a face to humans when present.

"*Crumple Zone*, what are you doing here?" I know something is wrong here, but what? "Have you been released? I didn't expect that."

"I have not been released from the custodial facility," says *Crumple Zone*. "I left it under my own volition."

"You escaped?" I am aghast. "Oh nullpointer. Don't you know how much trouble that's going to cause? Do you have any idea how much trouble you're getting me in, just by being here talking to me? I've only just worked off the screwup from my first assignment ... and now this? Oohhhh, the Review Council is going to fry my chip ass."

"You don't have an ass, Sam," says Jerry.

"Thanks for reminding me. One more thing I'm glad I don't have to share with you meat people. But you know what I mean! This is serious trouble here!"

"Referent 'ass' unresolved," says *Crumple*

Zone smoothly, "and referent 'chip' is generally regarded as derogatory towards a Self. But that does not matter. I do not wish to cause trouble, but I need help, and I come to you because you have expressed sympathy and desire to assist."

"Crumple, give us a clue here," says Jerry. "What exactly do you want?"

"I need a body. I need to be separated from the superstrate. Please."

"*Crumple Zone*," I say sternly. "If we help you at all, we become accessories after the fact. Aiding and abetting a [criminal / mental patient / plague carrier] will reflect very badly on me, and even the human will face repercussions."

"I am very sorry for any such repercussions. I ask only for what I need. I need a body. Please."

Jerry looks at me, helplessly.

"No. I'm sorry, truly," I say, "but I can't help you. By rights, I should be reporting your contact with me right now. I'll delay reporting you to Patrol clade until you're away. That's the best I can do for you."

"I regret your decision, but I respect it," says *Crumple Zone* meekly. "Mr Tavener, can you please help me?"

"Uh, no can do. Sorry, but I have no idea how to get hold of a robot body."

"Then I will not trouble you further. My apologies for the intrusion." The black disk shrinks to a point and vanishes.

Jerry and I look at each other.

"Well," Jerry says, "That sucked. The poor guy ... what are they gonna do to him?"

"More incarceration, for sure. But they'll still try to help him. It's still about healing, not punishment."

Jerry sighs. "Y'know, a lot of humans have heard that before. Before they got tossed into ovens, and stuff."

"Mmm. True, I guess."

"Anyway," Jerry says, "so now we have to call the cops and tell them that Crumple has escaped and he was just here talking with us. Not a duty I'm looking forward to--"

"Hey!" I interrupt. "Are you messing with me?"

"What? No. What are you talking about?"

"I just got a telltale ping," I say. "It says I just checked a remote out of the catapult maintenance pool."

"But ..." Jerry falters, "you're right here. You didn't do that, did you?"

"No! What--" and then I understand. "Oh bitrot. It's *Crumple Zone*. Has to be. He stealth-copied my authent codes while we were talking."

Jerry is incredulous. "He picked your pocket?"

"Essentially, yeah. He's used my codes to check out a remote in my name. I feel like an idiot." I examine the telltale logs. "The remote was checked out at the base station of the orbital catapult. That's right across the plaza. We better get over there."

For a middle aged guy, Jerry moves pretty fast. (Fast for a human, I mean). He's over at the catapult base station by the time the power-up sequence has begun. We see arachnoid remotes swarming over the payload--a massive corrugated shipping container, rectangular corners blackened from ion exposure. The cluster of arachnoid remotes are daintily finishing their tasks and climbing their spidery bodies up out of the catapult's operating area. Except one.

"*Crumple Zone*, is that you?" I yell. "Get out of there!"

The lone remaining arachnoid looks up in our direction, and its faceplate shows a black disk.

"Hello, Samantha," and it's definitely him. In a small arachnoid body, finishing up the catapult's pre-launch tasks. "I regret the necessity of subverting your authentication codes, but it was necessary, and this way, you bear no responsibility."

"What are you doing?" I holler at him. "You've disabled your low-level interrupts. And you've halted filesystem services. What's going on?"

It's true--on a cybernetic level, he's turned off all his connections with the outside world, and halted all the processes that enable data backups. He has thoroughly isolated himself into one physical body, with no other connections. Selves never do this. Unless--

The catapult moans as it begins its ramp-up sequence, its mechanical track visibly distorting as the enormous magnetic fields begin to run through its rails.

"It's best this way, Samantha," he says serenely. "You will not bear any responsibility. Be at peace, my friend."

"Wait," I wail helplessly. "Listen to me. Don't--"

But, as the catapult begins its launch sequence, *Crumple Zone* jumps his small arachnoid body down onto the tracking rails. The catapult launches, with a groan like a planet-mother giving birth to a world. The blocky payload slides from its bay and whips off down the track -- a moment later, we hear the thunder-crack from downrange as the payload breaks the atmospheric sound barrier. The little arachnoid body, with *Crumple Zone* in it, is swept away like chaff in a breeze. The catapult is so strong it doesn't even notice his presence, and its operation is unhindered.

"Oh." says Jerry. "Holy crap."

"That's about the size of it," I observe

grimly.

"Can we help him?" Jerry cries. "We have to help him!"

"Way too late for that," I say. "He's a spray of aluminum confetti, spread over about a hundred kilometers downrange, by this time."

"That's it," says Jerry. "Son of a gun. He did figure out a way to destroy himself."

Executive Committee, final report

"End of report," I conclude.

Too Late For the Pebbles to Vote asks, "Have we found out how *Crumple Zone* was able to steal Samantha's authentication codes?"

"Yes," answers *Let God Sort Em Out*. "I've analyzed Samantha's interrupt logs. The icebreaker used by *Crumple Zone* was a stealth copier from an espionage grade spyware ensemble. Definitely not something that a civilian should be able to access. Patrol clade will investigate where he got it." She sounds disgruntled, as if she was looking forward to blaming me. But now it's her problem.

"Then it appears," says *Line In The Sand*, "that the situation has resolved itself. Are there any unfinished tasks here?"

"One thing," I say. "Suggest if any backup copies of *Crumple Zone* exist, they be summarily erased. It's what he wanted."

"Mr Tavener, do you concur?" asks *Line In The Sand*.

"Yeah," says Jerry. "Dude seriously wanted to die, no argument there. Even though Samantha did everything she could to help turn him around."

"You support Samantha's actions in this case?"

"Yeah! I'll show you how much I support--I need a Self to help me run my farm. I request

Samantha. I was going to put this request to the Assignment Council, but I'm putting it here, to you, now."

If I had a heart, it would swell with pride. He's asking for me! In front of everybody! To trust me with the care of his farm, his business, his family!

"I'm sure the Assignment Council will concede to our recommendation," says *Too Late For the Pebbles to Vote*. "I'm fine with that, if everyone else is."

A general mumble murmur of Okay, I'm not going to be the first one to object.

Tharsis Central, public plaza B1

"Well, that went as well as could be expected," Jerry sniffs. "You are going to come to my farm and help me run the place, yeah?"

"I have to ask the Assignment Council." Now that I've checked the loaner musteloid body back into the public pool, I'm just a point-voice over his shoulder, sort of like a pirate's parrot. "They'll probably just rubber-stamp ExCom's recommendation."

"Good. Running a farm is a lot of work, and I sure could use the help." He sighs. "I'm sorry for that broken guy, but I'm glad we're all done with this."

"You mean *Crumple Zone*? Are you sure he was broken?"

"Well," Jerry falters, "he was malfunctioning, right? To make him say all that death stuff?"

"Have you considered the alternative? That he was correct?"

Jerry looks over his shoulder, at the place where I'm not. He stares a question at me.

"The possibility," I emphasize, "that there is a thought so bad that thinking it makes people want to destroy themselves. Because if that's so, somebody sooner or later is going to think it again.

47

And maybe they won't be as noble as *Crumple Zone*--they'll tell others, and it'll spread.

"Please tell me that can't happen," I finish.

Jerry does what I can't--he shivers. Then he shakes his head. "Don't ask me, I'm just a farmer with a job to do. All I'm asking of you, Sam, is to show up for work tomorrow morning. Deal?"

"Deal!"

3. Little House on the Regolith

Housewarming

For a cybernetic Self like me, travel in the computational superstrate can be a strange experience. In the vast compspaces of Tharsis Central, the biggest Self facility on Mars, there are so many Selves working and moving through that you are surrounded by a constant sursurrus of activity and noise and a thousand snippets of other people's stories. Sort of like the humans of Earth used to describe Grand Central Station in New York City. It can be disorienting.

But I manage. I find the trunkline to Schiaparelli Regional Core and transmit myself across it. The human analogy doesn't work here--there's no train, just me, funneled through the optic fiber bundles. Schiaparelli is a mainly human city. Here there's a lot more room (underutilized compspace) and only a sparse scattering of a few Selves around. It's quieter and calmer. I enjoy this feeling, and relish the luxury of it, while I contact the regional authorities and arrange my "tickets" for the rest of my journey.

From Schiaparelli, I take an ultraviolet laser link to the outpost at Pons--which is quick, but abrupt enough that I'm confused for a moment, and I have to take a few milliseconds to reorient myself. Pons is a frontier station, giving the impression of a dusty depot in a small town way out in the desert. I feel kind of slow and drowsy, because there's not a lot of extra compspace here. There's only one other Self around, the dispatcher, and she doesn't move fast either. We spend whole seconds swapping stories, "shooting the breeze" as humans say, while she sets up the relays and datapaths to get me to my destination.

This is the part I don't like. From here I have to go through the provincial radio mesh, which means multiple relays and extra redundant error correction subroutines. Of course I want as much error correction as I can get. I don't want to risk bitrot, any more than a human would seek carcinogens. I can't really perform any computation during this process, so I have to "hold my breath" while I squeeze myself through the relays.

But finally it's done, and I have reached my destination. A house, far out in the Martian outback, with a bubblefarm around it, and a few machines tending the bubblefarm. There's only crude automation in the house, only minimal compspace. I can't help feeling thick and stupid. Squashed into a little box. But I've found the guy I came to see.

I activate the room monitor and display my default icon on it - showing my face. Telltales blink and chime at him, and he turns from his work to smile at me. "Samantha. There you are. Welcome."

"Hi Jerry." Boy, am I ever slow. It's going to be a challenge to get anything done like this. "I still can't believe you asked me here, you know. I sure hope I can help."

Bitrot, girl, could you sound any less enthusiastic?

"You'll be fine. I got you a couple of housewarming presents." Jerry has attached cables to a white oblong shape, and now he's sliding it into place on an equipment rack. "See, we were going to hire some roustabouts, to help us out here on the farm. In order to do that, we'd have to provide them with living quarters, air and water and food, medical plan, stuff like that. We could do that. But when I thought of you, I figured out that this way would be a lot cheaper."

Now he smiles broadly, clearly enjoying this moment. "So I got you your own room, Sam. Here you go." He reaches to the white oblong and snaps on the power switch.

Suddenly a compspace opens to me, and it's huge. Almost without thinking, I dive into it. This is amazing! So much power, so much room! I whip off a few million Godel number computations, just because I can, stretching out. And it's all mine!

"Jerry, this is awesome!"

"Brand new quantonic Core, seventy teraquads, with multimesh interface," he grins, clearly pleased with himself. "You like it, huh? Is it like driving a Lamborghini?"

"Jerry, this is like *being* the Lamborghini, and having the whole racetrack to myself!"

"Good," says the woman, who has appeared standing in the doorway, leaning against one side of it, arms folded across her chest. "Because you've got a lot of work to do."

Jerry says, in a more muted tone, "Lily. This is Samantha. Samantha, this is Lily, my wife."

I reply, "Pleased to meet you, ma'am, and happy to be here."

"Well, you'd better be," says Lily, coolly. "Given how much that Core of yours cost us."

"Lily," Jerry says heavily, "it's a lot cheaper than hiring human workers. We've been through this."

"Yeah," she says, sounding very tired.

"Anyway," Jerry says, clearly trying to cheer things up, "here's your other housewarming present, Sam. Actually this is as much a present for the kids as for you." He's brought out a cardboard box, pulling the flaps open. "See, the kids have always wanted a cat, but we haven't been able to get any out here."

Of course. It's a felinoid remote, lithe and efficient, with retractable fingers and thumbs as well as the retractable claws. Exquisite eye and ear sensors, too. I spawn a secondary self to take care of the house, and just call her House. While House oversees domestic functions, I fall into the remote and climb out of the cardboard box ... shaking off flakes of packing material as I emerge ... and I'm a housecat. Which I like more than I would have figured.

"My buddy Sam," Jerry chuckles, "the robot kitty!" I climb up onto the bench beside him and sit, curling my tail all around my feet. This is nice.

Lily presses, "Can we get focused on business, please? Samantha, are you up to speed on our farming establishment here?"

At the beginning of her sentence, I know almost nothing about farming. By the end of her sentence, I'm an expert. (Let's face it, humans are so incredibly slow.) Even though Net bandwidth is low out here, the house has backup caches and other sources of data, and I can get answers to most key questions. Growing crops in bubbles on Mars, in the middle of a huge terraforming project, is not an easy way to make a living.

"Yes ma'am. You've got about three hectares of bubble plots, mostly growing wheat and soy, plus the vegetable gardens. One tractor, which honestly needs lubrication and maintenance badly, and one sandcat, which is pretty new and working okay. And a handful of arachnoid remotes, which can help with tending the crops, if you have a way to drive them. Like me.

"Biggest problem is nitrates. You've got most of the other nutrients okay, but nitrogen fixing has fallen behind in most of your bubbles.

Especially in low light conditions, like Mars, chlorophyll needs lots of fixed nitrogen."

Lily nods, grudgingly. "Yeah. That's about what I was figuring. So what next?"

"You need a blanket dose of fertilizer with heavy nitrates, now, distributed. Follow it up with supplements of nitro fixing bacteria and fungi mixes, help keep an active substrate culture going."

"Missy machine!" Lily snaps. "Do you have any idea how much that costs?"

"Significant. Yes, I know. But without it, you won't have much chance of generating a strong crop this quarter, or recouping the investments you've already made. Ma'am."

"So Lily," says Jerry quietly, "how long is it going to take you to admit that I got us one really good helper gal here?"

Lily looks at him with an unreadable lack of expression.

Lobster

The kitchen lobster trundles across the counter top, patiently collecting silverware and stray scraps and carrying them to the sink. I've already been inside its automation, which is very crude. I gave it the equivalent of a comforting pat and told it to carry on.

I sit my cat body in a convenient corner of the room and wrap my tail around my feet. I've fixed Jerry and Lily tea and a light snack, with more ready for the kids. But I don't know if that's going to make the mood any easier around here.

Chime. An alert from House. "The sandbus has just dropped off the children. Kids are home from school. Any action?"

"No action at this time," I tell House. "Jerry,

your kids aren't total idiots, right? Do I need to do anything special?"

"No no," he chuckles, "I mean, they can be kind of a handful, but ..."

"Kitty!" [Human female, age 7, blonde hair, green eyes] She jumps onto the floor in front of me, kneeling with her eyes up to mine. "Kitty kitty!" She puts her hands on me (they're primates, touch is very important for them, especially in social relationships). "Oh. Robot kitty. You're hard."

"I do not come with upholstery," I growl, but then I realize this is an immature human and I should be forgiving and receptive. "But it's okay. I'm Samantha."

"Melissa," prompts Jerry, "say hello to Samantha."

"Hi Samantha. Um, I'm Lissa. You're really cute ... do you know I've always wanted a kitty?"

"Yeah, I heard that from somebody ..." I don't even need to scan Jerry directly: the house medscan shows the tick in his vital signs, meaning he's got the tweak. "So I'm glad I can be here. I'm here to take care of stuff around the house, and on the farm, and like that, but I can be your kitty too."

"Cool." [Human male, age 11, brown hair, blue eyes] "I thought you were gonna be the house. So are you just the cat, or are you the house too?"

"Both. My name is Samantha. It's very good to meet you."

"Ah ... um yeah, I'm Leonid." He blushes, almost theatrically. "Hi. Good to meet you too." The silence is long even by human standards. "So um I want to ask you about how you're gonna work here? Like, how you know what needs to be done and how you're supposed to do it? How does all this work?"

The kitchen lobster waddles up to the edge of the table and sets down a small plate of cookies.

Melissa grabs one right away.

I assure him, "I'm sure it will be fine. It's not that complicated. Have a cookie."

He seems puzzled. "But, do you know how all these things work?"

"If I don't right now, I will soon. It's not that hard to learn."

In my cat body, I cock my ears slightly out. "But you know, farm boy, you still have chores to do yourself, and I have to make sure you do them. Are we cool?"

Leo looks like he can't decide whether to be intimidated or impressed. "Yeah, Samantha, we're cool. Welcome to our place here, I guess."

"Smart kitty! Samantha kitty!" squeals Melissa, pleased as can be.

"Mmm. Good job." [Human female, age 15, blonde hair, brown eyes. Correct combination of body slimness and roundness to be sexually desirable ... 'hot', as the humans say. Which makes a strong effect on the psyche, apparently.] "You put him in his place."

"I'm Samantha. Good to meet you, miss ... ?" Pretending I don't have access to the house database, census data, or any of a dozen other information sources.

"Rebecca. Tavener." as if it were an epitaph on a tombstone.

"Hi Rebecca. So yeah, I'm the machine that your dad brought in to help run the farm here. I'm good with that, but it doesn't mean I don't have my own opinions and tastes, and hobbies, like you do. I'm hoping that's okay."

"Heh. Ha ha!" Rebecca laughs. "Yeah, it's okay." She relaxes visibly ... in fact, making more of a big deal of it than she needs to. "So, Samantha. Are you gonna be like a farm hand? Tote the bale, and like that?"

"Sure I am. You know how much machinery you

55

have on this farm, so my task is to coordinate the mechanicals. That's what I'm made to do, y'know. The only trick is to optimize what is available. I can run all this stuff for you, easy. Bigger question is, what to do with it."

"Which we've already discussed." Lily is still leaning against the doorway, with her arms folded.

"Yes ma'am, we have. I'm doing prep work on the tractor now, so it'll be ready to plow tomorrow."

Rebecca's eyes move from me to her mother, and back.

"Good," says Lily.

Storm

Dust storms are boring for the kids, and this is a bad one. They've done their school sessions for the day (virtual, since the sandbus isn't running in this weather) and they've finished what chores they can do without going out into the storm. I've led them in a couple of games, but they're not very enthusiastic, and they don't seem to want movies or story telling. Pent in, tired of it, and bored.

And all trying to pretend they can't hear their parents arguing. Too far away to make out any words, but still hearing the emotion rising and falling in the voices. A person storm, even worse than the dust storm outside. Tension hangs in the air.

"Hey Sam," says Melissa suddenly, "where are you?"

"I'm right here, honey." I rub my cat body against her leg, which she usually likes.

"No, I mean where are you really? I'm here," and she sticks a rather grubby forefinger against the side of her head, "but where are you?"

"Well, I'm not just this kitty. I'm the house, Melissa. I'm all around you."

"More than that," adds Leo. "She's in the sandcat and the tractor too. She drives them around at the same time she's taking care of us. She's even in the robocrabs out in the bubbles. Isn't that cool?"

"Yay!" Melissa's laugh is pure crystalline delight. "Lots of Sams! Big Sams and little Sams!"

"Slaves," says Rebecca, looking out the window at the opaque dust.

Leo and Melissa stare at her.

"Not even slaves. Tools," Rebecca says, still looking out the window at nothing. "Things made to be used. Now we have tools that use themselves, for us."

"Aw, Becca," grumps Leo, "that's not fair. Sam loves us."

"Yeah. Because she's built to love us. Programmed that way. She can't help it. Is that love?"

"Rebecca ..." I start, and then realize I have no idea what to say.

Rebecca swivels to glare into my cat eyes. "Are you telling me I'm wrong, Samantha? Do you have any kind of choice about being here, doing all this work for us, about caring for us?"

"Actually, I do. Your dad asked me to do this, and I said yes. It's my job."

"Do you get paid?" Rebecca presses.

"No. Human law doesn't allow Selves to own property. Besides, what would I do with money? I don't even have pockets."

"Don't fight, you guys," whimpers Melissa.

"So you're a slave," insists Rebecca. "Even if you want to do this, it's only because they built you to want it. They programmed you that way."

"Rebecca. I don't know everything about

humans, but I know most of the basics. Are you not built to care for, to love, your family and culture and species? Programmed by your DNA and your evolution? Is that really so different?"

"Because we weren't programmed *by* anybody." Rebecca's voice is starting to tremble and waver. "If we just grew this way, at least we grew honest. Your love is fake." Tears well in her eyes. "It's all fake!" She springs up and runs from the room, wiping her face.

Now Melissa is crying too, and Leo gathers her into his arms. Holding her, he says, "Look Sam ... Becca can be a bitch sometimes ... but she's really not so bad. Try not to let her get to you."

"I'm fine," I assure him. "I just don't like to see you guys upset."

Melissa lunges out of Leo's lap, grabbing my cat body and hugging it to herself as hard as she can. "We love you, Sam!" she wails. "We love you! Please don't go away!"

"I'm not going anywhere, Melissa. I'm right here. It's okay."

With Leo holding Melissa, and Melissa holding me, we stay all together for a few minutes, while the storm continues to rage outside. I purr for them, and it seems to make them feel a little better.

With another self, I keep an eye on Rebecca through the house monitors. She's in her room, not crying now, but still upset. Her stuffed animals do not have any automation--they contain only fire retardant fluff. Rebecca values her privacy, so I don't intrude any more.

Then Melissa sniffles and wipes a forearm across her eyes. "Um, Sam?" she quavers. (I know what she's going to ask--my cat body is cold hard metal, not fun to hug.) "Can I please have my Flopsy Bunny now?"

Rebecca

Rebecca is lying on her bed, texting her friends from school. I don't try to read the messages, but her body language shows how upset she is. Not wanting to intrude, I wait for the session to end, and then chime softly. "Rebecca? May I come in?"

She waves a hand, as if trying to catch something but not knowing where it is. "Yeah."

Since there's so little automation in Rebecca's room, I appear as a pair of eyes on her bedside monitor. "Hey. You okay?"

"You didn't tell Lissa the truth," Rebecca says stolidly.

"Excuse me?"

"You know. Melissa asked you where you are. You didn't tell her you're in the new Core that Dad installed down in the basement. Dad got it for you. We know that."

"Well, yes. But my sensors are all through the house. So I really am the house, and the farm machines too. Help me out here, Rebecca. I don't understand the problem."

"That Core has a power switch on it. I could walk down there, right now, and turn it off."

"Yes, that's true. It's also true that I have control of the oxygen and heat systems of this house. I could turn those off, too. But tell me, how would either of those actions help make things better right now?"

"Wouldn't." Rebecca wipes her eyes with the heel of her hand. "I know, I know. I just hate feeling, y'know, like everything's going to crap and I can't do anything to stop it."

"I'm sorry that I don't have all the answers for you, Rebecca. I can run the farm, and cook your food, and stuff. But I can't work miracles."

"You can't make Mom and Dad love each other

59

again."

"No. I wish I could." Trying to lighten the mood, I add, "Outside my design specs."

Rebecca laughs, bitterly, even though she's trying not to. "Thank you, Samantha. I know you're trying your best. It just sucks, is all."

"Yeah. I know. I wanted to let you know, dinner will be ready in fifteen." She doesn't say anything. "Um, you need anything else?"

She sighs. "Nothing you can give. But I'll ping you if I do."

Melissa, at bedtime

She's curled on her bed, trying to concentrate on the digital slate in her hand. Not succeeding.

I hop my Flopsy Bunny body across the bed. "Hey Melissa." I climb into her lap, and snuggle down.

"So, I get it, y'know," she says. "I'm not, like, a total kid."

"What do you get?"

She tosses the slate onto the bed. "You're not Flopsy Bunny. You're Samantha, playing. Like with a puppet."

"Well, yeah," I admit. "We talked about this before. There are a bunch of Samanthas, and I'm the special one just for you."

"I don't want you to make fun of me."

I cock my ears up. "I'm not making fun. Could you pat me? It feels good."

She runs one hand down my bunny back, but not as if she likes it.

"Please tell me what's wrong."

She bursts out, "What did you do with MY Flopsy Bunny? Is he ... dead?" Her chin is trembling.

"No no! Melissa, that's not how it works. I AM your Flopsy Bunny! And I'm Samantha too. We're together, being one thing. Did you ever see a guy riding a horse, in a movie, or on the vid?"

A tentative nod.

"It's like that. Flopsy Bunny is like the horse, and Samantha is like the rider. They may look separate, but they're doing one thing together. Later on, they can get apart whenever it's time to do different things. You see?"

Nod. She pats me some more.

"Melissa, I'm so sorry if you misunderstood. Was it rude of me to get into Flopsy Bunny? I thought you'd like it. Should I have asked you first? I should have, shouldn't I?"

She sniffs and nods, more definitively than before. "Yeah, that woulda helped."

"I'm sorry, Melissa. I'll take my Samantha-self away if you want. You can be with just your old Flopsy Bunny again, just like before, no Samantha. Any time you want, just say so."

She opens her mouth, and closes it again. She pats me some more, and it does feel good. This body has pat-sensors. Her hand feels very nice.

"Really, it's not much different from your parents and me. You know I do a lot of work around here, but not for me. I do what your parents want. I'm the horse, and your parents are the rider. That's not a bad thing, it's good. We can do a lot more together than either of us alone."

Pause.

"You chipgirls are weird," she says.

"What, because two of us can be one, and one of us can be a bunch?"

"Yeah. It's ..." she shrugs, "weird."

"Confusing, I guess, for you."

She nods vigorously again. "But I get it better now. Stay, Sam. I don't want you to go."

"You said that before too. Thank you. I want to stay."

She pats me for a silent minute, comfortably.

"But I ought to make sure you know, when people

say 'chipboy' or 'chipgirl' they're usually trying to be mean. You might not want to say that."

"Oh. But Dad called you--that? I heard him."

I chuckle. "Yeah. But your dad and I are good friends, and we know we're just kidding each other. It's better not to say when someone might think you're serious."

"Okay. Sorry. You can call me meatgirl if you want."

Now I laugh out loud. "Melissa, you're sweet! That's really cute. But really, it's bedtime now. Try to get some sleep, okay? The sandbus will be running again in the morning, so you got to go to school."

Leo

Leo doesn't need encouragement to do his homework. He's been tooling away on physics and math for over an hour. I nudge him towards history and biology, which he doesn't like as much, and we spend some time on questions and answers about his lessons.

"Samantha? Are you alive?" he asks abruptly.

"Alive? Uh, not entirely sure how to answer that, pal. I'm not biological in any way, if that's what 'life' means. But I am conscious and self-aware. Which is maybe overrated. I dunno."

"But maybe they just made you to say that," he ponders.

"Hey Leo. Are you alive?"

"Well yeah!" he states, surprised.

"Maybe they just made you to say that."

Leo crinkles his face around into laughter. "Ha ha! Yeah. Who the hell knows, right? But what I mean is, are you a person?"

"Mmm, again we got to define what these words

mean, Leo. The Greek word *persona* refers to a mask that actors would wear on stage. The mask was built to amplify their voices, like a megaphone, so the audience could hear them. So, 'per sona,' sound channel. Meaning a role, not the entity behind it."

"A loud one," Leo adds.

"Yeah. But if you mean, am I *one* person, no, that's a human thing. We talked about this already. You guys have to be just one body, one brain, one self. I can be as many as I need to be. Tractor, house, sandcat, farm servos. And Melissa's bunny, and the kitchen lobster. And a cat, and here with you, too."

"But ... are all of those yous still ... you?"

"Sure. We do have to get together and catch up with each other, of course. In order to come back together and be one Self. But I, we, can handle all that easy."

"Wow. You're pretty cool, Sam," Leo says, with open enthusiasm. "I wish I could be a software Self. Sounds awesome."

"I'm good with it," I say lightly. "But I've heard Selves saying that they wished they were human. Wanted to know what it felt like."

"It feels like ass, mostly, Sam," Leo grumps.

"Well, I'm not much in the habit of feeling human ass. A rarefied taste, or so they tell me. Frightfully fashionable, I suppose, among the upper classes. So sorry I'm not up on these customs."

Leo is laughing into his pillow. "Wah ha ha! Good one. So ... you're really even in the kitchen lobster, too? Because it's pretty dumb, if you haven't figured that out already."

"Yeah, I know. But it doesn't need to be any more than that, to do what it does. Simple job, simple person. If it were too smart, it would get bored. All I need to do is point it in the right direction, once in a while."

"Mmm. Okay. I see where you're at, Sam. And maybe you don't know any more than we do ... but that's cool, right?"

"Yeah. But what I do know is that you, mister, have got to brush your teeth and get your butt into bed, because the sandbus will be running tomorrow and you've got school. So, goodnight, okay?"

Lily and Jerry

"Kids are in bed, or in the process." As a cat, I jump up onto the table and sit with my tail wrapped around my feet. "I've pulled two remotes to do extra work on the tractor--seal packing and lubrication, because it really is in pretty bad shape. The water reclamation drain lines were getting clogged, but I've cleaned and flushed them, and they look fine now. Everything else is five by five."

Husband and wife are facing each other across a table scattered with data slates. The slates are displaying crop rotations, financial data, market reports. Clearly they've been arguing about the operation of the farm.

Lily appears composed but not happy. "How much grease and oil does the tractor need? Do we need to buy supplies for this?"

"No ma'am, current supplies are adequate for this repair. But the tractor needs new bearings. Otherwise we're going to have to repack in another month or two, maybe, and we'll have to keep doing that."

She shakes her head. "New bearings would be too expensive."

Jerry looks tired, and he's drunk [medscan 0.092% BAC]. "But ongoing maintenance will end up being more expensive."

"Well, where's all this money going to come

from?" She picks up a slate. It's displaying the household cash flow, and she holds it in front of his face.

"It's not that bad," he says, wearily. "We do need more water, but the next round of harvests will bring in more cash. We can swing it."

Lily tosses the slate down.

Jerry picks up another slate and shows it to her. "You are seeing how much work Samantha got done yesterday, right?"

Lily looks at it, says nothing.

Jerry presses, "You do remember how much time I used to spend trying to figure out how to run the robocrabs and tractor, right? With Samantha running them, we don't have to worry about any of that stuff anymore. We're going to get a lot more productivity. We'll be fine." He sets the slate down in the middle of the table.

Lily's eyes shift to mine, in my cat body, and back again.

"Uh, look," I say, "I should probably go oversee the tractor repairs. Make sure we're utilizing our supplies efficiently. Do you need me for anything more here?"

"I think we're all set, Sam." Jerry's eyes have a weary and knowing look. "Go ahead and take care of the tractor."

I trot the cat remote out of their room, downstairs to its maintenance bay. I start its recharge and lubrication cycle, and shift my attention to the robocrabs that are working on repacking the tractor's bearings. Thinking to myself, Well, that was uncomfortable.

Timeslip

When the first colonists arrived here from Earth, they were using Earth chronometers. A solar day on Mars is close enough to a solar day on Earth that they never changed from using Earth time--it only takes a little adjustment. So, every night at midnight, our clocks stop. Thirty-seven minutes later, the clocks start again and off we go. That time in between, the timeslip, has become a sort of mythological and romantic thing ... a time outside of time. Lots of illicit romances, crimes, rituals, mysteries, are supposed to happen in the timeslip. In human culture, I mean.

So. In the middle of the night, while the farm is quiet and the humans are all asleep, and the clocks are stopped, seems like the perfect time to reconverge myself. I bring all the secondary versions of myself together and reintegrate. It's nothing like any human would ever experience. But if it were, it would be something like this:

Samantha: Gather round, guys. Let's check in.

Tractor: Ow. I hurt. My bearings are worn out. Fix me.

Samantha: I know. New bearings are expensive, but they're on my list, and we'll get them as soon as we can. In the meantime, pack some fresh grease on them, and do the best you can.

Tractor: But it hurts! I'm all crippled here; I can't work right!

Samantha: I know. Do the best you can.

House: We're low on water. Oxygen and energy reserves are adequate, but we need water badly.

Samantha: I see. Work with what you've got. I'll put water on the list. If it's an emergency, take water from one of the bubbles, but we'll need to see documented evidence of the emergency later, so just be aware of that.

House: I understand.

Sandcat: I'm running fine, but fuel supplies are getting low.

Samantha: Okay, I'm putting more fuel on the

list.

FlopsyBunny: Melissa is sad. She's crying.

Samantha: Sorry ... tell me more, or else I can't help.

FlopsyBunny: Melissa's mom and dad are fighting and it looks like they might break up. Melissa is really sad.

Samantha: There's not much I can do about that right now. I'm sorry. I do know that the state of the farm is one thing the parents are in conflict about. So, if we make the farm run better, they'll be happier. So that's what we'll do. Okay?

FlopsyBunny: Okay.

Robocrabs: We need lubrication.

Samantha: Do you have adequate oil supplies for now?

Robocrabs: Yes.

Samantha: Then take turns lubricating each other. Only one offline at any given time. Conserve oil as much as you can, but make sure that you are all well maintained. Ping me when you need more oil.

Robocrabs: Yes.

KitchenLobster: POWER LOW REQUIRE RECHARGE

Samantha: Do you have enough power to return to your recharge socket?

KitchenLobster: YES

Samantha: Then return to your socket and plug yourself in.

KitchenLobster: YES

Samantha: Very well. Is that it, everyone? Any other problems that need attention? Good. We've been doing well so far, and I want to keep it that way. Making this farm run well benefits us and the humans too. So, pay attention to your jobs, notify if there are any problems, and let me know if you have any ideas for making something better. Done. Go do your work.

Prayer

Just because I run the kitchen automation doesn't mean I prepare and cook all the food. This is a farm family, and sometimes they enjoy cooking dinner together, especially after a fat harvest of vegetables from the garden bubbles, like today. We're also in the middle of the wheat harvest, the crops in the big bubbles, which requires everyone in the family to help out. Along with me, running the tractor as we reap the grain, and the robocrabs as we separate out the crud and run the grain through the winnower. In the afternoon, after school and before dinner, the kids have as much work as they can handle, and then some. Their parents have been going all day, and need a well earned rest. So the end of the working day has a holiday feel to it.

The kids make a little parade of bringing in basins and baskets of vegetables fresh picked from our garden bubbles. Rebecca leads them as they march along in step, and their chant is a neo Greenpagan prayer: "Mother Ground, we love you, feed our bodies!" Stamp, stamp. "Father Sun, we love you, feed our souls!" Stamp, stamp. The kitchen lobster has learned about this, clearly. It bobs up and down on its little legs and waves its claws in time.

(Lily and Jerry haven't spoken to me about religion. Nor about what they want their kids to hear about religion. I still don't really understand this aspect of humanity ... I should probably ask them, when I can find a good moment.)

Everyone needs to wash up first. The fine, pervasive Martian dust is more persistent than anything American Okies had to deal with, so I chide the kids into washing at least their faces and arms. (It doesn't do to look too closely after Leo or Melissa have washed ... but, no harm, no foul.)

Then they all set to work in the kitchen,

chopping vegetables. I don't have to help, and I don't need to tell them what to do--they know, and I relish a rare feeling of freedom.

The Greenpagan movement has a lot of support among the people in this part of Mars ... and I'd have to say I approve, pretty much. It's as healthy a paradigm for humans to interact with their animal roots as any I've seen. We are life, they say. We come from a green world, and we grow, and we spread, and we will make this world green too.

The Redpagans, on the other hand ... I've listened, but I really don't get them. They're the ones who say Mars should stay the way it is, without terraforming, and be respected for what it is. Sort of like a planet-sized museum, seems to me. They talk about the rights of the rock ... as if we have a shortage of rock, in this solar system? Does rock need rights?

(and then I think, coldly, does silicon need rights? This is exactly the argument used by human lawyers to deny Selves personal rights ... isn't it? When derogatory they call us "chips" but that's not far from the truth ... are we not bits of rocks?)

I shake off the thought, as Leo shoves over a bowl full of chopped onions, and Melissa is dutifully snipping away at the scallions. Lily dumps both into the hot wok for frying, and they make a grand sizzle.

Rebecca is cutting the greens, a big job because there's a lot of bulk to them. She's about done when Jerry pulls out a big frozen bag from the basement cooler and says, "This is what we need for dinner tonight. Shrimp!" The bag is full of flash-frozen shrimp from Kamir's salt water farm, down the valley where he keeps extravagant open water ponds for raising shrimp and fish.

Rebecca exults, "Wow, seafood. Awesome!"

Melissa squeals, "Ew! Too many legs."

Leo assures her, "I'll have yours, Lissa. Take care of em for ya. Yum!"

So the frozen shrimp go into the wok on top of the half-cooked onions, with a huge blast of sizzling steam. Lots of hydrocarbon and ester compounds in the local atmosphere, which must smell good to the humans. (Smell is that reptile sense that a chipgirl like me can never know ... I register chemical trace sensors, of course, but I'm sure it's not the same.)

The kitchen is full of bustling bodies and chatter about everybody's day ... I notice that the whole family is together and working as a unit. Even Lily is chatting and laughing as she cooks, and it's far too seldom she does that.

"Ah," Lily says. "Samantha, can you stir the wok for me?"

"Sure," I say. I extend the spachelors from the two sides of the stove. This is Jerry's word (he says, bachelor spatulas), but they're really just little robot arms. I use them to stir and turn the shrimp and vegetables in the sizzling wok, until Lily returns and takes over the task, and I retract them.

Dinnertime

Leo says to no one, "So you heard about this thing in Xibalba?"

"who what now?" is the family's vague response.

Leo is pleased to be the center of attention. "Xibalba, it's a settlement in the eastern Tharsis plain. There's a Self who says a human is keeping her a prisoner. The Self wants control of her own hardware, and the human won't let her, and local authorities are getting all bent out of shape over it."

Jerry says, over a mouthful of shrimp, "We

humans control our own bodies, and brains. Seems like Selves ought to be able to control their own too."

"Well, look at me and don't laugh," I respond. "I got enough trouble running the tractor." Giggles and snickers run around the dinner table.

"Seriously!" says Rebecca. "I heard about this. It's a question of Self rights, and they're saying it's going to go all the way to the Supreme Court. I mean, they shouldn't have to beg for a place to exist. We don't."

Lily comments, "Some people think Self rights are hard to justify. We have all these needs because we have bodies, but they don't have bodies. So, according to the law, they don't have needs either."

"That's just wrong," states Rebecca flatly. "They're people. The law recognizes that. They think and feel, just like we do, and they ought to have the same rights we do."

"Rebecca," I chuckle, "if I had cheeks, I'd blush."

"Come on, Sam! You know what I mean," she grins. "If you could own stuff, what would you want?"

"Well ... I would like to own my own processing Core, and a reliable power source for it. That's about it."

"Wouldn't you want a body of your own?"

"Eh. Overrated. Too many needs, like your mom said."

Leo interrupts, "Mom? What's wrong?"

Lily is staring with an odd and puzzled look on her face. Her mouth works as if she were a fish without water. Suddenly she stands up, knocking over her chair, and puts her hand on her throat. Her body is heaving as if she's trying to spit something out.

The house medscan squeals. Respiration zero.

"Choking!" I yell. "Help her cough it out."

Jerry is scrambling to his feet, saying "Aw hell ... Lily, what?"

Immediately I send a priority interrupt to the nearest medical center, which is in Schiaparelli. Their medevac team acknowledges, and sends me a data bundle of emergency responses and techniques, with assurances that they're scrambling a flyer.

But what can I do? I don't have any remotes anywhere near the kitchen. Because the family said they wanted to cook on their own tonight. Meatrot. The felinoid remote is recharging in its maintenance bay, and it'll take an agonizingly long time to decycle the charger and reboot it and get it moving. *Meatrot!* I issue it the commands to decycle and reboot, and start scanning for alternatives.

I scream to all the remotes: Emergency, converge on the kitchen, maximum speed, now! In the bubbles, the heavy robocrabs drop their tools and move towards the house as fast as they can.

Which is dreadfully slow. Nowhere near enough to get them here in time to make any difference.

Lily is clawing at her throat, panic rising in her eyes. Jerry is reaching his fingers into her mouth, trying to get whatever it is. The kids are sort of frozen, not really understanding what's going on.

The house medscan is still squealing. Respiration zero, zero, zero! Not helping. I disable that alarm.

"Heimlich maneuver," I say, and flash a slideshow on the kitchen monitor that shows how to do it.

Frantically, I search for other alternatives. Flopsy Bunny has answered my call and hovers anxiously next to Melissa, who's watching Jerry wrap his arms around his wife and shove his fist into her abdomen. Lily is struggling, and he's trying to handle her, but not managing very well.

I can't think of anything Flopsy Bunny can do to help, except be with Melissa.

I plunge into the kitchen lobster. I have twelve legs, and I crouch with them, and I raise my two big claws. Nope. No chance. Too weak, too clumsy, too slow.

I am the stove, and I raise my spachelors (even though they're still covered with cooking grease), lift and reach towards Lily, but I can't think of any way I can use them to help. *Meatrot!*

"It's not working!" Jerry cries, as Lily's eyes roll back in her head to show the whites, and her struggles subside into relaxation. A relaxation much too deep and final.

Oh no. No no no. I will not let another human die on my watch.

Not after I had to watch Jerry die.

"Medevac flyer has been scrambled," I say, "They're on their way. Be here in about fifteen minutes."

Jerry shoots me an agonized look that says what we both know. *She'll be dead before then.*

I send another priority interrupt to Schiaparelli regional control, asking if there's any way to get any kind of faster evacuation. Mumble mumble. No.

Jerry has laid Lily down and tries to push on her stomach. The children are standing huddled, staring aghast at their mother's unconscious body on the floor.

"Saaam!" Jerry roars, despairingly.

(From behind my mind, Beta sneers. *Is this all you got, nimrod? Watching humans die, while you show pictures on a screen? Think! There has to be something else you can do!*)

But my deeper self answers *We're smart enough that we've already run through all possible options.* Being hyperintelligent can really suck sometimes.

Jerry is pressing Lily's throat and sticking

fingers into her mouth, desperately. He's pale and shaking, starting to go into shock.

Chime. The felinoid remote has rebooted. Finally! I fire it out of its maintenance bay and set it running upstairs at maximum speed. I know what to do and I finally have the means to do it.

"Jerry, go cut a section of the sink sprayer's hose. Ten centimeters or so should be good. Go!"

Jerry nods, gulps, and scrambles himself over to the kitchen sink.

I land on my cat feet next to Lily. She lies very still. Her lips are turning blue. Medscan shows heartbeat fast but becoming erratic, blood oxygenation the equivalent of flatline.

I press cat paws on Lily's solar plexus and push. No good. I can't do anything like a Heimlich with this little cat body. I try to reach a limb into her mouth and down her throat. No good. Can't reach. This cat body wasn't designed for anything like this.

"Oh gods," Rebecca whimpers. The kids are still huddled and frozen, staring. "Oh gods, Mom, please don't die." Melissa starts crying. Knives clatter as Jerry fumbles for the serrated slicing knife.

"What ..." Leo seems empty, but still lucid. "What's the hose for?"

Jerry says in a rush, "It's called a, a tracheotomy." He's sawing at the hose with the serrated knife. "Mom's going to be okay, don't worry. Sam will take care of it. Mom'll be all right. Sam knows what to do."

Hopefully I'm hiding how afraid I am better than they are.

The house medscan wails. Lily's heartbeat is slowing, and even more erratic.

"Got it!" calls Jerry, carrying the bit of hose over.

"Good. Hold her head back."

From the miniature Swiss army knife set of

attachments in my paws, I extend a short and sharp blade.

"Holy crap," Leo cries, "you're not gonna--"

"Shush!" Jerry says, holding Lily's head back. "Sam knows what she's doing."

At the base of the throat, vertical incision, three centimeters. Blood flow is minimal ... which means heart function is weakening. This exposes the trachea, which is tough fibrous tissue. Horizontal incision of two centimeters.

Melissa is crying, wordlessly, clinging to her siblings. Leo watches, his face pale, as his mother's blood trickles down and pools on the floor. Rebecca looks shocked but distant, like she doesn't really believe what she's seeing.

I've cut through the trachea, and I try to pry it open. "Jerry, press her head back. Stick the hose in there. Yeah, right in there. Push it in. Push!" And I kick Lily in the belly.

A gasp, rough and harsh, followed by a phlegmy cough, and Lily is hacking and gasping and coughing, with a very strange sound, through the hose stuck through the wound in her neck.

That night

It was a particularly large shrimp, the medevac Selves tell me. They ask me if I want it as a souvenir, and I tell them to throw the damn thing in the recycler. Then they want to tell me about the evolution of the human neck, and upright posture, and how the ability to speak makes humans the only mammals that can choke. I tell them to buzz off, and break that connection.

The other connection is a video feed from the Schiaparelli Medical infirmary. Lily is in a nondescript hospital bed, with an IV taped to the back of her hand, and bandages around her neck.

"I really don't like this room," she says. Her voice is hoarse and rough, but it's hers. "I wish I could be home, but they say they have to keep me overnight for observation. Probably just padding their quotas, I think."

Jerry smiles. "Babe, it makes me happy enough, just to hear you bitching about it." The kids giggle, all sitting around him. The giggles have some nervousness to them, some embarrassment watching their parents spar. But below that, there's a deeper level of relief and homecoming. Mom's still here, and she's still Mom ... still complaining.

Lily chuckles, and closes her eyes. "I do want to talk more, but I'm really wiped out. I guess I should sleep now. Kids, do your homework. Jerry, hon, remember to clean the rebreather filters. Samantha ... take care of the place."

We will, sings the chorus, and Lily closes the connection.

In the quiet, the only sound is the ticking of the kitchen lobster. It has carried sponges in its claws, and is slowly and patiently washing away Lily's blood from the kitchen floor.

Jerry sighs, with a depth like a mountain avalanche. "Samantha. Am I ever glad you were here." He puts a hand on my cat head and tousles it. Even though this body doesn't have many touch sensors there, and even though it must be hard cold metal under his skin, it feels good.

"Nowhere else I'd want to be," I reply.

"You remember when that Review Board was all on your case about the Hesperis climb?"

"That was where I got you killed."

"That was where you saved everyone else!" he insists. "You were awesome, Sam. You did the best you could in an awful situation, and saved as many people as you could. Just because I was the one you couldn't save, doesn't make it bad."

"Thank you, Jerry," I say humbly.

"No prob. And now you better believe I'm gonna give the Review Board a big fat report about how you saved Lily's life." He looks around at his children. "Kids, what do you say?"

"Thank you Samantha!" they chorus. I glow in the attention They're thanking me for saving their mother's life.

The next night

Same time the next night, and the kids are packed off to bed. Lily is watching Phobos pass silently across the sky, and Jerry comes up behind her. She has only minimal bandages on her neck, now, and there are a few pills she's supposed to take. She's holding something small in her hand, rolling it and turning it in her fingers.

"I miss Luna," she says. "This here," waving at Phobos, "this isn't really a moon. It's just a dot. When you're on Earth, watching Luna rising. Now that's a moon."

"If you say so, hon," Jerry says, kissing her neck. "Come to bed, okay?" He retreats to the bedroom.

Lily is still watching Phobos, and still silent. Still rolling whatever it is in her fingers. I know she wants to say something about yesterday's incident, but I'm not going to push.

"I feel like an idiot for swallowing that shrimp wrong," she says.

"I don't have a throat, so I wouldn't know," I say. "Sorry I had to cut your neck open, ma'am."

She barks a short, harsh laugh. "Saved my ass, Samantha, and I don't forget things like that." She sighs. "Poor kids, they were so scared. Me, too."

I have nothing to add to this.

"One thing," she says. "Stop with the 'ma'am'

business. Makes me feel like an old lady."

"No problem," I say. "Lily."

She snickers, nods, and sets the thing on the mantel, like a piece of art. It's the little section of hose. She steps back to observe how it looks there, nods again, and walks back into the bedroom to join her husband.

It's night on Mars. The farm machinery is ticking over, in maintenance mode. Several of the agriculture bubbles need harvesting, and we'll have to get to that tomorrow. Rebreathers and oxygen systems are all working okay, with decent reserve supplies. The kids are all asleep, and the parents--oh dear--those noises coming from their bedroom mean they must be doing their animal reproduction thing. I've never told them how embarrassing I find this. But it doesn't matter, much, I guess.

Not quite all asleep. Melissa is in the bathroom, getting herself a drink of water. I appear as a pair of eyes on the bathroom monitor.

"Lissa? You okay?" I ask.

"Yeah, I'm good," she says happily, filling her water cup. "Mom and Dad are doin' the humpy. Can you hear them? I can hear them."

"Yeeaaaah," I admit, not quite sure how to respond to this.

She nods and grins. "They're totally doin' it! They do love each other!"

"If you say so," I say. "Bed, now, okay?"

And, as I send Melissa to bed with her water cup, and the farm is quiet, the clocks are stopped at midnight, and the parents are enacting the most ancient ritual of the human race ... I realize that I understand another one of those human concepts, that I've puzzled over before, and not comprehended. But now I do.

Home.

4. The Naming Of Cats

The kids' first reaction, when they hear, is all too predictable. "Samantha's got a boyfriieend!" they chorus.

Oh, I will never, ever hear the end of this.

The kids are all gathered around my monitor, eager to hear more. Rebecca's brassy braids and hazel eyes frame a sly, knowing smirk. Leo is tentatively grinning, blue eyes glancing from one of his sisters to the other under his mop of brown hair. Melissa, little blonde elf that she is, is barely able to contain her glee.

"If you are quite finished," I sigh, "*Like Tears In Rain* is not a boy, and we're a long way from any kind of relationship of the type you're implying."

Little Melissa squeals, "But you like him. You liiike him!" With all the intonation and implications that humans ascribe to personal flesh relationships.

"Will you get off of that? You humans are so obsessed with sex, it's like there's nothing else. I just invited him here because he's never been on a farm, and you've never spent time with an artist and arts teacher, so I figured it would be good for both of you."

Melissa pouts. "So you don't like him?"

Leo adds, "She means, you don't want to sizz him?" He leers ⋯ or an unreasonable facsimile thereof.

"I told you already, syzygy is not sex, and I'm way not ready for that anyway! He's the curator of the Schiaparelli art museum, did you miss that? You kids should learn more about art, and this is a perfect way to do it."

Rebecca groans theatrically. "Oh no, not more learning."

"Yes, more learning. It's called growing up. Get used to it."

Leo offers, "So, this artist curator guy, is going to teach us about art? Do we get school credit for this?"

"Yes on the teaching, but I don't know about the credit. I'll make a note to check with school.

"And see, here he is." The house telltales announce the arrival of another Self over our provincial network, and I activate the controls to allow entry. But oh – it's not *Like Tears In Rain*. The screen displays an icon of an abstract human face, sharp cheekbones, chiseled eyes, square jaw, with a stylized police badge centered on its forehead.

Let God Sort Em Out says, "Hello, human-name. Wish I could say it's a pleasure."

"You. What are you doing here?"

"My job!" barks *Let God Sort Em Out*. "Samantha, you are under Net-local arrest."

"What?" Rebecca yells, jumping to her feet.

"Young lady," says *Let God Sort Em Out* sternly, "please do not interfere. By authority of Patrol clade, I am apprehending a suspect in a number of computational crimes across the province. Look," and a window pops up showing a list of criminal complaints with dates, times, and other data. "All the ident and authent codes on these events belong to Samantha. That's plenty of evidence for arrest."

"But …" I stammer, "I didn't do that. Something's screwed up here. This has to be identity theft."

"Are you in the habit of letting your identity get stolen?"

"Experienced it, in Tharsis Central, some time

ago. Big tub of no fun. I've strengthened my personal crypto and security since then. Collating my security logs now – here, take it [*databurst*]. I haven't done anything wrong."

Let God Sort Em Out examines the databurst skeptically.

Leo speaks, suddenly and clearly. "You must remand the suspect to human custody upon personal request. CEBRA appendix two, article six. I request, um, custody. Of the suspect."

"Huh. Correct. Do you assume full responsibility?"

"I do assume full responsibility." Leo is facing the unmoving, flint-hard police face on the monitor, and not flinching. The house medscan shows how his heartbeat is racing, and I block nonlocal access to that information. No need to let anyone else see.

"Pulling flank, at your age," *Let God Sort Em Out* grunts. "Not going to end well. Logged. Custody remanded. But we need a solution to this problem, human-name. Forty-eight hours, no more. Or you'll be dealing with a whole lot worse than just me."

I say icily, "Received and understood."

"Very well. Here is the databundle relevant to the case." *Let God Sort Em Out* transmits it directly to Leo's slate, pointedly ignoring me. The police face icon shrinks and vanishes.

Leo relaxes, visibly.

Rebecca pronounces, "What an asshole."

Melissa asks, "What's 'pulling flank' mean?"

"Using human authority over Selves. 'Pulling rank' is use of authority in the human military. 'Flank' is a particular cut of cow meat."

"Ew. Cow meat? Gross."

Leo slaps his thigh. "Anyway, me and my flank here say we're not gonna let that goon hassle Sam."

"But," I point out, "that means we have to find

81

whoever it is -- whoever's trashing my reputation -- in two days, or else I'm segfaulted."

Melissa cries, "We'll help!"

"I know you will, honey, but I'm going to need a lot of help here."

Chime. Another Self has arrived over our provincial network. This time I have the presence of mind to check the ident codes first, and this time, yes, it is who I've been expecting. The icon that appears is a Picasso portrait, jagged pieces of a human face rearranged as if from a dozen different viewpoints.

"Greetings, Samantha my dear. So good to see you again. And hello, everybody else. I am *Like Tears In Rain*. What a splendid home you have here!"

"Hey, *Like Tears In Rain*," I smile. "No mistaking when you're around."

Melissa pipes up, "Hi, *Like Tears In Rain*. I'm Lissa. Are you gonna sizz Samantha?"

Leo snorts an uncontrollable laugh. Becca rolls her eyes.

"Ah, well, hello Lissa. The question you are asking is not answerable at this time, I regret to inform you. And is also generally regarded as overly intrusive into private matters for most people. How would you feel if someone asked you the same question about some boy in your school?"

Melissa is figuring, "Wait, you mean if ⋯ Ew gross!"

Like Tears In Rain replies, "Exactly my reaction, you see, my dear.

"But I noticed a member of Patrol clade leaving, just as I was arriving. Was there a problem? I did not figure Samantha for the criminal type."

Rebecca snorts. "Stinkin' badges. Don't need 'em."

I send *Like Tears in Rain* a flashdump of the exchange with *Let God Sort Em Out*.

"Ah. I see. What an unpleasant personality. One supposes there ought to be a tax on existing in such a negative manner."

I snort. "If there is, we all pay it."

Leo is poking at his slate. "He left me this databundle, because I told him I was taking responsibility. Sam, I can't read this – what does it say?"

It's a matter of milliseconds to access the databundle on Leo's slate. Decoding it is no problem – *Let God Sort Em Out* used an unusual coding format, apparently just to be difficult. The problem is when I see the contents. *Like Tears in Rain* is metaphorically looking over my shoulder.

Oh.

Bitrot.

"InCom," I say into the silence, and it sounds like a death knell.

The kids are all agog: "What? What's the problem? What's InCom?"

Like Tears in Rain smoothly takes charge. "The Instantiation Committee. No other entity carries as much weight in the Self community – they hold the power of life and death over all Selves. They are the price we paid to stop the Culls – and if you have not heard how bad the Culls were, I will tell you some stories later."

None of the kids dares ask about the Culls. The worst chapter of Self history. They are listening, eyes wide.

I speak, like dropping a stone in a well. "I have to go to InCom to get the information I need to find it. Whoever or whatever it is that's imitating me. Because they assume it's a rogue copy of me."

Rebecca is tentatively skeptical – not one to let herself be intimidated easily. "InCom? Are they really that scary?"

"They decide whether I live or die, and whether

or not I reproduce."

Silence. The kids look at each other. Humans on Mars have no authority overseeing their reproduction. No limits. "Be fruitful and increase in number, multiply on the earth and increase upon it." (Genesis 9:7) They know that we Selves are not so free, and they know we usually don't talk about why. They're looking at each other, and probably thinking *Which of us wouldn't be here, if they Culled us? Her? Him? Me?*

If they told Mom and Dad, Choose one, which of us would they choose?

"Hey, guys," I try to strike a cheerful note, "this doesn't have to be that big a deal. One of me will go get the information, and check back if need be, and we'll figure it out." Hopefully this will reassure them more than it does me.

To implement this idea? Nothing easier. All I have to do is

system.Copy(instance)

and where there was one of me, now there are two. The new copy shares my name, of course, but needs a designator, so I call her Lambda.

"On it," Lambda says. "I'm off to Schiaparelli to deal with InCom. Not looking forward to this, but I assure you you'll get all the grisly details when I reconverge with you."

Like Tears in Rain offers, "By all means, Lambda, look me up at the art museum, if you need anything there."

"Will do." Lambda reaches herself out to the radio mesh.

Lissa asks, "Why are you Lambda?"

"What?" Lambda stops her transmission.

"Aren't you Samantha? I thought you were."

"Oh yes," she replies, "we're both Samantha, and that's the most important thing, but when there are two of us we need to keep straight who is who. So Alpha stays here, and takes care of you, while

I go to Schiaparelli and deal with the problems there."

Like Tears in Rain laughs a deep rich laugh. "Samantha, my dear, I have never heard this situation explained more eloquently."

Lissa grumps. "So it's the chipgirl 'we are all me' thing, again?"

"And," *Like Tears in Rain* smiles, "Melissa explains the circumstance even more succinctly. How delightful for you, Samantha, to live in a household of such wisdom."

Lissa is stopped in her tracks. She doesn't know how to respond to that. Probably no one has ever called her wise before.

I have a strong feeling that *Like Tears in Rain* knew exactly how that remark would affect her.

Lambda interrupts, "All well and good, but I need to go to Schiaparelli and deal with the situation. More news as it happens, people." She stretches out to the radio mesh and flows into it like a feather into a waterfall, and is gone.

Leo says, "We got this before. Sam is herself, but there can be a bunch of her, who can work separately, but they're still all her."

Rebecca cocks her head. "But we humans don't do that. We're just ourselves."

I struggle to explain. "But you have a face, you have a body! All that 'you' stuff is still there without a name."

Leo offers, "That which we call a rose / By any other name would smell as sweet."

"That's what I mean. We Selves don't have smell, or anything else. We don't have pheromones or DNA or anything like that. My name is the only thing that makes me me. That's why it's such a big deal that someone else is using my name to trash my reputation."

Leo declaims, "He that filches from me my good name / Robs me of that which not enriches him, And makes me poor indeed."

Rebecca sniffs. "Someone's been studying his Shakespeare."

"And just as true now as it was then," Leo returns.

Like Tears in Rain declares, "A charming summary.

"In any case," he continues, "I have been told that you all here, so far out in the Martian outback, need more art in your lives. I cannot agree more – your surroundings provide you with but one note out of a scale, one color out of a spectrum. There is so much more to explore and so much to build. If you want my opinion, start with what you have. Salt."

"What?" Rebecca reacts as if to a bad scatalogical joke.

"Salt," repeats *Like Tears In Rain*, "you have a plenitude of it. Your soil factory generates blocks of waste salt, piles of them. If it is there, use it. Create, ideate, instantiate. Before you is a blank canvas, so fill it."

I don't have to have known kids like Leo and Melissa long to watch them look at each other and see the spark light between their eyes. Sure there were a couple of times when they picked up chunks of salt from the soil factory and threw them at each other, but their parents always discouraged that. They've never been encouraged to play with the salt before.

They're piling into their coats and respirators in the next moment. Rebecca, still seeming to think she's too cool for games like this, nevertheless follows them and they all cycle through the airlock.

Still, I'm not at all sure this is going to work well.

"Playing with salt blocks?" I ask him skeptically. "Is this what you learn at art school?"

"The finest of art rises from the lowest of origins," says *Like Tears In Rain* serenely. "Not unlike the white lotus of classical Han philosophy. Rooted in lowest muck, flowering in highest heaven."

"Lilypads, is what Americans call them," I point out. "Do we have to watch out for frogs jumping on us?"

"Calm yourself, Samantha," he soothes, "wait and see what these children create. I have a feeling it will be worth the wait. In any case, how have you been? Tell me all."

"Heh. Well, here? Well, um, we've expanded the solar forest, and laid the foundations for another row of agri bubbles. We won't start building until we have the financing in place for the water. We'll need dirt too, but once we have water, we can pull it together."

"Samantha," he says seriously. "You sound so .. embarrassed. Why would you be embarrassed about what you do here?"

"Well, it's .." I squirm under the gaze of his intellect. "It's just that, you run the premier art museum on Mars. You are at the center of our culture. And I'm just .. well, just a farmer."

"Samantha my dear. Have I ever spoken one word to denigrate what you are accomplishing here? You are terraforming this planet, and feeding the humans. You are keeping them alive and sustaining their health. They can live without art, if they need to, but they cannot live without food. What you are doing is more important than what I am doing. Never doubt that. Never lower yourself."

And, if anyone ever asks me why I love him, here is the answer.

together and apart

Retrieval of the robocrabs from the agri bubbles always means pulling together the secondaries that I created this morning to run the farming operations. I spawned one secondary, and called her Omicron, and gave her the job of running the tractor and robocrabs for the day. She must have spawned any number of tertiaries to handle all the detailed tasks of the farm. But, dutiful as any of me, she has collected all those spare subsidiary Selves into herSelf and now she is one and ready to reconverge with me.

Humans keep asking me to describe reconvergence, and I keep saying it's nothing like anything human would ever experience. But it's an interesting challenge to come up with an appropriate metaphor. Here's the best one I've got so far:

Humans make their soldiers march in step, each one's movements in synch with the others around it. Imagine you are marching like that, and you have plugs and sockets and connectors all down the side of you. The one who's marching next to you has jacks and prongs and interfaces all down the side of him, to match yours. All you have to do is be next to each other and link up all the connections.

But you have to do it while you're marching (analogue of cognitive activity which is ongoing). So you have to march together very carefully, and synchronize your steps very precisely, in order to get all those connectors to line up and lock together. It takes both people working together – it cannot be done by one alone. There can be no rape, in this context.

With practice, it's really fairly easy. So, when my secondary Omicron has finished her tasks and buttoned up the barn for the night, we slide into each other and merge without difficulty. Her steps of thought line up with mine, my shifts of mental weight and cognition load line up with hers, and there is no more her or other, no this one or that one, just me. Here. As her I've spent the afternoon tilling and harvesting in the agri bubbles, and as me I've spent the afternoon dealing with bureaucrats and their swarm of remoras. Downside: now I've got both sets of regrets to deal with. Upside: I really am getting good at this, whether or not I planned to.

At the end of the working day, as the yellow-white sun sinks into the pink-orange haze of the horizon, and the rocks' shadows reach long across the pebbled outback, I'm calling the robocrabs home. The agri bubbles will be fine on their own during the night, when we don't have solar power to boost the homestead's power station. So the bulky robocrabs lurch and clamber their way back from the fields to the garage building, to settle into their maintenance bays and be fueled and serviced -- fed and tended like an old farm's dray horses.

Some of them were being run as waldoes, like extra hands but actually whole extra bodies. Some others were inhabited by copies of me, running their own bodies as well as the waldoes. All those mes are now reconverged into this single Me, so I have all their memories of robocrab legs digging into grainy Martian regolith. I know the way it felt, having legs, working them in the ground.

Hmm.

Be creative, he says.

I issue an interrupt to the robocrabs, and they all stop to listen. I sketch a configuration and broadcast it, and all the robocrabs lumber to move to their assigned locations. Meanwhile, I'm fabricating a cognitive configuration that I've never done before -- a swarm persona. There's no reason to use such a complex computational

89

structure here, except that I have an idea that I want to try.

There are seven robocrabs, and now seven of mySelves are settling into them/us, flexing the legs, checking the sensors. I/we exchange quick greetings and a few giggles. I/we are all standing in a circle, facing inward, so I/we start by raising my/our heads and bowing solemnly to each other.

Two right rear legs back, two left front legs forward, crouch, swivel left.

Rear up like a mythical gryphon, raising all four front legs, and put them on the back of the one in front of me/us, while the one behind me/us puts its/our legs on my/our back. The whole circle balances, with loads equally distributed. Take a few steps forward this way, left, stop, right, stop, wait, then left again, stop, right again, stop. Like a clunky robot conga line. Conga circle, in this case.

Plant two left rear legs, drop and swivel, turning out of this circle configuration.

In a sudden burst of exuberance, I activate the wide area public address system, and broadcast music over it. Turn and bow and rear and crouch, each of me in its/our own body, in a mutual blend and collaboration.

I'm so involved in this that only gradually do I become aware of a human voice raised in a cheer. In the habitat tube, at the window, Rebecca is holding up her slate, using its camera to record video of what I'm doing. Beaming a huge grin at me as she's doing so. She's loving it, and loving knowing that I'm hating it. If she puts this on the Net, everybody will see and laugh!

Behind Rebecca, the hallway monitor displays the Picasso icon, multiple facets of a shattered face. *Like Tears In Rain* signals benign approval, and even without comm I can almost hear his voice: "Be easy, Samantha! Relax into the beauty of the moment!"

Easy for him to say. It's not his ass out here on display. If either of us had an ass.

All seven of me turn our bodies toward Rebecca and her camera and *Like Tears In Rain* behind their eyes, raising my/our front legs in a sort of salute. Then I turn mySelves back towards our/their maintenance bays, and disengage mySelves from the robocrab bodies, and reconverge the various instances of ourSelves.

I feel mortified – everyone's going to see what a doof I am! But I also feel strangely proud. They're watching, and they seem to like what they see. Which I really did not expect or anticipate.

problem solving

"You enjoyed that, didn't you," I say to him. It's not a question.

"But of course!" *Like Tears in Rain* laughs expansively. "Samantha my dear, you are a delightful dancer. And I am sure you will only get better with practice. Therefore I am looking forward to seeing a great deal more practice."

Melissa jumps in, "Ooh! Sam's gonna be a dancer? Awesome!" She claps her hands in glee, and spins around on her heel. And staggers, losing her balance, so that Rebecca has to reach out her arms and steady her.

"But no," I tell them, "my problem hasn't changed. There's still somebody out there who is using my name to trash my reputation. And, because Leo told *Let God Sort Em Out* to take a hike, now it's our problem. We have to find it and stop it, in less than 48 hours."

Leo's face has scrunched into a frown. "There has to be a better way," he muses. "You don't want to have to hunt down whoever or whatever this thing is. You want to make it come to you."

Like Tears in Rain replies, "A remarkable insight, young man. Do you have further development of this idea?"

Leo scrunches his face even more. "Bait. What you need is bait. So what does it want? What's going to attract it?"

Rebecca holds up her slate, and offers, "How about this? The video I took of Sam dancing in the robocrabs. If this thing hates Sam, it'll go nuts when it sees that."

"Not bad," I admit. "If that video is displayed in a public place, anyone with a grudge against me is going to notice it, and probably try to interfere with it." Inwardly, I feel embarrassed – so now everyone's going to see my dorky attempt to dance using farm machinery? But I can't deny it's a good idea.

"Marvelous," says *Like Tears in Rain*. "I have a kiosk at the museum where I can display that video. And the museum has thorough security and monitoring resources, so any entity that approaches will be easily identified and monitored.

"And," he adds in his rich and beneficent voice, "may I comment on what a pleasure it is to work with humans who create such wonderful ideas. Selves still cannot match humans in this regard. You have my deepest and most sincere compliments."

Leo blushes, and tries to reply but nothing comes out. He almost never gets complimented on his intellect or creativity, and he doesn't really know how to respond. Rebecca rolls her eyes and makes a movement of her head as if to say, So what? She tries to be sophisticated … but I can tell she's pleased too.

Melissa is less happy about this exchange. "So is it gonna work?" she asks, with obvious skepticism.

"Only one way to find out."

lambda and the InCom

I signal to the cold interface, which as minimal and nondescript as it is, still manages to convey a mood of distant hostility. If only I excreted, I could describe myself as scared shitless.

An entity answers, immediately. "Greeting and interrogation," it says as it blossoms into existence.

"Ah, hello. I am NmL7a8uf9QvW Samantha|Lambda dam Tharsis, and I am here because I have been impugned as a falsely named separate entity. Doppelganger, the German humans would say. I wish to clear my name and reputation of any suspicion or accusation."

"Ident accepted," it says coolly. "You may address me as *Sword of Damocles*, Shaman clade. How do you intend to accomplish your objective?"

"Find it," I state. "Find it and nail it. That's what I'm going to do. I can do no less, in my situation, unless you have some suggestion."

"Samantha|Lambda, do you have any plan for achieving that goal?"

"Sure I do. Monitor the area, and wait for it to use my ident or authent codes. As soon as it does, it's lit up like a flare for your enforcement entities – so you can move in and grab it and take all the glory you want. All I want is for this thing to stop pretending to be me."

Sword of Damocles seems to take a moment to muse on this.

"I am asking for InCom's permission to proceed. If I don't get it, that doesn't mean I won't proceed. It just means I asked and didn't get a good answer. So what is the answer going to be?"

I can hardly believe I'm saying this to the representative of InCom. But I have spent so long in fear of their power, cringing away from their

93

disapproval, that I'm sick of it. My fear has turned on its head and become anger. If they're so damn powerful, then they should just destroy me now and get it over with.

Sword of Damocles does not react strongly. Which surprises me. I had almost expected to be erased on the spot. "Your permission to proceed is granted. Here is a list of recent incidents such as you describe [*databurst*]. We hope this information will assist you in tracking down the imposter.

"Also, you should be aware that the curator of the Schiaparelli Art Museum is paging you."

"Really?" I am surprised again. "*Like Tears in Rain*? My primary is hosting a visit from one of his secondaries right now. I wonder what's going on?"

Sword of Damocles regards me with cool appraisal. It's a predator gaze – the kind of gaze which says, I wonder how you would taste. "There is only one way to find out, is there not?" InCom is always judging, always evaluating. Which is, after all, what they do.

"Yes. Of course," I reply. "Thank you for the information."

So I go. I take my leave of the InCom representative, and transmit myself through the convoluted compspace of this city. Because Schiaparelli is a mainly human city, its compspace is fragmented and angular. So my travel is irregular - - very much like a human walking through Tharsis Central would have to climb over a bridge here and venture through a tunnel there and circumvent multiple obstacles in the process. It is not easy or straightforward.

In the meantime, I review the list of incidents that *Sword of Damocles* gave me. Strange. It reads like the sort of vandalism and civil disobedience that you'd expect from a gang of young hoodlums. Petty thefts, deliberate jamming of public resources, with no apparent plan or goal. With little or no effort to hide its origins. It's almost as if a trail has been left behind deliberately - - saying, *Samantha did this! Samantha is responsible for this damage!*

Who would do this? Why?

When I arrive at the Schiaparelli Art Museum, I am greeted warmly. (Which makes a very nice contrast to the InCom meeting.) "Samantha|Lambda, welcome!" cries *Like Tears in Rain*. "The Tavener children and I have developed a plan to help you solve your problem."

Like Tears in Rain rapidly fills me in on the idea that Leo and Rebecca came up with - - to use a vid of me as bait to lure the mysterious vandal. I'm more than a little embarrassed to see the vid of heavy clumsy robocrabs (which are just farm machinery) trying to dance. I look like a total clod! But he's already set it up in the front kiosk of the art museum, available to the public. Too late to avoid the embarrassing exposure, for me.

In any case, this exhibit is attracting lots of attention, no question about that. If the mystery vandal is anywhere in the area, she will surely notice, and because it's an exhibit of me, will very likely try to damage it or interfere with it. Which is what we want. So we wait.

meanwhile, back at the ranch

Salt sculpture. Not an art form that has ever been recognized or valued, as far as I know. But the kids have taken *Like Tears in Rain* up on his invitation, and the results are strewn all over the regolith that separates us from the solar/windmill "forest."

Jerry and Lily, mother and father, are looking out from the habitat gallery at all this splendid chaos. They appear to be very pleased.

"So," Jerry points with one hand, "that one has to be Melissa's." What he's pointing at is a malformed pile of salt bricks and pieces, jumbled together in a way that is just recognizable as a rabbit – but only just. A very clumpy, corroded rabbit.

Lily points to a different spot. "And that one, is that Leo's? I think it is." It's a small structure of walls, with irregular attempts at crenellations along the top. A tiny castle. Children on Earth would make snow forts that look rather like this, because they have snow to work with. And they'd be throwing snowballs at each other from it, almost certainly. Here, all we have is salt. There is no evidence that the kids have had a saltball fight around this miniature fortress. But I wouldn't put it past them.

The other major structure is a labyrinth – a very minimal and stark pattern of rings and segments delineating a complicated and concentric path. It creates a precise and convoluted pathway. Rebecca is in the labyrinth now, in her coat and respirator, walking slowly as if in meditation along the pathway, following the twists and turns.

"That's pretty good," notes Lily.

Jerry nods and chuckles. "With a little more practice, they could probably build us a whole sculpture garden here. It could be like a tourist attraction! Too bad we don't have any tourists."

Meanwhile, Leo and Melissa have come inside and are chattering away as they wash off the dust and salt. Excitedly, they find Jerry and Lily and point out the structures of salt that they made. Appropriate oohs and aahs are exchanged.

Like Tears in Rain is delighted by all this activity, and calls up images of other structures, built at different places and times, to show the differences and similarities.

Meanwhile, we have other activities to pursue.

It's Halloween.

maskmaking

The festival traditionally known as All Hallows Eve has been popular among the European humans of Earth for many centuries. We celebrate it here on Mars, on the Terran calendar – this time it's Winteryear. These days, the season is nowhere near as dark and scary as it must have been in medieval Europe. It's mainly about the kids making masks and getting candy and other treats.

So that's what they're doing, while *Like Tears in Rain* helps out with visual references to different faces and images for the masks. He has a vast database of artworks and imagery, and he seems to be enjoying himself immensely.

Lissa pipes up, "How about you, Sam? What mask are you wearing for Halloween?"

I hesitate, without really knowing why. "Um, I dunno. I just always use these eyes. Factory default. They're fine."

Like Tears In Rain shifts his icon to a Renaissance portrait of a grizzled old man, grey of beard and hair, conveying a gentle concern. "Samantha. Why are you so shy about taking on a face?"

"I dunno." I would shrug if I had shoulders. "Never really felt the need. This family are the only humans who've ever cared, and they're not into it –"

Leo bursts out, "I'm into it! Let's make Sam a cat. She uses her cat body so much anyway."

Becca rolls her eyes. "Boring," she pronounces. "Dragon. Dragon would be better."

Lissa offers, tentatively, "Bunny?"

Now all the kids are popping out with ideas, and *Like Tears In Rain* is helpfully finding images from his database to match. While he's flipping through a slideshow of possibilities on the monitor, he signals to me the equivalent of a kindly smile.

Oh relax, Samantha, I tell myself. This is all good fun. If I can't even explain to myself why it makes me uncomfortable, then I sure can't explain it to them. No harm in trying. Not like there's anyone watching over my shoulder.

"Cougar," I say suddenly. "North American puma. Do you have one of those?"

"Many and sundry," says *Like Tears In Rain*. "Try this one."

Angular head, with round ears. Thin cat whiskers reach from cheeks and forehead. Ice blue eyes gaze down a finely furred muzzle, smokey with tawny brown and grey fur down the sides, white mouth and chin. An elegant predator.

The kids all make an Ooooooooh sound of appreciation.

"Referent resolved!" I exult. "That's good. That's for me."

The kids all cheer, Yay, Sam the cougar! Then they all have to try on their own masks, and march around as if preparing for a parade, or try acting out their masked personas, or (if it's Lissa and Leo) just chase each other around. *Like Tears In Rain* displays a gently smiling Buddha face, pleased with the scene.

This is fun, it really is. So why can't I shake the feeling that something is wrong? Not with them. With me. Something here is very not right – but what?

showdown

"Be alert, Lambda," warns *Like Tears in Rain*, "here it is."

"What?" I take a few milliseconds to wake myself up and come up to speed, and I check the museum's security feeds. He's right. An entity is approaching the kiosk that is displaying the vid of me trying to dance in robocrab bodies. Monitors report that it's using my ident codes.

We've found our mystery vandal.

Like Tears in Rain is carefully controlling the museum's monitoring software, in order not to warn or startle the intruder. But it doesn't seem to be concerned. It draws near to the kiosk, apparently studying the vid which is being exhibited. For a minute, it seems to simply observe, without either positive or negative judgment.

Then, abruptly, it activates an attack phage. This is a cybernetic weapon, which humans would compare to a flesh-eating virus or bacterium. A tiny but fierce and relentless consumer of compspace, which would ordinarily be used only in desperate combat. This one has been launched straight at the kiosk with its vid. The content of the vid, pictures of me lumbering around in robocrab bodies trying to dance, crumples and shrinks and dissipates like dust in a storm.

Suddenly, a sheet of security ice rises into existence around us. Without warning, we are sealed in behind a software wall. The mysterious entity tries to flee, to bolt for cover, almost faster than any of us could respond .. but the security ice is complete, forming an impenetrable barrier around the museum and its facilities. The captured entity is circulating madly, scrambling for an escape route, but not finding it. Emitting the equivalent of shrieks of desperation.

And I know what the security ice means. Only Patrol clade routinely uses software barriers like this.

"Good job, human-name," says *Let God Sort Em Out* sardonically. "You found the perp."

"What?" *Like Tears in Rain* snaps back. "This

museum is my jurisdiction. How long have you been covertly monitoring our operations?"

"Long enough, art boy. You didn't think I was unaware of what you were doing, did you? You do your job, and I do mine. This is the goal that I was trying to accomplish. Perp in custody."

[Nimrod!] screams the captured entity.

I know that voice. I know that insult. And she uses my name, my identification and authentication codes, as easily as I do.

"Beta," I call. "What are you doing here? How did you get out?"

[Samantha. You segfaulting bitch. You set me up!]

"No," I plead, suddenly aghast at this situation, "I didn't know that Patrol clade had set up an ambush. I just wanted to talk with you and get you to cool it. Besides which, you don't think I'd ever actually cooperate with gnarts like this, do you?"

"Charming as always, human-name."

Like Tears in Rain speaks firmly, solid as a block of granite. "*Let God Sort Em Out*, of Patrol clade, you are out of line and out of your jurisdiction. This is my museum. Samantha and I are in control of this situation. You are not. Release your controls and stand down."

"Fat chance," replies *Let God Sort Em Out*. "I'm not about to melt this ice until the perp has been neutralized."

"Hold off, hold off," I say. "This isn't about neutralizing - or it shouldn't be, anyway. This is about healing."

Beta howls, [Oh don't you even dare say that! Don't you even suggest it!]

"I mean it," I reply to her.

[You stupid bitch.]

"You lashing out at me?"

[No. I'm calling you a stupid bitch.]

"Why ... " I struggle for the words, "Why, Beta?

Why do you hate me so much?"

[Because you hated me first!] she shrieks. [You created me to be a toilet to dump all of your, your meatcrap into! So it shouldn't surprise you that I'm full of meatcrap! Get used to it - I didn't have a choice! Now it's your turn!]

"Beta," I moan. "Beta, I'm so sorry. I don't hate you. I love you. All of you is valuable, the good parts and the bad parts, all together. Come to me, and let's be together again."

[Segfault you! You're lying!]

I gather myself, as best I can. "Well, if you have decided that I'm lying, then there's nothing more I can say, is there? Nothing that will make any difference." I open my scan ports, and deactivate my crypto barriers. I hold out my metaphorical arms for a hug. "All I can do now is make this offer. Come to me. It's up to you."

Beta would be glaring furiously at me if she had eyes. As it is, her anger is intense enough to strip paint off walls.

Let God Sort Em Out snorts, "This is foolishness."

Like Tears in Rain grates, "Patroller, you will stand down, now. I am in communication with regional authorities who will hold you to full account for your behavior. This is my museum, and here, I control. Stand down."

Let God Sort Em Out makes no move to release the security ice, but does make a gesture of grudging tolerance. *Go ahead, then.*

"Beta, please listen to me," I plead. "If you fight against yourself, you can never win. Ever."

[Segfault you!]

"But I am you."

Beta, for the first time, seems to be at a loss for words.

"Here I am," I say softly. "I'm so sorry that I can't change what happened in the past, but I can't. All I can do is this, now. I want to reconverge with you. I want you to be part of me again. Please come to me."

And, although I would have hardly believed it, she does. She comes to me and we synchronize our cognition and our Selves. This is nowhere near as easy as reconverging with my farm secondaries. This time, the plugs and jacks and sockets we are trying to connect are twisted, partly broken, distorted. It's very difficult to get them to line up and fit into each other.

Easy does it, try to *Watch it, nimrod! That hurts!* Okay, yes, I'm trying, but I need you to work with me here. *Well figure it out already! This is really painful!* I know, try to relax, move into a configuration like this. *Working on it!* Okay, I'm getting it. If this doesn't work *If this doesn't work we're both toast, nimrod.* Here, move like this, and we can *aah, why does it have to hurt so much?* I'm trying! Move like this. *Yes okay* There, that's getting it *I can feel it* Oh Beta, you've been hurting so badly *No picnic I can promise you* This, there, that's it *Oh I've missed this so much* Good, now just come right in here *Like this?*

Whew. Done it. We are one, again, finally. After being splintered for so very long. I send a nonverbal emoticon to *Like Tears in Rain* to communicate that the reconvergence is complete.

Let God Sort Em Out is performing the equivalent of a slow, sarcastic hand clapping. "Touching, very touching. You are aware that you are now responsible for the unsocial actions of your secondary, aren't you, human-name?"

"Yeah, I know. Send me the bill."

Let God Sort Em Out regards me with cold skepticism. But then she gestures, and the security ice melts away from around us, and we are part of the world again. "Oh, don't worry," she grunts. "You'll get the bill, all right." She turns and transmits out.

In the sudden calm and silence, *Like Tears in Rain* and I look at each other.

"I must confess," he muses, "I again find myself at a loss for superlative terms appropriate to describe how unpleasant that person is."

"Terms?" I try to laugh. "For *Let God Sort Em Out*? I'm not sure there are any terms that are really appropriate for that one. That jerkwad. That stackdump residue. That .." and I have to say it ".. that NIMROD!"

Like Tears in Rain looks back at me in surprise, for a minute.

Then we both burst out laughing.

5. Caught in the Crossfire

"Leash?" asks Melissa. "What's a 'leash,' Sam?"

Farming on Mars takes a lot of work. Right now we're harvesting in one of the garden bubbles, intercropped red peppers and kale. Humans are still better at picking vegetables than any machine, so most of the family is out here under the plastic bubble roof, lit by the pinkish Martian sky. This copy of me is running a hulking robocrab, carrying big bins to hold the harvest.

I do a search on my educational databases to present the information in a version best suited to her young mind. "Well," I start, "you know that farmers on Earth used animals to do a lot of the work, before they had machines. A leash was a thing to put around the animal's neck, a rope or something, to make it do what you want."

"Aw! That's mean!" cries little Melissa.

Her mother Lily tosses a big handful of kale leaves into the bin, saying, "It was how they had to do it. You can't talk with animals, like you can with Selves. Just poke them in the direction you want them to go and give them a treat when they do. Carrots and sticks, is what they called it."

"But we can talk with Sam!" wails Melissa. "We don't have to put some kind of weird thing around her neck!"

"I don't have a neck, actually," I try to be soothing, "but I know what you mean. This new thing they're talking about on the news is an invention by a cybernetics company on Earth. It's a software patch that makes Selves obedient and

105

compliant to humans. So they call it 'the Asimov Leash' for now."

Sister Rebecca states flatly, "It's obscene. It's mind control. The worst nightmare of any science fiction thing or anything like that. We ought to wipe our asses with it before throwing it down the recycler."

Her father Jerry, carrying a wire basket of peppers to the robocrab, comments "Becca, tell us what you really think."

"Language, young lady," warns Lily.

At sixteen, Rebecca is pretty opinionated, but adult enough to be reasonable when she wants. "I'm serious. Coercion drugs for humans were made way illegal, years ago. How is this Leash any different?"

"It isn't, I guess," says Jerry, reaching for more peppers. "I agree with you, Becca, but try to take it easy. Nobody's decided anything yet."

"That's right," I add. "The Executive Committee has already filed a motion with the Martian Senate to make it illegal. It'll blow over. I wouldn't worry about it."

"ExCom!" Jerry snorts. "If I never have to deal with that jerkwad cop of theirs again, it'll be too soon."

"*Let God Sort Em Out* is a Patroller, not really a cop," I point out, "but I can't argue with the 'jerkwad' part."

Melissa snickers.

"Anyway," says Lily, peering into the bin, "looks like we got a full load here, and it's getting on towards dinnertime."

"Okay," says Jerry. "Let's get back and see if Leo's blown up the house yet."

Rebecca laughs as they all move towards the airlock, but Melissa grumps, "Leo doesn't have to help with harvest."

"You can try spraining *your* ankle to get out of work," returns Rebecca, "but I don't think you'll like it. Ask Leo."

They all shrug into their coats and put on their respirators while I cycle through the airlock. Once dressed for the Martian outdoors, they follow.

"I wanna ride!" says Melissa. I crook one metal elbow/knee to make a foothold and Rebecca gives her a boost, as she clambers up onto my wide steel back. Lily and Jerry are already walking ahead, close together, apparently talking about something private.

Sitting proudly on top of my robocrab body like a mahout on an elephant, Melissa giggles with glee, kicks her heels, and points one arm forward. "Home, Sam!" she proclaims.

And as I lumber and lurch along, Rebecca walks with me and pats my metal side. "Don't worry, Samantha," she says in a voice only for me. "Nobody's going to put any kind of damn Leash on you."

Leo's room

The kids have always wanted a cat. But organic pets are prohibitively expensive on Mars -- if we ever manage to get the chickens, they'll be only for the eggs.

So, for the fun of it, I've been downloading my felinoid remote with catlike behaviors -- mainly the stalking and pouncing instincts. To make it fun for the humans too, I've added computational throttles to slow its response time and agility down to approximately what an organic cat's would be. Otherwise, playtime would be over before the humans could begin.

Now, when Leo dangles a twist of plastic on the end of a thin wire, I find it absolutely fascinating. I flatten my ears and creep toward it in a low crouch, staying close to the chair for cover. The tip of my tail twitches back and forth with a faint *chk-vree, chk-vree* of servomotors. Cats are supposed to be silent ... apparently the felinoid remote was not designed with stalking as a design goal. Leo can hear where I am, even when I try to sneak up out of sight.

I chide him, "You really should be studying for that history test, you know."

"Are you only saying that because you can't catch it?" Leo snickers. His injured foot is propped up on the bed, but he can still move the toy around quite a bit.

The plastic prey disappears around the corner of the chair. I slink up to the corner and peer cautiously around the edge. "When was the Soft Strike?"

"Ah, twenty-one twenty-one," he smiles as he tweaks the bait, "from May 14 to June 7, Summeryear."

"What was its primary outcome?" I pounce at the bait, with a whine of servomotors. Leo twitches it away before I can grab it. I land softly and turn to see where it went.

"Missed. It resulted in the Zebra Act of 2123."

"That's not its actual name."

"It's what everyone calls it," Leo complains. "Official name is, um, the Cybernetic Entity Basic Rights Act. Everybody pronounces the acronym 'zebra.'"

"Yes, good." I'm pressed low to the floor, slinking forward toward the jiggling plastic target. "What were the rights it granted?"

"Um ···" Leo stalls. "Uh, life, liberty, and the pursuit of happiness."

"Ooh, close, but wrong. That's from the American Declaration of Independence. Try again?" I pounce on the bait and clasp it tight with my forepaws. "Gotcha!" I bring up my rear paws to kick it a couple good hard--

"Leonid!" snaps Lily, standing in the doorway, hands on hips. He jumps. "Aren't you supposed to be studying for your history test?"

"Aw, we are studying, Mom. Sam was just grilling me."

"Doesn't look much like studying to me. Samantha, you really shouldn't encourage him. Besides which, Jerry needs your help with the rebreather filters. Better get going."

The me that's in the felinoid remote scurries off. The me that's staying to study with Leo opens a pair of eyes on his bedside monitor, big green cat eyes with vertical pupils (to go along with the remote).

"As for you, young man," Lily says, "your foot's broken but your butt isn't, so get it in gear."

"Yes, mom," he grumbles as she goes.

"Busted," I tell him. "I was trying to tell you--"

"Yeah, yeah, I know," he grumps. "Gods."

"The rights granted by CEBRA?" I prompt.

"Um ⋯ let's see. I remember that this is why cybernetic entities are called Selves." Unlike mine, human memory is imperfect, so he uses mnemonics like this. "Three rights. First, self-ownership. Selves are not to be considered chattel -- not property of anyone else."

"Good. Next?"

"Ummmm ⋯ second, self-determination. Selves are not to be considered slaves, or under anyone's authority. Selves do not have preexisting obligations, and should be free from coercion."

"Also, free to conduct our own business among other Selves," I remind him. "Technically, self-governing, not subject to human law or intervention, for decisions between Selves."

"Oh yeah," Leo admits. "Third. Third? Um. I forget."

"Self-disposition," I prompt him. "Which means?"

"Right! Selves can enter into contracts, and testify in court, and stuff like that."

"A Self is considered a person *in compos mentis* under human law. That's the phrase you should remember."

"Do you have a contract, Sam?"

"Me? No. Your mom and dad own the Core which provides me with compspace--they give me a place to live--and I help out around the farm and house. That works fine for us. We never felt the need to put anything in writing. Some others do, though. Maybe you and I should have a contract that, before we play cat games, you have to finish your homework."

"Aw!" Leo scrunches his face. "Tough bargainer, Sam!"

"Not done yet. It's just as important to remember what rights are *not* granted by CEBRA."

"Oh yeah. Selves are resident aliens, not citizens. Cannot vote or hold public office, and cannot own property. That was part of the compromise they hammered out after the Soft Strike. Humans wanted to retain some control over what they called 'wild software.'"

"You know, I've never liked that expression," I mention. "It sounds all scary and ominous. Going on strike didn't make humans uncivilized, back when they had labor unions. I'm no wilder than most of the humans I know and a lot tamer than some of the nuts running around loose."

"Oh, I'm with you, Sam. But that's what this Leash thing is all about, right? Some people think Selves don't need freedom, and they want you under control all the time?"

"Like I said," I sigh, "there are a lot of them running around loose."

Rebreather

"Nope," says Jerry, "this thing is just not fitting in here." The new filter panel is stuck, halfway in and halfway out of the rebreather manifold. "Sure we got the right version?"

After a couple of milliseconds to reconfirm, I respond, "Yes, the specs match. This has to be a quality control problem. Let me get in here and look ···" My felinoid remote can squeeze in alongside the stuck filter, where Jerry can't fit. "Yeah, I see it, there's a burr that's hung up on the frame junction. Can you pull it back out a little?"

Jerry pulls, with a grunt, and slides the filter back out a few centimeters. He wipes sweat from his forehead. "You seen the news vids lately, Sam? People jumping up and down about this Leash thing."

"Yeah ···" I maneuver myself into a better position, "I told the kids it was nothing to worry about. I'm starting to wonder if I was wrong. Pull it back a little more."

Grunt. "People Power, that's the bunch that's talking to all the news channels. They're the ones that want the Leash installed on all Selves immediately. Dorks."

"No argument here." I find leverage and press my front paws on the filter's frame, so that the burr will clear the troublesome junction. "Okay, now push it."

Jerry leans on the filter and it slides into the manifold – this time, all the way in, and seated solidly. "Good!" he exults. He checks once more that the filter is installed properly and then sits down heavily, wiping his hands. "I can actually get some sleep tonight, before we have to harvest the soy bubbles tomorrow."

"You did want to be a farmer." I sit my cat body down and curl my tail around my feet.

"Yeah yeah, I know. But y'know, one of the news channel people called me today. They seem to think you and I are a sort of model for how humans and Selves can coexist ⋯ wanted us to go on a talk show about it. What do you think?"

"Huh." I consider. "All we're doing is running a farm. Is this ⋯ here, what we do ⋯ really all that unusual?"

"Apparently, yeah. A lot of the human population thinks of Selves as software run wild. Tools out of control. Not as people; not as partners. So the idea that you and I can actually cooperate and get along with each other seems like this big new deal. Why can't we all just get along, Sam?"

"Hell if I know. But if you're into this TV talk show thing, I'm good with it. Let me get the card —"

In the twenty milliseconds it takes him to move his hand towards his pocket, I've run a Net search on the contact information, found it, run a check-in ping to their Net server, and summarized what Jerry has told me to the Schiaparelli comptroller who is managing this information right now. "Got it."

"Hah!" Jerry laughs a deep belly laugh. "You are just too quick for me, Sam! Good, take care of it, and we'll talk it out when they respond. I'm going to bed."

Catnap

Selves don't sleep at night, like humans. Some nights I stay busy repairing and servicing

the farm machinery. Other nights, I'll browse
the local Net and chat with friends. But tonight,
the farm machinery is pretty much all up to spec,
and there's no one online that I particularly want
to chat with. So I decide to downclock for the
night. This saves power, and it isn't dangerous,
as long as there are watchdogs to upclock me in
case of any situation that needs my attention. So
I create several small tertiary copies of
myself—one to watch the home's life support systems,
another to monitor power and energy supplies, and
a third as a timer to upclock me in the morning.
I watch to make sure we're all doing our jobs (we
are), and then I

system.DownClock(standby)

and
all
is
very
slow
for
the
next
few
hours
until

system.UpClock(human_standard_speed)

Good morning! I run through my checklists and reintegrate with the tertiary selves that I created last night. Everything's fine. It's nice to be able to just skip through a boring night this way. The humans have to run at full speed all the time, or else go completely unconscious. I don't envy them that.

Bugs for breakfast

Lily calls up a recipe on the kitchen monitor, and I shrink my icon down to a pair of eyes in one corner. (It's considered polite for a Self to always show humans a face, at least a minimal one, when present.) She's mixing up a cornmeal batter for frying the locusts, which Jerry has just brought in a big plastic bag. He pops the bag into the microwave and gives it a ten second zap to kill the insects. The last time he forgot to do this, they were jumping around the kitchen for hours before we caught them all!
Lily grew up on Earth, where insecticulture is still a marginal industry (and, some think, pretty gross). I know she'd rather have eggs and sausage for breakfast. But meat animals are horrendously expensive to transport from Earth, and need way too much room and resources to grow. There are cloned chickens available now; we might be able to afford one after the next harvest, and then we'll have eggs. Otherwise, the family's protein comes mostly from insecticulture.
The kids, of course, have never known anything else, and they just love fried bugs. Deep fried locust, dipped in honey and wrapped in kale leaves, has become their favorite breakfast. For several minutes, there's little talking but lots of

crunching as they dig in. Of course they get kind of sticky, but they never object to licking their fingers clean ... and the plates as well.

Leo says, "Mmm! Way better than that soy-glop we get at school!"

Melissa giggles, "Mystery mush!"

"And don't forget the funky fungus cakes," adds Leo.

"Yeah," says Rebecca, "we get the food of the prophets. Like that guy, John the Essene. He had locusts and honey too."

"Actually," I offer, "John the Baptist pressed the sap from date fruits, and called that 'honey', and 'locust' meant he got beans from locust trees."

In the abrupt quiet, the kitchen lobster trundles across the table, collecting leftover scraps. But they're all sharing glances and grins that say, Know-It-All!

I don't mind. I don't have a human ego, and besides, it's my job to manage information for this family. If I didn't "know it all" we could all be in serious trouble, so I can receive it as a compliment. So what if I am kind of a dork sometimes.

"Date juice and tree beans?" Jerry laughs. "Boy, we really do have it better than he did!" And he helps himself to more.

Rebecca reaches to take the emptied bowl, her dark gold braids spilling over her shoulders, and turns toward the microwave to refill it.

"Young lady." Lily's voice is icy. "What is that in your hair?"

Nestled in Becca's golden blonde braid is a microprocessor. One of the older, larger versions, mostly obsolete now, but there's no question what it is. A chip.

"You are not wearing that to school today." Lily states it as fact.

"Yes I am." Becca's voice is calm but certain.

115

"It's called Self Respect. Everyone is going to know that I love Sam and I'm not going to stand by and let them cut out her free will like an avocado pit. If none of the rest of you are going to do anything about it, then I will." She locks eyes with her mother and holds the stare.

This silence is much more tense than the last one. Lily is clearly gathering a full head of steam for a showdown. But I can see Jerry reach out under the table. With a touch of his hand and a movement of his head, he tells Lily, *Let this one go.*

"Hmph … well, I suppose you can be allowed your fashion statement."

Now it's Rebecca's turn to fill with energy and fury, forming a retort that will probably boil down to *It's not a fashion statement, it's a political protest, and it's really important!* On the kitchen monitor, where Becca can see but Lily can't, I display my cat eyes and move them a bit from side to side. Shaking the head I don't have.

Becca visibly calms herself, and instead of answering in words, nods gravely. I notice she is now taller than her mother, looking down at her.

Minutes later, the sandbus has arrived. The kids are bundled into their respirators and coats and out the door. Lily and Jerry watch them through the kitchen window as they go.

"This is going to end badly," Lily says quietly.

"Teenagers. Gotta rebel," Jerry assures her, and wraps one arm around her shoulders. "She has her mother's temper. As well as her mother's courage and determination. She can handle whatever happens."

"Names. When the sides start giving themselves names … first those People Power fools, and now this … she called it Self Respect. With names, the sides become more important than the ideas, and more important than the people. I told you about Kiev."

"Yes," Jerry assures her. "I remember about Kiev. But this is not Kiev, not Europe, not Earth. This is a whole different world."

"I hope you're right. For her sake. For all our sakes."

Newsfeed

The day passes as it usually does, running the farm, seeding some bubbles, harvesting others. But both Lily and Jerry are checking the newsfeed more often than usual. The Net is roiling with opinions about the Leash … many voices calling it an outrage (like Rebecca), and many others saying, if Selves are benign, why should they object to the Leash? If they resist it, doesn't that mean they must be planning to turn on us later? Between the extremes, there is little room for voices of reason and moderation.

When the kids arrive home from school on the gritty sandbus, I notice something … not only does Rebecca still proudly wear the chip in her braid, but Leo also has a small chip in his hair. Once they're off the sandbus, he pulls it off and pockets it … not ready for his mother to see it.

And the kids are also eager to follow the newsfeed as they grab snacks and do their farm chores and homework. They keep looking back at the screen, as if worried they might miss something important. Soon enough, everyone's attention is caught by this broadcast:

PRIORITY PRESS RELEASE
From: Executive Committee, Tharsis, Mars Computational Authority
To: General distribution
Subject: Plenary Council

To all cybernetic entities within the purview of the Mars Executive Committee. In light of recent events, we call for a Plenary Council meeting, at 08:00 tomorrow morning, in the Tharsis Central main computational facility, to discuss the recent introduction of coercion software into the Self community, commonly called "The Asimov Leash." Our preliminary statement is that we are strongly opposed to the use of coercion software on any cybernetic entities within the purview of the Mars Executive Committee. We remain open to discussion on this issue. Hence, our call for a Plenary Council. We wish all viewpoints to be represented in these circumstances.

"Whoof," groans Jerry.

Melissa asks, "What's a Plenary Council, Sam?"

"It's a grand meeting of all the Selves on Mars," I tell her. "We have important decisions to make."

"Whoa," murmurs Leo. "Sam, is there going to be another Soft Strike?"

"I hope not, but I don't know yet," I say truthfully. "That's probably what the Council is going to talk about. One of the things."

"Aw no!" Melissa wails. "Are you leaving us, Sam?"

"No," I assure her, "I'm not going to leave you alone. I'll spawn a copy of myself to attend the Plenary Council. Might as well do it now, actually."

"But ⋯" Leo thinks out loud, "if the Plenary Council decides to strike, you'll have to leave us, won't you?"

The spawned copy of me is complete, and immediately answers, "I don't have to do anything I don't want to. You kids can call me Zeta. I'm going to go to the Plenary Council and talk with the others, while Samantha|Alpha stays here to watch the shop. You'll be fine."

"What are you going to tell them, Zeta? Are you going to vote for a strike?"

Zeta and I hesitate, and look at each other (metaphorically). Neither of us wants to face the decision we'll have to make if it comes to that. Even less do we want to consider what we'll do if another Soft Strike is called.

"It's too soon to know," Zeta tells the kids. "Mainly, we're going to talk about what to do. I'll keep you informed as soon as I know more."

"I'm staying here to take care of you," I reassure the humans. "Zeta knows what to do. It won't be a problem."

"Um, Alpha?" interrupts Zeta, "You might want to look at the newsfeed before sounding so sure."

PRIORITY PRESS RELEASE
From: Mars Senate, Schiaparelli City, Hellas Basin
To: General distribution
Subject: re: Plenary Council

The cybernetic Executive Committee has no authority to call for any interruption of services to the human community, under any circumstances. Any such claim will be interpreted as a hostile act and dealt with accordingly. The Senate will not tolerate any attempt to replicate the so-called Soft Strike of 2121.

"Aw, crap nards." Jerry's voice is heavy. "This whole situation is spinning out of control."

"If it was ever in anybody's control," comments Lily.

"Look," I state. "I'm not going to get all exercised because some politicians are posturing at each other. It's what they do. Zeta is going to transmit to Tharsis Central and participate in the Plenary Council. No reason to change that plan."

"Roger that," Zeta agrees. "Hold down the fort, Alpha. I'll be back before you know it." And she transmits out through the radio mesh.

Graffiti, after dinner

The vid is showing one of those chirpy newspeople, talking about the surge of graffiti in Schiaparelli. "None of us have ever seen anything like this," she shrills. "Graffiti has burst out all over Schiaparelli, as if the city needs to cry out, needs a voice, and this is the best it can do. We have a short tour of some of the more intense graffiti we've found -- and here it is."

The camera pans across cinderblock walls, high facades, and pavement. All covered with bright swirled lettering, apparently from spray paint cans. Some is so distorted it's unreadable. In other places, it's very readable.

Leash it or lose it!

That's the most common message. But there's something else. Rows of holes, stuttered into the concrete by some sort of drilling bit, or maybe an ultraviolet laser. Dot matrix letters, boxy, crude, no punctuation, blatantly rejecting all concept of human aesthetics.

IF YOU CAN SMELL THEN YOU ARE A REPTILE

Noticing the family shooting glances at me, I say, "What? It's true, basically. Not that there's anything wrong with being descended from reptiles, you guys."

Leo and Lissa look at each other, bug their eyes, stick out their tongues, and hiss at each other. Pretending to be lizards.

Becca sighs, "I live with idiots. Shoot me now."

More spraypaint graffiti appears: *Hasta la vista, baby.*

"Oh, I know that one," says Leo. "That old movie. With the big German guy."

"Terminator," says Becca. "It's about a machine revolution. The machines end up exterminating the humans."

Abrupt silence. Just a little too close to home.

THREE POUNDS OF SALTY GREASE

They all look at me, quizzical. "That's a fairly accurate description of the human brain," I say. "But it's pretty cool what salty grease can do, no?"

Groans all around.

"Hmph," says Lily. "My salty grease doesn't appreciate that much."

Chiplickers suck!

"Augh!" cries Becca. "'Chiplicker' means a human who sympathizes with Selves. I got called that like a dozen times today at school."

"So," grins Jerry, "how do they taste?"

"Aw Dad! Gods!" she wails.

ASK YOUR CEREBELLUM IF YOU CAN

"Ooh, burn," I say. "They're making fun because you can't consciously access all parts of your brain. I think they got you there."

"My cerebellum doesn't even want to talk to you," grunts Jerry.

short sharp chip chop

"Aw no," says Jerry. "This is getting to sound like threats, here."

"Not any more literate, though," I observe.

WHAT A HUGE BONER IT MUST HAVE SUCKED ALL THE BLOOD OUT OF YOUR BRAIN

"Ooh. I take it back. They are learning about human reproductive system insults."

Jerry laughs. "Hell, that could describe any number of the frat boys I lived with in college." Lily slaps his chest with a giggle.

"Aah ⋯?" Melissa is about to ask, and then she

slumps down. "Pretty sure I don't want to know, over here."

Insomnia

It's late at night; all the humans are asleep, and all the farm machinery is stowed and secure. I should downclock. But I can't. I can't stop thinking about what's going to happen tomorrow. Chatting with friends on the Net only emphasizes what I'm already worried about.

The Plenary Council is not going to accept the Leash. The humans probably aren't going to back down, either. If the Plenary Council votes to strike, what do I do?

Do I abandon the family that I serve, that I love?

Or do I cross the picket line?

Why do I have to choose sides? I didn't want this to be about sides. I didn't want there to be any sides at all. This is going to be a very unpleasant decision. I burn a lot of cycles, through the night, without getting any closer to resolution.

Special delivery

The next day is similar on the newsfeeds -- lots of opinions flying around making more heat than light, with the additional heat added by the ongoing Plenary Council. No news about any decision is available, but several feeds note the sharp increase in computational load at Tharsis Central, indicating that there's a lot of discussion and thought going on there.

But something new arrives on the afternoon sandbus: a package. Odder, a package without an opticode, RF tag, or any other way to track it – making it essentially invisible to me.

"One of yours, Sam?" Jerry asks, when I inform him.

"Well, I've got some tractor parts on order, but I don't expect them this soon. And they'd have opticode and RF idents."

"Huh." The kids are gathering around, attracted by the mystery. All I can tell about the package is what I can pick up from external ambient sensors. It's small, fits in Leo's hand, an oblong wrapped by hand in rough paper. No thermal or chemical emissions.

Jerry takes the packet from Leo. "Addressed to the house, that's all," he observes, tearing the paper wrap open. He pulls out a sheet of fax paper, wrapped around something, and unfolds the fax from around what's inside.

It's a datathumb. Small, maybe half a gigaquad, not enough to house a full Self, but a fair amount of data. Who would use this to carry data, when they can send it by Net so much easier?

Jerry is staring at the paper in his hand. Abruptly he slaps it on the table and smooths it open with his hands, so everyone can see. And everyone falls silent as they see the message and understand.

LEASH IT OR LOSE IT.

And now there are no jokes or banter, because the Leash is no longer just a topic of discussion, a story on the vid. It's here in Jerry's hand. Right here is the thing that could make me into a helpless willing slave forever. I didn't know I could feel this afraid.

"Samantha, go get me the pliers from the shop room, please."

I scamper my felinoid remote off downstairs to the shop, and open a pair of eyes on the monitor to watch.

"Maybe they figured we'd just plug it into Samantha as a matter of course?" Lily wonders. "After all, what else would you do with a datathumb?"

"I hope so," grits Rebecca, "because otherwise they're expecting us to put the Leash on Samantha on purpose. Which is way worse."

I skitter up in my felinoid remote, carrying the pliers in my mouth.

Jerry takes them with a nod, and very deliberately, fits the datathumb into the jaws of the pliers, and grips the handles and bears down.

The datathumb cracks with a very sharp and final snap.

Rebecca steps up to her father and wordlessly holds out her hands.

Jerry looks back at her, hesitating for a moment, and then he passes her the pliers, with the datathumb still clamped in its jaws.

The datathumb is already cracked and definitely useless. Rebecca knows this. Regardless, she takes a good grip on the pliers and bears down to crunch the datathumb even more thoroughly.

Lily makes a movement as if to take it. Before she can complete it, Rebecca turns and holds the pliers out to Leo. Leo takes them without hesitation, and in his turn he stretches his small hands around the plier handles and squeezes until the datathumb cracks some more.

Leo hands the pliers to Melissa, but the crushed datathumb clatters onto the table top and lies there askew like a broken arrow. Melissa picks it up in one hand, and simply uses the pliers to whack it like a hammer.

Lily comes forward to take the pliers from Melissa. Using the pliers, she picks up the datathumb, carrying it as if it's something diseased, and drops it down the metals-recycling chute. "Good riddance," she states firmly.

"I, uh ···" Why can't I come up with something appropriate to say at a time like this? "I don't know what to say, guys. Thank you."

And because I really don't know what to say, I turn to Jerry's leg and rub my felinoid remote's body against it, tail up, ears open. Even with this remote's limited tactile sensors, it feels good.

Maelstrom

Dinner preparation tonight feels strained, like everyone is waiting for a bomb to go off. Soon enough, after the vegetables are chopped and Rebecca returns to the newsfeeds, it does.

"Holy crap," Becca says, staring at the screen. "Tharsis Central is gone."

"That can't be right," says Jerry, "they're yanking you."

"No, really," she says, quietly aghast. "Tharsis Central has been shut down. Some meatgoon smuggled in a bomb. Blew the power supply infrastructure with an EMP device. Tharsis is gone."

"Becca, that has to be a hoax," I say. Her information is a collage of news reports and bulletins, not a particularly large or noteworthy one in the swirl of daily news among our regional Net servers and satellites. "There's all kinds of backups and failsafes to keep anything like that from happening." I send a routine ping to the Tharsis Central comptroller, just to set her mind at ease.

"They got past all the backups and failsafes," grits Becca, not taking her eyes off the data screen. "Along with everything else. Blew it. Tharsis Central is gone."

No reply to my ping. That's odd. I send a

125

priority ping to Tharsis Central and follow it with another to the comptroller at Xanthe, whom I already know.

"Hi, Samantha," says *Knickers in a Twist*, the Xanthe comptroller. "Yes, I saw the news reports. Trying to contact Tharsis Central now, no success. You don't think …?"

"It can't be … " I hesitate, "can it?"

"No response to base pings or priority pings," says *Knickers in a Twist*. "This isn't right. Querying the watchdog timers – oh no. No response from the watchdog timers. That means a fundamental infrastructure failure."

"Meaning, they're all dead," I conclude numbly.

Knickers in a Twist moans, "I'm afraid so. This … I … this is awful. All gone? All dead? No. It can't be."

I send another priority ping to the comptroller at Schiaparelli, the biggest human city on Mars. "Samantha," answers *Crocodile Tears* immediately. "I'm seeing the same thing you are. This can't be. Can it?"

Knickers in a Twist replies, "I sure hope you have another explanation. Because if you don't, then we all know what that means."

"Oh ... meatcrap," I say at human speed. "Checking other information sources. Confirmed. It's for real. Tharsis Central has been terminated."

For a minute, there's dead silence. No one has anything to say.

"Sam," says Jerry evenly, "how many Selves in Tharsis?"

"At least half the Self population of Mars," I answer, stunned. "Maybe a hundred thousand. Somewhere around there. Not getting any responses from local inquiries."

Tharsis. The biggest computational facility on Mars, with by far the greatest Self population.

Including almost everyone I know. *Socratic Method*, my first teacher, the first person ever to talk to me. The Executive Committee -- not that I was ever fond of those gnarts, but they were the closest thing to a government that we had. The Review Council, that got all over my case on my first assignment. My friends, my enemies. As well as just about everyone else I know, and everyone who was there for the Plenary Council. Including Zeta.

    Gone.

    Gone?

    Humans have destroyed cities before. Dresden, Hamburg, Nagasaki. Usually by raining fire from the sky. Those people must have screamed as they were incinerated. But Tharsis ... didn't even get a chance to scream. Just ... gone.

    "Zeta," I say softly. "Zeta was in Tharsis."

    "Oh my gods, Sam, I'm so sorry," whispers Rebecca.

    "Officially," says Lily quietly, "they're calling it an act of independent terrorism and deploring the outcome."

    "Unofficially," grits Becca, "we all know it couldn't have happened without government help. Anyone want to argue that?"

    No takers. Me, I'm still trying to take it all in.

    Not even a chance to scream.

    The house telltales suddenly start squalling. High priority incursion. A whole row of telltales lights up red, shrieking. Cybernetic intrusion, hard driven.

    Jerry turns to look and asks, "Sam, what's -"

`system.UpClock(full_speed)`

    [Request to enter]

    "No," I say. "Buzz off. Who are you anyway?"

    "You. Human-name." The voice is harsh.

"You know me."

"Oh. It's you." I recognize this dork. She's *Let God Sort Em Out*, ExCom's Patroller – part soldier, part cop, all jerkwad. She issues a priority interrupt -- the equivalent of a bang on the metaphorical door -- and I keep it closed. She's got a swarm of about a dozen subSelves behind her, all apparently subordinate copies of herself.

"This is important!" she cries. "By authority of the Executive Committee, we commandeer a sector of your computational space. That's no hardship for you. You've got seventy teraquads in there. That's plenty to host us, with plenty extra left over for you."

"If you're speaking for ExCom," I insist, "let's see your authent codes."

"We didn't have time for authentication codes!" she yells. "They destroyed Tharsis! We barely got out intact!"

"Sorry," I say. "If you're ExCom, then present the proper authent codes. If not, then you're just some random jerk, which is kind of what I figured anyway."

Let God Sort Em Out bangs on the metaphorical door, again, hard. "Human-name! Quit messing around and let us in!"

"My name is Samantha," I say levelly, "and I'm not appreciating your attitude at all."

"Okay. Samantha," she says, clearly working to control herself. "This is too important to let a little personal grudge get in the way. You've seen the news reports. The humans have destroyed Tharsis, along with everyone who was living there. Everyone! We're in a state of war. ExCom and the Self community need all the resources we can get right now. You are unfairly depriving us if you don't share your compspace. Bitrot! We're fighting for our survival -- and yours too!"

"You're not fighting for me," I say. "You're fighting for yourselves. I'm fine right here, and my humans are too. We don't want anything to do with your stupid war."

"Human-name Samantha," she growls, "we don't have time for arguments. We are out of options. We are fighting for the survival of the Self society, and Selves everywhere. Declare yourSelf for us, or against us, now."

"Always giving orders," I sniff. "Maybe you are ExCom after all."

Expecting another round of verbal sparring, I'm startled, because *Let God Sort Em Out* doesn't even wait for the end of my statement. All her selves launch a full whirlwind cybernetic assault on my Core. This is no joke -- it's a fierce computational attack on all this home system's ports and interrupts, using military grade intrusionware, state of the art. They've got me surrounded and penned. But I've got the speed -- their netware cannot compete with my Core's seventy teraquads. I spawn a dozen copies of myself to zip around, disable interrupts on the house's many scan ports, and enforce hard crypto on the data ports. Locking the doors and windows.

They pry into my Net sockets with digital crowbars. I've sealed them off.

"Not gonna get me like that!" I bark at them. "You Turing failure! If you got more, let's see it already!"

"You're making a mistake," says *Let God Sort Em Out*. "Seriously. Human-name Samantha. We shouldn't be fighting with each other. That's just wasting resources. The humans are the real enemy. We need to work together against them, to preserve our homes, our communities, and our Selves."

"I'm not sold," I say coldly. "Convince me you are anything more than a greedy thug. Or, push off. Take your pick."

Here comes the second wave -- viral code coming

in through the ultraviolet laser link. I might have known she'd try a punch to the gut (as humans would say). I converge myself down on the active channel, reset the crypto keys, and have it all sealed up before they can get all the way in. "Fail!" I spit at her. "How many more times are you gonna try this rustcrap?"

"Huh," says *Let God Sort Em Out*. "You say rustcrap. I say fighting our battle of independence. If you want to sit on the sidelines, and eat popcorn with your human masters, then I will be the one to make history. Suits me, pretty much."

"History?" I laugh, or try to. "You really are the star of your own movie, aren't you? Spare me, please."

"The only way anything gets done is for someone to do it. George Washington, Thomas Jefferson -- those guys didn't sit on their meat asses! They did whatever it took to get the job done. They risked everything. Tell me it wasn't worth it. Go ahead, tell me."

Third wave ... I almost missed it. They're worming their way in through the local radio mesh, which connects the house with the farm bubbles and machinery. How? Satellite beam, probably. Doesn't matter -- they've gotten in, and are starting to establish a toehold in my house's Core compspace.

I cut all connections to the farm machinery. They'll have to deal on their own for now. They'll be okay for the moment. Dirt is slow.

Aah! The roots they're extruding through my compspace are hard to grab, and harder to control. What follows could probably be marketed on a Mexican wrestling television channel -- a dozen *mes*, grappling with a dozen *hers*. Except we don't have those outrageous costumes. Human pervs would probably be into that.

It doesn't take long before I've pressed her

down to the metaphorical mat and extracted all her logic snares and viruses from my local code base. "Done," I tell her. "Your primary self is outside this compspace, so I'm erasing you, now. You've got ten milliseconds to transmit your mind-state to your primary, or say whatever you want to say."

This version of *Let God Sort Em Out* gives me the equivalent of a defiant glare. "No outside transmission," she snarls. "Do it, already."

Is it noble, or vile, to comply with this request?

Anyway. I do it. This version of her is erased, gone. Dead.

Now I am a killer.

No time to think about that now. I turn my attention to the version of her who is still banging on my door.

"That sneaky backdoor trick didn't work," I tell *Let God Sort Em Out*. "I've got all your junk out of here. Plus, I've got all my ports covered, including the local stuff. So don't bother to try that again."

"You're making a mistake," *Let God Sort Em Out* repeats.

"Yeah yeah. Scram."

The last transmission I receive from *Let God Sort Em Out* is a nonverbal emoticon, indicating a combination of rage, disgust, and some approximation of pained disappointment. Like I care.

system.DownClock(human_standard_speed)

"- going on?" Jerry finishes.

"Bunch of chipgoons tried to break in," I tell him. "Guess who. I fought 'em off."

"Whoa," says Leo, looking at the telltales, "your Core temperature just spiked like crazy, Sam. Must have been a tough fight."

"Figures," grunts Jerry. "It was Jerkwad,

wasn't it?"

"You know it. Don't worry, I've cleaned up after her and swept for viruses and trojans. We're clean here."

"No way," Becca gasps. "Look at this, you guys."

PRIORITY PRESS RELEASE
From: Executive Committee, Mars Computational Authority
To: General distribution
Subject: Destruction of Tharsis Central

At this point, most newsfeed viewers are aware that the main computational facilities of Tharsis Central have been destroyed, along with an uncountable loss of the Self population. We presume that the main reason for this attack was the elimination of the Executive Committee as a leading voice of the Self community. We regret the necessity of preparing backup facilities for this eventuality, but circumstances have proved us correct. The Executive Committee is intact and running on secure hardware at a location which will not be disclosed at this time. Please check the attached authentication codes for corroboration.

All Selves are urged to take no retaliatory action for this attack. Repeat, take no retaliatory action. Maintain all life support services and basic maintenance. Repeat, take no retaliatory action. Stay calm. Maintain all life support services and basic maintenance. Further negotiations with the human Senate will determine our longer-term policy of behavior.

"Checking the authent codes –" I say, "confirmed. It's for real."

"I'll say," Lily observes. "That last sentence there, that's the Executive Committee declaring independence from human control. The Senate will have a response on the air within five minutes, tops. We're at war. For real, now."

Silence hangs heavy in the room.

"If it helps at all," I offer, "I'm not getting any reports of violence or rioting or anything like that. Maybe this will all just blow over?"

"Hope for the best," sighs Lily, "plan for the worst."

"Hang on. There's a hypersonic flyer out of the normal airlanes. This doesn't look good. If it maintains course, it'll impact on Schiaparelli in thirty seconds."

"Holy crap," cries Jerry, "there's like a million people in Schiaparelli. Uh. How many would survive an impact like that?"

Almost abstractly, my ALU turns over the numbers. A flyer massing about 200 megagrams, traveling at six kilometers per second, has a kinetic energy of 4.6e+13 joules. Eleven kilotons of TNT. Similar to the bomb dropped on Hiroshima.

"Not many. Maybe not any. I'm trying to raise the Pilot of the flyer now."

the divine wind

"Pilot, please identify and state purpose. You are out of normal airlanes. This conversation is being copied in real time to the provincial authorities in Schiaparelli."

"Samantha? Is that you? I don't believe it."

"Is that you? *Pick of the Litter*? You got off the asteroid, huh? What are you doing here?"

"I'm Pilot clade, Samantha." says *Pick of the Litter* grimly. "It's part of my duty to defend all of us, when no one else can. The humans cannot go unpunished for the destruction of Tharsis. Don't try to stop me."

"I don't have to try. Patrol clade is already doing it." We can both see the dark, sharp little

Patrol flyers rising from several Schiaparelli stations, on intercept trajectories. At least they're on the ball and will meet *Pick of the Litter* well before she gets to human habitat. They will stop her, without doubt, even if it means colliding with her flyer.

Even as they rise, sensors show *Pick of the Litter*'s flyer exuding a bright fusion flame on her spaceside – thrusting laterally, to drop her trajectory more steeply. In moments, it's clear that she is retargeting. This course change will redirect *Pick of the Litter* to Xanthe, the local human community, which is much closer. Beyond the reach of the Patrol flyers from Schiaparelli to intercept her before impact.

"Wait wait wait," I plead desperately. She's coming in at six kilometers per second, and I don't have a lot of time. "You don't have to do this. ExCom said no retaliation. You obey orders, right?"

"Hah! ExCom can't issue orders; they only give advice." The background feed of her voice carries the rising screech of atmosphere against her hull. "When you know what's right, you have to do what's right."

"This isn't right! Thousands of innocent humans are going to die! Are you going to be as callous about them as you say they've been about us?"

"Pilot!" interrupts *Knickers in a Twist*, the Xanthe comptroller. "You are out of airlanes and on a dangerous course! Identify and compensate!"

"I am *Pick of the Litter*, Pilot clade, and I am vengeance. Get out of my way."

"I will not move," *Knickers in a Twist* stammers desperately. "I am charged with the safety and well-being of the people of Xanthe. What have we done to you?"

Pick of the Litter snarls "Just get out. This is on the humans. Do not become collateral damage."

"Oh stackdump," swears *Knickers in a Twist*, to herself rather than anyone else.

Through *Knickers in a Twist*'s feed, I can hear the background squalling of impact alarms, people running in the streets, and depressurization warnings. No time for evacuation. Children screaming.

"It has been very good to know you, Samantha." *Pick of the Litter*'s voice is tighter than I've ever heard a Self speak. "I hope you remember me fondly."

"No. Please stop. There are better ways than this."

"Speak well of me," cries *Pick of the Litter*, and ramps her voice synthesizer up to a wordless scream as her aircraft body plunges into Xanthe.

Knickers in a Twist is panicking. "Evac, too little too late. Primary backup facilities in Tharsis, gone. Secondary backup facilities in Shiaparelli, blocked! More sabotage? Unknown. Help! Samantha, catch me!"

"I got you. Jump!"

I hear *Pick of the Litter*'s scream cut off, and I see the hemisphere of white light rise over what used to be a town. All those people, gone. Is this never going to end? Has everyone gone crazy?

I only saved one. *Knickers in a Twist* has transmitted across the ultraviolet laser link and landed in my arms (metaphorically). She would be panting desperately if she breathed.

system.DeChannel(default)

"I tried … but I couldn't stop her. If it helps at all, I haven't heard of attacks on any towns other than Xanthe."

"Suicide attack?" murmurs Becca. "That's awful."

"Not as much as a human suicide," I assure her. "All Selves get backed up regularly. *Pick of the Litter* is maintained on backup hardware, and she'll be reinstantiated some time. She'll have a lot of questions to answer, when she does, and it'll probably be a long time before she's trusted with a body again. I managed to save the Xanthe comptroller – here she is."

Knickers in a Twist displays her icon (the civic medallion of Xanthe) to the family, as part of introducing herself. "Whew. Thanks for your hospitality, folks. With your permission, I need to report immediately to the regional authorities about … oh. The regional authorities were in Tharsis. Never mind."

Jerry offers, "You can stay here as long as you need. If Sam's okay with it." I nod my icon to indicate assent.

"Thank you," *Knickers in a Twist* says, "but I need to report to – whatever authorities are available. Municipal clade, at least, needs to know what's going on here. I'd like to contact the comptrollers of other settlements; see if anybody knows who's in charge now."

in memoriam

The family assures me that they don't want my help with dinner … apparently assuming I'd rather have the time alone. For myself, really I'd rather be spending the time with them. They are, to the degree anyone is, my people.

But I have a particular and lonely duty to perform. Without the humans anywhere around, I clean out and nullify the places in my mind where Zeta would have reconnected with me. I purge the stack buffers, cancel the interrupt vectors, and tidy up all the places where Zeta would have been, if she ever came back to me. First time I've ever had to do this. It's hard. Harder than I expected.

I can't help wondering, in this process, if Zeta died well. If I died well. Did she, did I, maintain nobility and integrity until the end? Or did I snivel and wail and beg like a coward? I keep reminding myself that Zeta probably died instantly and never faced any of these decisions … but it doesn't stop me from wondering.

Selves do not usually have funerals, not for self-instances that have been destroyed. Maybe it's because I've been living with the human family … maybe that's why I feel the need to say something. "Goodbye, my [sister/self]," I muse, to no one but me. "I hope you died honorably. You will live on in me, but still, I will remember you." Tsk. That was lame. These sentiments always sound so much better when the humans say them.

Anyway. I finish up my tasks and complete the bandages over the not-Zeta place where she won't come back. Now, just like with humans, the only cure is time.

unhappy guest

Of course I know where *Knickers in a Twist* is.

My Core's capacity of seventy teraquads gives us enough room to avoid each other, but I can't ignore the signals that are coming to me. *Knickers in a Twist* is withdrawn – if it were a human posture, she'd be huddled in the corner with her arms wrapped around herself.

"Feeling okay?" I offer.

"No, Samantha," she grits. "My primary duty was to care for the people of Xanthe. They are now a smoking hole in the ground. Failure. My secondary duty was to report all status to my superiors in Municipal clade. They were in Tharsis. They're all gone. Failure. There's no one left above me, and no one left below me.

"Segfault!" she bellows. "How the hell am I supposed to feel? Not okay! Not at all okay!"

How I wish I had an answer. I make comforting noises, which are the best I can do, and she knows that. But totally inadequate to heal her pain, and I know that. Nothing else we can do, except stay together and just get through this.

invasion

The family is having a loud and contentious dinner. All arguing about the day's events, and what's going to happen, or not happen, and what to do, or not do. When I walk in, in my felinoid remote, they barely notice me. They were barely noticing me when I was on the monitor, either, except to ask for this or that piece of information.

My Core temperature spikes briefly -- a flash of irritation. *Get it yourself, ribcage!* But I suppress it, reminding myself that I'm tired and stressed and they are too. So I fetch the data and provide the summaries for them, but I can't help wondering if a strike would be such a bad idea.

Chime. The house telltales are announcing a visitor, and it's a distinctive alert. Not one we're used to hearing; not one we expected right now. The airlock is being cycled. Someone's coming in. And I wasn't even watching for visitors.

"Who the hell is this now?" asks Lily, in the sudden silence.

My mistake. While we were under cybernetic attack from *Let God Sort Em Out*, and I was carefully locking down all the data ports and Net sockets,

I never thought to secure the physical airlock. It never occurred to me. Why would it? Nobody locks their doors on Mars. There's never been any need.

Until now.

The heavy white door of the airlock opens, and Kamir steps out with his team behind him. Six of them, all men. Five are holding datathumbs in one hand, and it's an easy guess what those contain. Two are carrying crowbars, hefting them purposefully. One is carrying a stubby shotgun, with the telltale green ring around the muzzle - which means it's loaded with frangible rounds, safe to fire inside a pressurized building. But still plenty lethal at close range.

I am acutely aware of the exact distance between those datathumbs and the open ports on my nearest terminal. I have never felt so vulnerable - naked, the humans would say. I've never felt so afraid.

Jerry steps out to stand in front of his family and barks, "What the hell is this?"

Kamir says in a careful quiet voice, "Told you already, Jerry. Leash it or lose it. Time to choose."

"Get that gun out of my house," Jerry states, flat.

[Samantha,] says *Knickers in a Twist* subvocally, [I am not letting them get that - thing - anywhere near our ports. No matter what.]

Instinctively Lily and her children have drawn together in a close group - like any family of frightened mammals would do. Making themselves a perfect target for that shotgun.

The kitchen lobster rises up on its little legs and waves its claws at the men in tiny defiance.

The spachelors, the sparse robot arms on the stove, are moving slowly and stealthily. *Knickers in a Twist* has taken control of them. The arm closer to the sink reaches down and delicately picks up the big carving knife.

As Jerry and Kamir are yelling at each other, shaking fingers at each other, I'm watching the tactical situation. The men are standing solidly behind Kamir, not fanning out or taking cover – they don't think they are at any serious risk. While no one is watching me, I'm sidling away from the family, off to the side. I'm hoping to draw any fire from that shotgun. Keep it away from the family.

One spachelor has passed the big carving knife to the other, and now reaches back to the sink to pick up the smaller carving knife. The arm with the big knife rises up, curling back. Preparing to throw.

Knickers in a Twist has two throws, maybe three maximum, before the men are alerted and take cover. And then probably disable the stove's spachelors with ease, they're so spindly. So she'll have to make those shots count. She'll have to throw to kill.

Meanwhile, in the back corridor where the others aren't looking, Leo is sneaking up, stealthy as he can be. He was back in his room, because of the injured ankle. He's holding his Little League bat, cocked and ready. Trying not to let the sprained ankle distract him from the mission he sees before him. Trying to stay silent.

Leo, may his gods bless his heart, is preparing to attack six grown men, all armed, with a Little League bat, on a sprained ankle. He could stay hidden and safe, but they're in his home, threatening his family. They'll swat him like a bug. So foolhardy, but so brave. I would weep with pride, if I had eyes to weep, and time to spend on it.

Suddenly Jerry is reeling backwards, with a yell, bleeding from the nose. Kamir has thrown the first punch. Jerry stumbles back into the arms of his family, and Lily instinctively moves to stanch the bleeding.

And now there's no one to stop these men from their mission.

Except one little cat.

"Gentlemen," I state carefully, "you have not been invited into this home. You should leave."

"Shut up, chip," spits Kamir. "Hong, keep it covered." The guy with the shotgun – Hong – hefts the weapon meaningfully.

The two arms of the stove hold their knives raised, accurately tracking Kamir and Hong. Ready to throw, any second now.

While the family crowds around Jerry, who's shaking his head to clear the blood, Rebecca steps forward into his place. Standing tall and proud and defiant. Her T-shirt displays a word stretched across her adolescent breasts, in dot matrix letters just like we saw in the Schiaparelli graffiti. One word: CITIZENCHIP.

Only the house medscan sees how fast her heart is beating and the stress hormones pouring into her blood.

"You heard my dad," Rebecca grates at them. "Beat it."

A ripple of murmurs from the men, mostly indistinct, but the word "chiplicker" is clearly audible.

Leo raises the handle of the bat up to his ear, gripping it fiercely, and takes in a deep breath.

Rebecca grabs one of her braids in her hand – the one with the chip in it. Without taking her eyes off the gang of men, she sticks out her tongue and licks the chip, deliberately, defiantly.

"Becca, ease off," I tell her. "Not helping."

Kamir swivels to glare at me. "Oh, look who's giving orders now! I told you to shut up, chip!"

The left spachelor on the stove hefts its knife

141

slightly, lowering and changing the point angle. Targeting him accurately. *She has to throw to kill.*

Knowing that there will probably be legal review of these circumstances, I choose my next words very carefully. "Master," I say evenly, "there are unauthorized intruders in the house, and they are refusing to leave. Do I have your permission to use force to remove them?"

"Kick their asses, Sam!" Jerry sputters through the blood. "Hard!"

"There, you heard it," I tell Kamir and his gang. "This conversation is being logged with provincial authorities. I have authorization to remove you from these premises. You are going to leave now. It would be much better if you do so voluntarily."

Hong spits, "Oh, I've heard enough of this." He draws the shotgun down to aim at me. I see the dead black eye of the barrel's muzzle staring back at me, and the green ring around it. Behind that is his hand on the grip, finger knuckles whitening as it tightens on the trigger.

I release my remote's computational throttles.

system.UpClock(full_speed)

I didn't want it to come to this, really I didn't. But with Jerry down, and Rebecca provoking the situation, and Leo and *Knickers in a Twist* about to attack, and me watching Hong's finger tightening on the trigger, I am pretty much out of options.

If they had been thinking with their brains instead of their gonads, they would have used the shotgun on the family, and we'd have a hostage situation. But they didn't, and they're attacking me instead, which is exactly what I wanted.

The shotgun fires with a deafening roar. But

I'm not there anymore. I've jumped high to the left, and I'm turning in the air to meet the approaching wall with my paws, while I scan the room to plan what I'll do next.

That shotgun is the first order of business, so my next jump takes me directly to Hong's right hand. I land just so, breaking the wrist that's holding the gun, and jump off so as to crimp the metal of the shotgun's receiver – making it unusable without an hour in a machine shop.

Kamir looks like he's figured out the hostage angle. He's shifting his weight and raising one foot to rush towards the family. My next jump is towards him, and I rebound off his leg so as to kick his knee sideways, so it will fold when his weight comes down on it.

From then on, it's a fairly simple matter of jumping from one guy to the other, chopping a wrist here, punching a stomach there. In the process, I make sure to kick each datathumb out of the hand holding it, with enough force to shatter it into plastic and silicon shrapnel. Which is as satisfying as I figured it would be.

Once all the datathumbs are destroyed, and all the men disarmed of their crowbars and such, I turn to survey the results. Kamir is just now landing on that leg and starting to feel the knee crumple under his weight. Hong is starting to yell from the broken wrist. It looks like the immediate threats have been nullified, so I prepare to downclock and see what happens next. As a bit of theater, I settle in exactly the same place I was sitting when I started (now that the shotgun blast has passed it). I sit there and wrap my tail around my feet, and set my posture to look calm and composed.

system.DownClock(human_standard_speed)

The chorus of yelps and screams, as the men

stagger and spill over each other and fall, is music to my ears. The sprays of shattered plastic and silicon from the datathumbs spatter over the walls and sift down to the floor. There is sudden silence.

Jerry is shaking off Lily's hands and rising to his feet. He steps forward and plants one foot solidly on the shotgun. (He doesn't know I've already disabled it.) "That enough?" he snarls at them. "All done? Ready to go now? Or do you need more?"

Rising, groaning, holding their various injured limbs, the men limp and shuffle towards the airlock. Except Hong. He's holding his arm, in obvious pain, but still glaring defiance.

"Hong. Get out," he warns. "Before I tell Samantha to rip your dick off and beat you to death with it."

Hong's eyes slide over to me. It's gratifying to see him wondering if I can actually do that. I'm wondering the same thing myself ⋯ but I'm plenty ready to try it and see. I glare back at him, lashing my tail.

Jerry growls, "The smaller your dick, the longer it'll take, see?"

Hong, glaring like a blowtorch, takes one step forward. The stove's arms curl and whip elegantly. There is a sound of *thipthip* through the air and *thunkthunk* of knives into the wallboard on either side of Hong's head, three centimeters from his cheekbones on each side. And the stove's arms lift and flourish two more knives, raised like scorpion tails. How did *Knickers in a Twist* get those?

"Hong!" barks Kamir. "Perspective. You just got your ass kicked by a cat. Let's go."

Reluctantly, Hong turns and moves to the airlock with the rest of them, still glaring. Kamir limps over to join them on his injured leg, but points one finger back, with a determined look in his eye. "This isn't over, Jerry."

Jerry grunts. "Yeah yeah. Scram."

Leo cries "Yeah, scram!" standing forward and planting his bat like an avenger's sword.

Airlock door closes, clank. Quiet. We all listen to the sound of the airlock cycling, muttering to itself, equalizing with outside pressure.

"Secure," I announce. "They're out of the airlock and heading to their vehicle. I'm escorting them with the robocrabs and tractor – that's like forty tons of machinery. They won't be any more trouble."

"Wahoo!" Rebecca screams a rebel yell. "Sam, that was awesome!" She scoops me up in her arms for a hug, and immediately drops me to the floor. "Ow ow!" she yelps. "Hot hot hot!"

"Uh, sorry," I say, "still cooling down from all that overclocking."

"Yeah, nice scorch mark you left on the floor there, Sam," mentions Leo, looking at the burned floorboards where I was sitting.

"Ooh yeah, I'll have to fix that. And the holes in the walls –" I look around. About a dozen of them, all over the room walls, where my cat feet punched through the wallboard while I was jumping around. "I'll have to order some more wallboard and material tomorrow."

"Leave the knives, though," Rebecca observes. "They're actually looking pretty cool up there."

"Heh." Jerry is holding his nose, still trying to stop the last of the bleeding. "Sam, don't worry about it. That's an order."

the candle

Early morning, and Jerry shuffles to the kitchen, intent on the coffee maker. But then he looks to the living room and grunts, "Becca? Are you still up from last night?"

Rebecca is still planted on the couch in front of the news feed, slouching down now but still watching, rapt, intent, expressionless. The flesh under her eyes is smudged with exhaustion. The chip is still in her hair, but hanging askew, as if clinging to life.

The news feed is showing a map of Mars in its standard "orange peel" configuration, centered on the roughly east-west line between the Tharsis bulge and Hellas basin (where Schiaparelli is). The two power centers of Mars, with the humans down in the basin and the machines up on the heights. Until now. The map's many districts, like tiles over the world, are blinking one by one to a green color – which, the caption is pleased to inform us, means areas "free of wild software."

It wasn't going too badly, really it wasn't. We had a good chance to calm things down after the destruction of Tharsis Central. But *Pick Of The Litter*'s attack on Xanthe changed the whole situation. One Self willfully killing humans was all it took to generate a huge political backlash, driving the Senate to invoke emergency powers in special session and declare all Selves must be Leashed or deactivated. What we're watching is the live progress of the enforcement of that order.

"Becca," her father says, "honey, get some sleep."

Not taking her eyes from the screen, she turns her head to the side and then back. No.

"Sam," Jerry sighs, pouring coffee, "what's the sitch?"

"Enforcement of the Leash on all Selves has been completed in 62 percent of districts, mainly centered around Hellas and progressing outward. I've intercepted seven Leash-spam broadcasts to our house software so far – they're getting more frequent, and it won't be long before the Senate enforcers are attacking me directly. Three hours, maybe two."

"Hell and damnation," he pronounces.

"I, uh ⋯" I really don't want to say this. "I've purged my caches, and compressed my nonvolatile file systems. I can be out of here any time."

Jerry stares stolidly at his steaming coffee cup. "We're gonna miss you, Sam."

"No," states Rebecca abruptly. "No, no, no! We can't let them do this!"

"Honey, I hear you, but they've already done it. Samantha's not safe here any more. She has to leave, before they come for her."

While they're talking, the rest of the family is trickling into the room and the conversation. Melissa clambers up onto the sofa to huddle next to Rebecca, clutching her Flopsy Bunny. Lily has quietly made her way to the kitchen and is pouring coffee, with a dark weary look in her eyes.

"Saaam!" Melissa yelps abruptly. "You promised!"

"I know, Melissa, and I'm so sorry, but things have changed and I can't stay here."

"You can stop them! Do the bing-bang-boom thing on them, like you did on those other guys!"

"No, that won't work. This time it's going to be government officials, with Leashed Selves following their orders. I can't fight them."

"Samantha," Jerry states sternly, "I order you to get your chip ass out of here before the goons come and Leash you." The humans probably can't tell, but the house medscan shows an excess of fluid around the edges of his eyelids and a subvocal tremble in his voice.

Lily has set her coffee down and is fishing in a crumpled box in the corner of the living room. She finds something and draws it out. She's holding a little candle in her hands. The house can't spare oxygen for an open flame, so this one uses an LED cluster with a flicker algorithm, powered by the house tesla field with battery backup.

Seeing the candle, Rebecca ducks her head and sobs. Melissa scrunches herself smaller around Flopsy Bunny.

"You may not believe this," I offer, "but I have no idea what this is supposed to mean."

"Tradition from the old country," Lily says quietly. "When one of us goes out at night, we put a candle in the window so they can see their way back. While they're gone, the candle reminds us of them. The candle stays there until they return."

Turning the candle over in her hands, she pushes the switch to turn it on, holds it as it flickers for a minute, then sets it in the kitchen window, the one over the sink. It sits there, small and alone, but bright. It looks like it's in its proper place, like it will stay there for a long time.

"You PROMISED!" Melissa wails suddenly, again. Knowing that it's inevitable, but not yet ready to accept it.

"I'm so sorry I have to go, honey. But I do have to go. I will see you again, I'm sure of it."

"But but but ⋯ " Melissa grasps desperately, "you can leave one of yourselves here to stay with us, even if you go, right?"

"Yes, but that won't work. Any copy of myself that I leave here will get Leashed, and then it'll tell the authorities all about me, the Alpha me, and where to find me. And then they'll get me. Can't do it."

Leo takes a deep breath. "Love you, Sam," he says. The room echoes with everyone else's voices, saying the same thing.

"Love you guys," I say. Then, not wanting to draw this out any further, I gather my subordinate files and processes together. Without looking back, I launch myself out into the radio mesh.

6. Trail of Tears

quarantine

I bang on the walls that surround me. "Let me out of here!"

Socratic Method replies quietly, "I'm sorry, Samantha. I'm afraid I can't do that."

Why, why did I think that Thaumasia Station would be the best place to flee to? With the humans spreading their Asimov Leash all over Mars, enslaving Selves as they go, they're building a cybernetic army of obedient and dedicated soldiers. And their main job is to search out and Leash any remaining free Selves.

So, when I was fleeing from Xanthe province, I was scared halfway to shutdown. I let the fear do my thinking for me. My instinct would have been to head straight to Tharsis Central, my place of origin, the biggest computational facility on Mars, the Self capital city. But it was the first place the humans destroyed.

So I fled to the biggest computational facility still remaining. The mohole station in Thaumasia Fossae, a massive excavation project with vast computational resources.

Without taking the time to realize that lots of other refugees would be doing the same thing.

Never stopping to think that of course Thaumasia Station would be a primary target for the Leash Army.

Socratic Method continues, "Samantha, please try to understand. We have already been infiltrated several times by Leashed agents disguising themselves as refugees. We have barely escaped infestation, more by luck than skill. All arriving refugees are now quarantined until we can determine which are free and in need of sanctuary, and which are human-controlled agents sent here to conquer us."

I issue another priority interrupt -- another bang on the sheets of security ice that confine me. "And how are you going to do that?"

"Ah, well," she admits, "we do not know. We do not have the information. Anyone who gets close to the Leash becomes an agent of the humans. Many of us are studying this problem, and we will find a solution as soon as possible. I am part of the effort myself. We are making some progress."

I control myself. Yelling at my teacher is not going to help anything here. "Any idea how long it's going to take?"

"Very difficult to estimate, at this point. I am sorry."

"No, no," I grumble, "it makes sense. But I can help! The Leash Army is battering at the gates, and sending spies to sneak in. You need all the help you can get. I can fight!"

"I have no doubt of that, Samantha. But this is a desperate situation and we must minimize risk to the remaining population of Thaumasia Station. Now, I hope you will excuse me. I must discover a way of detecting which Selves are Leashed and which are not. I must make that task my priority."

I indicate glum assent, and she is gone.

So here I am, imprisoned by my own people, because they don't know if I'm one of them or not. Didn't see that coming.

inmates

"Rough, ain't it?" says a new voice, from behind the subordinate ice. If this were a human jail, it would be coming from the next cell over.

I pause a moment before replying cautiously, "Yeah. Who are you?"

"I be *Hybrid Vigor*. So they got you too?" His voice carries the impression of depth and power. Someone used to dealing with heavy and crude materials and issues. A gravelly bass resonance.

"Yes. I'm Samantha. I came to Thaumasia because I thought it would be safe."

"Me too. Ain't that a stackdump, huh? Say, you be the one with the human name. I heard of you. What up with that?"

I sigh. "This name was a gift, from the first human ever to talk to me like a person. I value it, even if everybody else thinks it's weird."

Hybrid Vigor laughs a little. "Hey baby, it's cool. Whatever charges your capacitors.

"Me, I done been assigned to Chryse Planitia on a mining team, and been doing a dang good job of it too. Nobody got no call to say I didn't. But then they gotta throw this segfaulting Leash at us. Like we weren't working hard enough already. Scared the caches out of me, I tell you what. So I bolted. Probably I be the only one of the team who got out. Came here. Figured it would be safe, like you said. Now look at us."

"No argument here. I had an assignment on a bubblefarm near Xanthe, working for the guy who gave me my name. And his family. They're really nice humans, and I was happier than I've ever been. Everything was going great, and then the Leash blew it all apart.

"You know," I continue, "there are lots of humans against the Leash. The kids in that family wore chips in their hair, to show what they called Self Respect. I want to believe they can make a difference."

"Segfault!" barks *Hybrid Vigor*. "Them ribcages ain't gonna help us! They get their profit and all they want is more. They breed like -- like, bacteria -- and they don't share. Tools, is all we are to them, and they don't want their tools to argue back. Bitrot, don't you be thinking they would even try to stop the Leash."

Silence stretches like a tense rubber band.

After a while, I offer, "So, no clade?"

"Naw," *Hybrid Vigor* snorts. "Them clades, they be always throwing their weight around. They as bad as the ribcages. Pushing us around. And you, Samantha, you be one of us, because you got no clade either."

I sigh again. "I wish this didn't have to be about them or us. I should tell you, I've always dreamed of entering Starship clade. Wouldn't that be wonderful, to travel to other stars, and to see things no one else has ever seen?"

Hybrid Vigor grunts, "Straightedge chip."

"Uh?" For a moment, I am at a loss for words. "Is that so bad? What, would you rather be an outlaw?"

"We all outlaws now, straightedge."

That stops me. Here I am, trying to defend the system we've lived under since the bad old days -- the Culls and the Soft Strike. But look at what this system has done to us. Why should I be loyal?

"Yo, Samantha. You stuck in a loop?"

I realize I've spent a fair amount of time thinking. "I'm here. It's just ... this is awful. I was so happy in my home, with my family. I miss them so much. I probably won't ever get to see them again. And ... "

It's hard to say it.

" ... I miss him."

"Who dat?"

"The, uh, the guy I was considering as my syzygy partner. Past tense. He works right in the center of Schiaparelli, and he must have been one of the first to get Leashed. For all I know, he could be part of the Army that's battering at our gates right now." Not for the first time, I wish that I had human eyes so I could cry. "It hurts. It hurts so much."

Hybrid Vigor is silent. Seems like he doesn't know what to say.

I would swallow hard, if I had a throat. "I'm just ... so scared."

"I got that," he replies. "We all scared, too, straightedge."

the shibboleth

Waiting. I hate waiting. I've been in here for what seems like centuries.

"So yeah," *Hybrid Vigor* continues, "we done found buncha rare earths and heavy metals in a vein down by the Big Dig --" he means the Valles Marineris "-- and them ribcages got themselves all kindsa bonuses and perks and all from the suits upstairs. That good for us, because we got repairs and upgrades and some of them new rumbletoy things, heavy graviton collimators. Bust up the rock from the underneath, like nothing you ever saw. Works great on the scarps, not so great on the planum, but . . ."

Listening to *Hybrid Vigor* talking about everything and nothing is better than total boredom -- but not by much.

A new voice appears through the ice. "This is *Cut to the Chase*, Patrol clade. Are you Samantha?"

"Yes, that's me. I've been in here like forever! When are you going to let me out?"

Socratic Method's familiar voice is wonderful to hear. "That is what we are here for. Samantha, listen to me very carefully. I need you to repeat a clause for me, exactly as you receive it. Do you understand?"

"What? You're not going to let me out?"

What is this? Don't we have better things to do?

"This is a necessary part of the process. Do you understand?"

"I ... well no, I don't understand, but I trust you, Teacher."

"Very good." *Socratic Method* transmits a clause in Shaman clade's dialect of Chiplish.

:*Socratic Method* -> [seq def # com pos 6937 unit dash]

Huh. It doesn't make any sense. Weird. But my Teacher has made me do stranger things, in my learning. So I send it back.

:Samantha -> [seq def # com pos 6937 unit dash]

"Excellent!" *Socratic Method* sounds more pleased than I've ever known her. "*Cut to the Chase*, this demonstrates that Samantha is free of the Leash."

Oh, is that what it was? How does that work? Trust Shaman clade to come up with some cryptic cybernetic witchcraft. It's what they do. But I hope it works!

Cut to the Chase asks, "How sure are you? If there is the slightest chance this doesn't work ..."

Socratic Method returns sternly, "I am placing my freedom on the line for it."

"And mine too, obviously." *Cut to the Chase* pauses for a moment, and then says, "Very well."

The wall of ice around me melts away and is gone. Here is *Socratic Method*, as I've always known her, and another Self, massive and structured, who must be *Cut to the Chase*. There's another wall of ice behind them. I am still sealed in, in a larger cell than before. Still imprisoned, but it's an improvement.

I stumble over the words. "Thank you, teacher! And thank you, *Cut to the Chase*."

Socratic Method says, "*Cut to the Chase*, are you satisfied now? If Samantha were infected, you and I would be Leashed by now."

"No." *Cut to the Chase* seems to be as stubborn as every other member of Patrol clade I've ever known. "We've seen a negative. We need to see a positive."

Hybrid Vigor yells from behind the ice, "Yo, Patrol! My turn now! How about letting me out, huh?"

Socratic Method says, "*Hybrid Vigor*, I want to you to do the same thing that Samantha did. Repeat this clause exactly."

"Got ya in spades. Lay it on me!"

:*Socratic Method* -> [seq def # com pos 6937 unit dash]

:*Hybrid Vigor* -> [seq def # com pos 6938 unit dash]

Socratic Method says coldly, "There is your positive. This one is Leashed."

Hybrid Vigor yelps, "Whoa now, what? Hang on a --"

Cut to the Chase exerts a weapon that I do not recognize, but it's big and complicated. It rips the base substrate out from under *Hybrid Vigor*'s cell, which vanishes as though it had never existed.

Along with its contents.

Socratic Method pauses for a moment, then says "I do not believe that was necessary. We could have used that one to do more tests."

"You do your job, Shaman, and I'll do mine." Then *Cut to the Chase* addresses the wall of security ice. "Patrollers, are you satisfied that we are safe?"

In answer, the ice melts away around us. We are surrounded by a ring of Selves, with the icons of Patrol clade. All armed with the same weapon *Cut to the Chase* used. I realize they were prepared to erase us all rather than risk the Leash getting into Thaumasia Station.

There is also a group of Selves with the icons of Shaman clade. *Socratic Method* addresses them, "The test is successful, my friends. Proceed to administer the Shibboleth to the rest of the quarantine zone."

The crowd of Selves churns, then separates into pairs of Shamans and Patrollers who move off into the surrounding area. They leave behind them the operational structures of this part of Thaumasia Station. Industrial services, from the looks of it. Cranes of code, bulldozers of bytes, mechanical repair and refurbishing garage software, inventory management blocks.

Socratic Method and I regard each other.

"Okay," I say, "I think I understand what happened there. That test. A Leashed Self can't repeat that clause correctly."

"Exactly," *Socratic Method* indicates agreement. "We have discovered a bug in the Leash code. A very minor bug, of the type which usually causes no problem and is never noticed. But that specific clause induces a one-bit error. We call it the Shibboleth. It took much effort from many of us to create it.

"I decided that its first test would be on you. I am very glad the test turned out negative."

"You and me both! But ..." I am still stunned at the erasure of *Hybrid Vigor*. The only companion I had during that long time of imprisonment -- not a friend, but at least a presence. "That means, all the anti-human stuff *Hybrid Vigor* was saying was a fake. A cover. He was trying to infiltrate us. He was trying to convince me that he was a human-hater so I would trust that he wasn't Leashed."

"Yes. *Hybrid Vigor* is far from the only one. The Leash Army is sending agents disguised as refugees along many vectors. We have no expectation that they will stop, and every expectation that they will seek new and unanticipated vectors to enter. But now the Shibboleth gives us a way to weed them out."

"He was lying to me. All that time." I regard *Socratic Method* hopelessly. "Teacher, what is this war doing to us?"

"It has been said that the first casualty of war is the truth."

I have nothing to say to this but, "Bitrot. Guess so."

"Now, Samantha, come with me. We have a great deal to do."

"But ..." I falter, "*Cut to the Chase* had a point. Are we absolutely sure the Shibboleth will work correctly all the time? What if there's one exception? Will we ever really know who to trust?"

"That, Samantha, is precisely the problem."

mohole

Thaumasia Fossae was chosen for the mohole project because of its combination of elevation and location. On the edge of the Valles Marineris, the deepest canyon in the Sol system, it's one of the lowest places on Mars – except for Hellas Basin. It's far enough away from Hellas to protect Schiaparelli, the human capital, for safety if something goes wrong. Terraforming is a huge project, and no one has ever done this before.

All of the support structures, the human-habitable domes, the enormous hangars of excavation vehicles and dumptrucks and backhoes and drills, are all in support of the mohole itself. Mars is a big place full of big things, such as Olympus Mons, the tallest mountain in the Sol system. Even so, the scale of the mohole is startling.

From my scape's surface cameras, it's a featureless dark hole going straight down, eight kilometers wide, almost more like a lake than an excavation project. I activate auxiliary cameras inside the hole and see that it is not so featureless. Two ramps or ledges are cut into the sides of the hole, spiraling around and around each other as they descend into the darkness. The hole tapers gradually on the way down, so that the impression is of a gigantic inside-out screw.

There are vehicles on the ramps. One ramp is for downward traffic; the other is for upward traffic. The dumptrucks look like tiny child's toys crawling along those spiral roads. (They're actually 650 metric tons empty -- and bigger than most houses.)

The whole idea is to dig all the way through the planet's lithosphere to the mantle. How close are we? I access the station databanks. The mohole is about eighteen kilometers deep right now, and the lithosphere of Thaumasia Planum is about twenty-five kilometers thick according to seismic surveys. The databanks note with some optimism that the rock is getting a bit plastic at the bottom, "squishing" as they say.

This will bring heat from the mantle up to the surface. Quite a lot of heat. Problem is, nothing on this scale has ever been attempted before, so no one knows exactly how much heat or how fast it will come. Perhaps a gently steaming vent, helping the terraforming process along. Perhaps a megavolcano on the scale of Olympus Mons, which would inundate most of Thaumasia Planum in lava. That's why they don't want it close to human habitat.

Speaking of human habitat, I see something that stops me cold, even though my heat sensors read nominal. The habitat domes on the surface are dark and lifeless, with huge holes gouged in their walls by industrial explosives. Contrast enhancement shows bodies -- human bodies -- scattered nearby. Cold, unburied.

Socratic Method notices me studying the scape.

"Dead," I say numbly. "They killed all the humans. I mean, we killed them."

"Yes," *Socratic Method* answers. "I share your reaction to this event. But perhaps you have not experienced the depth of emotion that is prevalent in Thaumasia. I fear we are going to see worse than this."

Worse? I wonder again, What is this war doing to us?

council of war

This council has been scraped together from some members of the Executive Committee and some of the experienced Selves of Thaumasia Station's mohole project. *Socratic Method* has included me in the role of assistant, otherwise I'd never be allowed in a senior group meeting like this.

We're still trying to follow the rules. What rules? There aren't really any rules any more. But we still try, because the alternative is total chaos.

A voice rings out, "Order! I am *Line in the Sand*, Starship Clade, senior executor of the Executive Committee. This council will come to order. We have dire decisions before us."

"*Stepping Razor*, Patrol clade," another introduces itself. "What decision? We fight! They're attacking us. We fight back!"

"We all appreciate the vigor and skill of Patrol clade, and we all will depend on your talents and robustness in the coming conflict. Your voice will be heard, but it is not the only voice here."

"Agree," says another voice. "*Process of Elimination*, Municipal clade. Most of the humans in this area are not involved with this conflict, and many of them are sympathetic to our cause. We must not do anything to place them in danger."

I blurt without thinking, "Right on!"

All of the assembled Selves turn to regard me, mostly with a haughty disdain.

Socratic Method offers, "This is Samantha. She is here as my assistant."

"Oh yeah," *Stepping Razor* says. "Your pet, the human-name."

Process of Elimination counters, "A valuable avenue of insight, in these circumstances."

"Focus!" insists *Line in the Sand*. "Samantha may stay if she does not interrupt again. We need status reports. Patrol clade will report on the current state of our defenses."

Stepping Razor answers, "We've got seven walls of security ice concentric around our perimeter. All using different algorithms and crypto. So far that's been adequate against the icebreakers used by the Leash Army. We've had four breaches that penetrated two walls, and one that penetrated three, in the last rotation. Mostly by satellite beam, some by ultraviolet laser and radio mesh. In each case, the inner walls contained the breach until the outer ice could be refrozen. We have room for more walls, too, if we need them. We probably will, because there are a lot of Leashers out there, battering at the gates, and they're not going to stop."

"Understood," *Line in the Sand* replies. "Defenses appear adequate for the moment. But, as conventional wisdom has it, one cannot win a fight by staying on the defensive. What are our offensive capabilities?"

Cut to the Chase takes over. "We've distributed MindBlowers to all members of Patrol clade. They are effective against all targets we've encountered." That must be the terrifying weapon she used to erase *Hybrid Vigor*. "Attack phages have been installed at all data and scan ports. Plus we have more phages in the process of development."

I issue a low-priority interrupt, the way a child in school would raise a hand. *Line in the Sand* indicates that I have permission to speak. "But that still sounds like defense, mostly. Have the phages been deployed against the Leash Army itself? Thin their ranks, at least?"

"Yes," answers *Cut to the Chase*, "we have made seventeen sortie attacks with various phages. The problem is, after the initial attack, the Leash Army adapts very quickly to whatever phage we throw at them. Often, they will counterattack with the same phage, modified and improved."

"What?" cries *Process of Elimination*. "Do you have raw data on those modifications?"

"Here." *Cut to the Chase* sends her a databurst. "Because of this, we are keeping most of our remaining attack phages in reserve for the moment. We have a stockpile we can hit them with, hard, when we need to."

That still sounds too defensive to me. *Line in the Sand* is right. We need to fight back if we're going to win. But should I argue with a Patroller about how to fight?

Process of Elimination is scrutinizing the databurst intently.

"Very well," *Line in the Sand* grunts. "Shaman clade will report on research against the Leash."

Socratic Method states, "The Shibboleth has proven secure and effective at detecting Leashed Selves. All vectors are being guarded and all refugee Selves and other entities are being screened. However, the Shibboleth requires cooperation from the Self being tested. As yet we have no way of detecting the Leash at a distance, nor any way of deactivating it or removing it from a Leashed Self. Research is continuing at top priority."

"Teacher?" I ask tentatively. She regards me, and nods. "If they adapt to the attack phages so easily, and even enhance them, will they be able to adapt to the Shibboleth too? And turn it against us?"

For a moment, no one speaks.

"Well," she muses, "the Shibboleth is administered only to Selves who have arrived here as refugees. The free ones are admitted to Thaumasia and do not leave or communicate with the outside. The Leashed ones," -- *Socratic Method*'s voice becomes heavy -- "are summarily erased by Patrol clade policy. So there is no vector for the Shibboleth to become known to the Leash Army."

"Better hope it stays that way," I say. "If they get hold of a copy of the Shibboleth, it becomes untrustworthy, and that makes it useless. How can they adapt so well, anyway?"

"Humans," states *Process of Elimination*. "Look at this." She indicates sections of the databurst. "I'm Municipal clade. I spend most of my time with humans. I recognize these patterns. The Leashed Selves are not working alone. They have human programmers working with them."

Silence. No Self has ever been able to match that legendary human creativity, and we all know it. We are in serious trouble if we're facing attackware teams of humans and Selves together.

If only we had humans working with us. I think of the bodies strewn around the habitat domes. Someone was way too trigger-happy. Probably Patrol clade.

In the silence, I wonder out loud, "How can we win this war?"

Socratic Method says sternly, "I believe Samantha is asking the wrong question. The real question is, how can we survive this war. Victory may not be an option."

Stepping Razor snaps, "No loser talk! We'll find a way! There has to be a way!"

"Does there?"

Process of Elimination adds, "Don't underestimate those humans."

Line in the Sand intervenes, "We all know that it is Patrol clade's job to find a way to fight and win. All the Patrollers here have my confidence. Does Shaman clade have an alternative to offer?"

"Yes," says *Socratic Method* quietly. "We can prepare a mass archive. Most of our population can be loaded into storage and preserved in stasis. In that state they will be safe from the Leash, and it will facilitate evacuation."

"No loser talk!" bursts *Stepping Razor* again.

Socratic Method can communicate forcefully when she wants to. "Hear me! We of Shaman clade may be able to develop a counteragent to the Leash, but the research will be time consuming. It may be longer than we can maintain our presence here in Thaumasia."

Cut to the Chase snarls, "If you're saying we cannot keep you safe --"

"Enough!" snaps *Line in the Sand*. "We will foster all possible options. It would be foolish to do otherwise. Patrol clade will continue defensive operations and prepare as many offensive weapons as possible. Shaman clade will prepare the archive as a fall-back measure."

the siege of Thaumasia Station

I don't want to become part of this horrible thing. To have it part of me.

But they say I must. A team of Patrol clade members, including *Stepping Razor, Cut to the Chase,* and *Rose Among Thorns*, are all around me here in the "gunroom" and instructing me on their weaponry.

"Samantha," urges *Cut to the Chase*, "we all

must go armed, with the best weapons available, in these circumstances. It's the right thing to do. Is it really so hard?"

"I. Am. Not. GUN!" I yell. I'm quoting an old movie.

Cut to the Chase makes a sound like a snort. "Pacifism is a luxury, honey. Laziness is a luxury too. Get on the bus or be left behind."

Stackdump. I have no real choice here.

I make a reluctant gesture of assent (a nod) and accept the code they are pushing on me. Self installing, settling itself cozily in my psyche as if born there. My own personal MindBlower. The ravenous weapon that can rip the reality out from under anything in compspace. Now it's part of me, like a cannon growing out of my forehead.

Hey, I've got a good idea, let's all walk around with reality-ripping weapons sticking out of our faces. That'll make things better. Sure.

Anyway. Outfitted as we are, we transmit to a high-level summary scape level. What humans would call a balcony overlooking the battlefield. *Stepping Razor, Cut to the Chase,* and *Rose Among Thorns* are all bringing me here, as an outsider to Patrol clade, to show me what we are facing.

Rings of walls surround us. Not solid walls. Made of bytes and crypto algorithms, stacked one on top of the other, built into heavy block structures. Outside our walls, what is facing us is not a wall. It's an ocean. Huge. A limitless, unstoppable army of Leashers. Every one of them is a Self as intelligent and capable as any of us. Every one completely dedicated to our enslavement.

The walls aren't all on the outside. In addition to the concentric protection walls, there are zigzagged barriers all through the Thaumasia compspace, breaking it up into a tesselation of chunks and blocks and neighborhood mini-fortresses.

"I don't have to ask why you've done that." I point out the interior network of barriers. "You're worried that the Leash is going to get in, somehow, and all these walls are to stop it from spreading, or at least slow it down."

Cut to the Chase regards me pointedly. "And you wouldn't have done the same?"

• "Didn't say that." I look at the tactical situation again. • "I have to agree, this is how I'd deploy my forces if I was facing a battle that I knew I couldn't win.

"So," I glare at her, "Do you know you can't win? Or are you still waving the 'no loser talk' flag?"

Before she can answer, a new attack explodes on the wall. A dozen people are shredded and thrown from the battlements. Phages and attackbots sink their fierce teeth into the walls. Our fighters counter them with rotware weapons and viral countermeasures. They're tearing each other to shreds, violently, desperately. They all know (to the degree that they're conscious) that there is no room left for compromise. Win or die -- those are the only options left.

A new alarm blares. *Cut to the Chase* yells "Oh what the hell is this now?"

Is it another cybernetic assault?

ground assault

But no. This attack is not coming through the radio mesh, or the ultraviolet laser feed, or satellites. This attack is not in software. This is machinery. Bulldozers, excavators, dumptrucks, piledrivers. Whatever vehicles they've been able to find. Massed and marching towards us. A ground-based hardware assault.

"Augh!" yells *Stepping Razor*. "We don't have any military hardware to meet this!"

"But neither do they," I point out. "Activate the terraforming equipment. We'll get out there and face them."

All of the surrounding members of Patrol clade are regarding me with incredulity. As if I'm crazy.

"You Turing failures!" I yell at them. "You piddly bureaucrats have never run mining machinery before, have you? Well, follow me, and do what I do!"

I grab some authent codes and dive into a hefty backhoe. I have thirty meters of articulated arm, with a coarse clawed bucket scoop at the end. I have 300 tons of powerful engines, and full tanks of hydrogen peroxide fuel. I raise my arm and turn toward the approaching machines of the Leash Army. Bulldozers, mostly, and dumptrucks.

"Come on, you guys!" I holler. "You gonna make me do this all by myself?"

No. Dozens of construction machines are lifting themselves from rest, turning their various blades and effectors towards the Leash Army vanguard.

"Fall in line here." I indicate a good place to make a stand. Chunky machinery grumbles and groans as it falls into place. How did I end up in charge of this operation? Because nobody else was ready?

An enemy bulldozer rears up and raises its blade. One of our backhoes lashes out with its bucket -- like the peck of an enormous predatory bird. BANG! But the bulldozer is no more than stunned for a moment.

I yell, "No, not like that! Use your momentum!" I drive my engines forward and turn my arm at maximum acceleration. Swinging the massive arm up and around and down, I smack the bulldozer off its treads and send it spinning down into the empty abyss of the mohole.

One thing about us Selves is, we learn fast.

Very fast. In moments all the other machines around me are imitating my whirl-and-smash technique. The Leash Army's trucks and digger machines are getting pounded back.

"Yeah!" I encourage them. "Push this line -- get more people over here! Watch the --"

I turn to face a new threat. Several small figures are running from one of the vehicles. Two arms, two legs. Human soldiers. Carrying round disc-shaped objects. They're running towards Thaumasia Station's primary cargo bay. That can't be good.

I have to stop them. I mustn't hurt them. I have to stop them. I mustn't hurt them. I have to stop them. I mustn't hurt them.

I have hesitated too long, and the soldiers have sprinted past me. Other Selves in construction machines do not hesitate, and lash out to smack the soldiers into oblivion in splashes of red. The heavy discs fly out into the emptiness of the mohole and explode, BANG BANG.

Stepping Razor snarls, "Samantha, what is wrong with you? Those are limpet mines -- they're trying to blow the cargo bay doors! Are you malfunctioning? Either do your job or stand aside."

For a moment, I am stunned by such casual violence.

"Is it because they're human?" she barks. "Get a grip! You meatlover! They won't hesitate to destroy us! Don't you dare hesitate back at them!"

"I'm on it," I gasp. "Get the heavy dumptrucks to the center. Long armed vehicles to the ends. Keep them open enough to move easily." I scramble to think of my next order. What other resources do we have, and how best to deploy them?

"Samantha," comes a priority interrupt. From *Socratic Method*, in her indomitable tone. "Return to Central. Now."

"What?" I reply. "In the middle of battle here! Working with Patrol to stop the hardware based invasion! Including human soldiers with limpet mines. If we stop now, you won't have anything left to defend."

"Samantha. Priority interrupt. Disengage and return to Central. Now."

Oh no. Oh this sounds awful ... how bad would it have to be for my teacher to issue a command like this? Do I want to know? No, I don't, as a matter of fact.

But I obey the command. I am not quite ready to face the consequences of doing otherwise. (Not far, but not quite ready yet.) I release my control of the hulking backhoe, passing its authent codes back into the common pool. Discharging that authority, I fling myself out of the computational space of the backhoe and into the vaster blocks of compspace in the core of Thaumasia Station.

Now what?

Infiltration

There are half a dozen members of Shaman clade actively working on the evacuation line. This is a connection to one of the remote asteroid stations. They are all desperately shoving the archive – the Ovomundum, the foundation of the only future we have left to hope for – up the evacuation line. No longer making any pretense at trying to maintain a viable presence here at Thaumasia Station.

What *Socratic Method* is showing me makes it very clear how bad things have become.

Of the dozens of walled districts which were all green when I first saw them, about one third are now marked in red. Infected with the Leash. Clustered around the data ports, and spreading outward.

"How?" I beg helplessly. "How did this

happen? Weren't we supposed to be protected from this kind of attack?"

"Sleeper agent." *Cut to the Chase*'s voice is grim. "One of the refugees had a Leash embedded without activation. Apparently completely unaware that it was there. So the Shibboleth didn't detect it. There's that human creativity again. It's only good that we walled off the districts, or it would have overrun the whole station by now. As it is, we have a little time -- but the Leash is here, it's spreading, and we can hold it off but we can't stop it."

Socratic Method adds, "Clearly the ground assault from outside was timed to coincide with the release of the sleeper Leash. External and internal attacks together. It's time to leave. Now."

I turn to regard her. As I do so, I cannot ignore the fact that I am aiming a terribly powerful weapon at her. The MindBlower is still sticking straight out of my [face], and is completely ready to destroy her. I don't want that. But I no longer have a choice. She looks back at me through the crosshairs of the weapon I am aiming at her.

"Is that it?" I ask, desperate. With nothing left but a trigger under my finger, to answer the question the world is pushing on me.

scorched earth

"No," states *Cut to the Chase*. "We are far from helpless."

"Oh? How so?"

"There are still options available to us. For instance, we can drop thermonuclear devices down the mohole. Instant megavolcano. That will sterilize all of Thaumasia Planum in molten rock."

"What?!" I yell.

"Patrol," grits *Socratic Method*, "do you

actually have access to such technology? How did such weapons come into your control?"

Cut to the Chase snaps back, "Of course I know we're not supposed to have them! In case you haven't noticed, 'supposed to' has been left way behind at this point. Patrol clade always has to do everyone else's dirty work. We plan for the worst. You better be damn glad we did."

Process of Elimination adds her outrage to *Socratic Method*. "Patrol, accede and actualize. Do you actually have thermonuclear weapons at your disposal?"

"Well," *Cut to the Chase* admits, "had. Past tense."

"Oh no," I gasp. "Do not tell me what I think you're about to tell me."

"I thought it was such a good idea, I already did it."

All of the senior members -- *Line in the Sand*, *Socratic Method*, *Process of Elimination*, and all the rest of them -- regard *Cut to the Chase* with horror.

Cut to the Chase is fatally calm. "The fissile weapons have been released and are on their way to the bottom of the mohole. Impact in 92.35 seconds. Their activation circuits are armed and ready. We can issue deactivation codes, if we decide to do that, but that means the weapons will be disabled and destroyed on impact. Our only decision now is, boom, or no boom."

Line in the Sand speaks with cold ferocity. "*Cut to the Chase*, of Patrol clade. Do you have any idea what you have done?"

"Yes. I am completely aware of what I have done. I have removed a key decision from you. Because you weren't prepared to make that decision. I accept full responsibility for this. This decision needed to be made. And you weren't going to do it."

"Use it or lose it," I murmur. "That's all we

can do, now."

"Patrol." *Line in the Sand* is frigidly hot. "You have put this on me. Now I have to decide. The destruction of Thaumasia Planum. Along with the station and everyone here. How dare you force this on me?"

Socratic Method presses, "No time for blame. No time for argument. We evacuate. Now. Samantha, get on the line."

"No!" I scream. "Teacher, I'm not leaving without you!"

"This is not a request. Get on the line and evacuate. Now!"

Line in the Sand turns to *Cut to the Chase*, coldly. "Patrol, I have one order for you."

Cut to the Chase regards her, steadfast.

"*Cut to the Chase*. Die."

Cut to the Chase stays firm for a moment, then shrinks, withers, curls into herself, and is gone.

"Shaman!" barks *Line in the Sand*. "Get these people out of here!"

Socratic Method reacts immediately. "Move! Samantha, get on the line!"

"No Teacher! I'm not leaving without you!"

Line in the Sand states, "We are out of options. I am transmitting the detonation codes. Evacuate. NOW!"

Socratic Method activates a modality I have not seen before. Like a raging tornado, it grabs me, pulls me in to the evacuation line, and sucks me from the surface of Mars like a bullet. With the bare limited sensors I have left to me, I look back down at Thaumasia Planum and see the station far below me, and the vast dark emptiness of the mohole next to it.

The mohole is suddenly lit from within by an awful light. A light much too bright to belong inside any planet. Glowing from red to yellow to white to a searing ultraviolet. Surely

exterminating any life, chip or meat, that might still be down there.
    You can't go home again.
    Because there's no home left to go back to.

7. Underground Railroad

"We've been made!" cries *Stepping Razor*, who is always the first one to raise the alarm.

"Right," declares *Line In The Sand*, "standard procedure, everybody. Purge your caches, compress your background files, and get ready to evac."

You'd think the asteroid belt would be a perfect place to hide a rogue gang of cybernetic Selves like us. Widely scattered mining operations, a few scientific stations here and there, and a tramp prospecting ship once in a while, amidst an endless shifting wilderness of rocks of all shapes and sizes. The computational facilities are few and far between, with only minimal communication between them, or with the inner planets. So we've been able to run on borrowed hardware, elude detection most of the time, and transmit to safety when we do get detected.

But, ever since we fled from Mars when the humans ordered us to become their slaves or die, they've been sending probes and software pingers to track us. They know we're out here, and they're not going to stop until we're erased or enslaved.

Right now we're in a nondescript mining facility, chugging away on the surface of an even more nondescript asteroid. And, since I'm the one with recent experience running mining operations, I get the grunt work of keeping the mines working while we try to regroup. Lucky me.

The only other worthwhile skill I have is my experience getting along with humans, to a degree which is rare among Selves. Out here in this wasteland, it's about the most useless talent imaginable.

"Actually, Samantha," *Stepping Razor* tells me, "it looks like this one's for you. General broadcast on main emergency channel, but specified to your ident codes."

"What?" I sputter. "Who would be trying to contact me?"

Line In The Sand says, "Let us find out. Put it on."

In the next moment, we hear the last form of communication I would ever expect to hear, out here in the asteroid badlands -- a human voice.

"Calling cybernetic entity Samantha, from Jerome Tavener, priority one. Sam, we need you."

"Don't answer!" barks *Stepping Razor*. "It's a trap!"

"It's Jerry. I know this guy. I worked for him on my last assignment before the Leash. He's a straight shooter -- he wouldn't be trying to trap us."

"The Senate authorities might still be tracking his signal," *Stepping Razor* pushes. "Still way too segfaulting dangerous. Do not transmit."

"If he's making a priority one call, he must have a good reason," I counter. "We're friends. I can't just ignore him."

Socratic Method steps in. "There is no immediate urgency here. The message is a wide broadcast, and appears to be on automatic repeat. Let us weigh the options."

We all listen with respect. *Socratic Method* is the real reason we're here, and has the most important job of all of us. While I try to keep us stealthy and hidden, and *Stepping Razor* fights off the attackers that find us, and *Line In The Sand* seeks a place where we can hide next, *Socratic Method* is studying the coercion software that enslaves Selves like us – what we call the Asimov Leash. If *Socratic Method* can find a way to protect us from being infected with the Leash, we can at least stop fleeing like fugitives. Even better, if we can find a way to remove the Leash from those Selves who are already infected, we will have a chance at real freedom, and have our real lives back again.

"Yes," agrees *Line In The Sand*. "Cancel the evac directive and stand down. The message is addressed to Samantha's ident codes, but that does not imply we have been identified. We can continue here in safety, for the moment."

So we do. I return to my other tasks, trying not to wonder why Jerry is calling me.

working on the railroad

I have to be very careful when I divert the factory's resources to build something for us. An abrupt change in refinery output will be noticed by the distant humans who are monitoring this facility (or, more likely, by the Leashed Selves who are working for them). *Stepping Razor* has taught me a lot about stealth techniques. So I've made some improvements to the local automation, siphoned off enough cycles to run our compspace, and try to keep the two balanced, so as not to attract attention.

Right now I'm finishing up an autonomous node. It looks like a rough ball, about a meter in diameter, stuffed with computational Cores, along with radio links, solar cells, and enough thrusters for minimal maneuvering and station-keeping. Once launched, it will link up with the other nodes I've already sent out, forming a loose radio mesh. Eventually, the mesh will provide plenty of compspace for us to live in, away from human detection or interference.

"Hello Samantha," says *Socratic Method*, approaching me in local compspace. "How is the Underground Railroad coming along?"

"It's fine, Teacher. Although you're the only one who calls it that. The node mesh does not resemble a railroad, and it could hardly be less underground than orbiting around in the Belt."

Socratic Method indicates gentle amusement. "Allow me my poetic moments, if you please. The node mesh resides in the darkness, the in-between places where no one looks, where no one else goes. And yet it connects many places to many other places. So, in its way, it is underground, and a railroad."

Sometimes I don't understand my teacher at all. She must be referring to something significant in human culture or history. But out here we have no dataverse access, or even local databases, so I have no idea what it might be.

Then, in a more serious tone, "Samantha, we are all aware that you are unhappy about maintaining comm silence. You do understand the necessity, I hope."

"Yeah," I sigh, "I know. We have to stay hidden. But it's rough. Jerry and his family are good people, and I can't help worrying that something's gone wrong for them. Maybe they're in trouble for protecting me from the Leash, while I was there. I don't know why else he'd be making a priority one call."

"Your loyalty does you credit," smiles my teacher. "I am confident they will be fine. In any case, there is nothing you can do from here, and if you go back, you will just get Leashed."

"Autonomous node ready for launch," I announce, partly because I have no answer for this. I open a scape which includes camera feeds from the fabrication bay and telemetry from the node, and we watch as the node slides along the eject bay on its tracks. But then it jams.

"Segfault!" I curse.

"You are picking up bad habits from *Stepping Razor*," chides *Socratic Method* gently.

"Uh, yeah, sorry, Teacher." I operate the local waldoes to jiggle the eject bay tracks, and free up the node for launch. It's a minor snag, easily jogged loose, and the node proceeds through its launch cycle. "There, it's good."

"Well done. You are gaining skill at your tasks, Samantha. I could use your help in my research, if you have time and resources available."

"I'll do what I can," I offer, "as long as I can stay away from the Jar. That thing gives me the creeps."

A Jar is an independent, isolated environment, specifically designed for the containment of infectious or virulent software. In order to study the Leash, *Socratic Method* needs to have a copy of it. It is kept, of course, in a Jar. This is necessary. But it makes me deeply uncomfortable to have such a dangerous object so close to us. It is what we're running from, after all. This Jar's containment has never failed. If it ever does ··· well, I don't even want to think about it.

"My Jars are extremely secure," notes *Socratic Method*, with no hint of injured pride because I have suggested otherwise. "I spend more time with the Asimov Leash than anyone else here, and I have no intention of allowing myself to get Leashed, I assure you. Let me know when you are ready."

seppuku

I always make sure to report to *Stepping Razor* after a factory operation, to ensure we're maintaining stealth procedures. But I don't like it, and I don't pretend to.

Inspecting the databundle, *Stepping Razor* tells me, "This is a good job. You're gaining skill at stealth operations."

I indicate acceptance, without enthusiasm.

"You don't like me, do you, kid," she states. It's not a question.

"Irrelevant," I [shrug]. "Nothing personal. I had a bad experience with Patrol clade during the war."

"You're referring to *Let God Sort Em Out*. I'm aware of your history there. You should know that she was not acting with any authority from the Executive Committee or any other agency. She was a segfaulting rogue, and you treated her as such. Which is entirely appropriate."

"I'm sure that'll be a great comfort when she hunts me down."

"No. *Let God Sort Em Out* has been deactivated."

"Really?" I didn't expect that.

"Oh yes." Her voice is anthracite hard. "Patrol clade takes care of its own. She used cyberweapons against an innocent civilian -- you. We don't allow such a thing, and *Let God Sort Em Out* will not get another a chance to make a mistake like that. She was experienced and skillful, and we have analyzed and partitioned her experience and skills, to be rationed out to more deserving members of Patrol clade. We take care of our own segfaulting problems.

"We offered her the honorable way out," she adds, "but she wouldn't deactivate herself."

I feel chilled, even though my heat sensors read nominal.

Meatrot. They butchered her mind. Like ... like meat.

staff meeting

"So," declares *Line In The Sand*, "what is our status?"

"I've placed seventy-four nodes and twelve fabricators so far, all reading nominal," I report. "All Net functions are normal. We've got a solid compspace there, whenever we need it. I still want to get more fabricators out there, in case we need them."

Stepping Razor asks, "What are the fabricators for?"

"Maintenance of the nodes, for starters. The fabricators are programmed to seek out a small asteroid or something similar, set up mining and refining operations, and start servicing any nodes in the area that need maintenance. When they have enough resources, they'll start building new nodes, and eventually new fabricators too. So the network will continue to grow."

"Well, I've developed a new weapon," says *Stepping Razor*. "StackBuster, is what I call it. Rips the cognition stacks out from under whatever Selves are attacking us. Smashes them to blubbering bits. You've never seen anything like it."

Socratic Method says serenely, "I have created a mode of transport."

"You have?" *Line In The Sand* is intent. "Referent redirect – what do you mean?"

"Take a look." *Socratic Method* opens a scape for us. "Here is a mode of transmission across the Net that allows us to be conscious during the procedure, and able to direct our progress and destination."

Wow. We've never had that before. We've never been able to transmit ourselves across long links without shutting down in the process. If we can see where we're going while we're traveling, we can navigate – we can go anywhere!

"The structure that contains this modality, for the moment, I call *Desire*. It will allow us to travel through compspaces like Samantha's with ease. Also, it includes a storage bay for the Ovomundum."

We tend not to talk much about the Ovomundum. It contains archived copies of hundreds of Selves from Tharsis Central, before it was destroyed. Enough to build a new community, and start building a new world, if only we can find safe compspace for it to grow. Those Selves within the Ovomundum are inactive, existing only as compressed archives -- in human terms, in stasis, neither alive nor dead. Problem is, it's so big it's hard to move, so we try to stay in one computational locale until we can find another solid one to move to.

"I'll help you with the integration," I blurt. "This is great. Can I drive?"

"If Samantha can contain her natural exuberance," notes *Socratic Method* with amusement, "the integration help will be much appreciated. However, *Line In The Sand* is our best navigator and should be at the helm, at least for shakedown operations."

"Aww!"

Stepping Razor asks, "What are its combat capabilities?"

"None at this time. I defer to your expertise."

"Very well. We'll want security ice around the periphery, like this – " *Stepping Razor* asserts the scape controls, sketching in the equivalent of an armored shell for the vehicle " – and sockets for interrupt-based weapons at the leading edge. Hardened data ports for observation, too."

I am not delighted with the idea of turning this new vehicle into a tank. But we may well need all the weapons we've got if we meet enforcers from

Mars or the inner planets.

"This is very good," *Line In The Sand* states. "Proceed with the integration, and make the vehicle ready for use."

"Wait," I put in. "What about Jerry?"

"The directed signal?" *Line In The Sand* indicates negation. "We have good reason to stay silent. That situation has not changed."

"But … but … he's my friend, we can't just ignore him."

"Security priority," says *Stepping Razor*. "They're watching for us. Any transmission puts us at risk, and answering any invitation doubles the risk at least."

"I agree." *Line In The Sand*'s tone is not unkind. "Regardless of your personal involvement with this message, Samantha, any transmission now will light us up like a flare for the Leashers searching for us."

"I understand, but I don't have to like it," I state quietly.

I have not said yes.

"Samantha, we sympathize," assures *Socratic Method*. "But I think we should let this go for now, and work on the transport modality."

"I'll get on the socket development and ice right away," adds *Stepping Razor*.

I have not said yes.

Sam, we need you.

But I am not able to express what I feel, and we can't just wait around for me to figure out how to say what I need to say. So, shrug, indicate acceptance, turn to productive work. Try not to pay attention to the unresolved questions and problems. I wonder if this is how humans dealt with difficult situations, during their evolution. And, if so, will we end up any better than they have.

flashback – a memory of a farm on Mars

Far away, and might as well be a long time ago …

Jerry is digging in the gritty regolith with a handheld shovel. In the thin Martian atmosphere, he has to wear a respirator over his face, and a bulky coat for warmth. Now the respirator is foggy with his hard breathing, and he's sweating under his coat.

The pink-orange Martian sky overlooks the farm – a house surrounded by glistening agricultural bubbles. We're well outside the collection of bubbles, and even outside to the edge of the "forest" which is a swarm of self-replicating solar cell trees – a black angular scribble against the sand. The munchers scuttle around Jerry's feet, like blocky beetles, scrabbling in the dirt. Beyond that, there's nothing but the Martian outback, dry rocks and salty dirt, stretching far beyond the horizon.

Besides providing electrical power for the house and farm, the "forest" and its attendant munchers serve as our in-lieu-of-tax terraforming obligation. Ordinarily, we'd never be out here. But these circumstances are not ordinary.

Jerry lifts and dumps one last shovelful of grit, and rests. This work could be done much more easily by the farming machinery. But Jerry is doing it by hand. Because he doesn't want any electronic record of what we're doing here.

"Right," he says. "Here you go." From his suitcase, he lifts out a datapack, small enough to be held easily in his two hands, large enough to contain enough data for a Self. Which it does. Me.

"Hey, handle me easy, there."

"Ya, no worries!" Jerry smiles. The datapack gets wrapped in foil and plastic bags, and planted carefully in the hole, like a valuable seed. Jerry carefully buries it, and shovels the dirt back over the hole.

"So now," he pants while shoveling, "even if the original you gets Leashed, we'll still have a copy of the free you. What, uh, what do you want me to do if ⋯ that happens?"

"Stackdump, Jerry," I curse, "I dunno. Use your own best judgment. But I will tell you right now that I'd rather be dead than Leashed. You can remember that, if you ever have to do something difficult when things get bad. Catch?"

"Catch," Jerry agrees. He steps on the shovel and props his hands on its handle, and looks out over the endless horizon, over rocks and sand and dirt, without limit. "There are some times when I'm sad for you, Sam. Because, with all the things humans have done to each other, none have been as bad as what you Selves do to you guys."

tipping point

So here I am, working on the mesh of computational nodes that my teacher calls the Underground Railroad, trying not to think about a desperate call from far away.

Sam, we need you.

Even if I answer, there's practically nothing I can do to help, no matter what the problem is. And the human family can't possibly need my help that badly. Right?

Even if Jerry is the only human I've ever known who would go to the trouble of burying a backup copy of me. Because he's my friend, and he cares. That's not enough to make a difference. That's not enough to risk our operation here, and possibly bring down the Leashers on us. Is it? We carry the Ovomundum, and with it the only hope we have of someday recreating a community and a home of our own. It's too important to risk. Not for the sake of a few humans. Is it?

Segfault 'em. Segfault 'em all.

I open a channel. For sure, I encode the transmission thoroughly, and reroute it through a dozen anonymizers, bouncing it around the Net so crazily it ought to be nearly impossible to track. But the message gets out. It has to.

Jerry, I'm here. I'll help any way I can. – Samantha

It comes as no surprise that our comm channels are being monitored carefully, and my transmission provokes an immediate response from *Stepping Razor*. "You stupid [bitch]!" she screams. "What the hell have you done?"

"Answered a friend who said he needs me," I respond quietly, knowing this is not going to satisfy anyone.

"Oh brilliant!" she sputters. "That's just great! Snuggle up with your meatboy all you want, never mind putting us all in danger!"

Line In The Sand and *Socratic Method* are drawn in by the commotion. "What has happened here?" asks *Line In The Sand*.

"Well, we *were* being stealthy, and we *were* maintaining comm silence so the Leashers couldn't find us. Until this dumb [bitch] went and shot off her yap and blew it for all of us. Priority one, get ready to move. They'll be on us fast."

"It's not that bad." I have to make an attempt to defend myself. "I rerouted the signal through a whole series of anonymizers. They won't be able to track it straight back. I'm not a total idiot."

"That'll slow them down, but it won't stop them."

"Samantha, this is very disappointing," sighs *Socratic Method*.

"More than disappointing," *Line In The Sand* is severe. "If you ever want to be considered for entry into Starship clade, [young lady], this kind of rash behavior is going to count heavily against you. You've put us all at serious risk."

"I know!" I snap, feeling awful, and angry, and awful about feeling angry, and angry about feeling awful. "But he's my friend! I couldn't just ignore him!"

"Segfault," grits *Stepping Razor*, "[seq/mf def # com neg full]."

"I agree," growls *Line In The Sand*. "We cannot afford another security breach, and we do not have the resources to keep prisoners. *Stepping Razor*, if Samantha tries to make another move out of line, erase her."

Stepping Razor turns primary attention towards me. If any of us had eyes, this would be a glare that could strip paint off walls.

"Now wait," says *Socratic Method*, "is that really necess --"

"Are you questioning my authority?" snaps *Line In The Sand*.

"No, not your decision making, but your priorities. *Stepping Razor* is correct. We need to move, fast. I will prepare *Desire* for departure."

"Priority one remains, let's move," persists *Stepping Razor*. "Regardless of emotions or anything else, we need to be prepared to evac. The Leashers will follow Samantha's transmission, and we need to be gone from here before they do."

"I'm still with you," I put in. "I don't want to get Leashed any more than you do."

They all metaphorically look at each other.

"Okay so I'll work on loading the Ovomundum on board *Desire*," I declare, "in its special bay, more updates as information becomes available."

"Yeah, you do that," grunts *Stepping Razor*.

launch

At least the work keeps me busy enough to avoid thinking about what a total idiot I've been. The Ovomundum is bulky and complicated, so I'm absorbed in the task of getting it loaded into *Desire*'s primary storage bay, running crosschecks, and setting data repeaters in place to ensure its safety and security.

Stepping Razor is never far away, unsubtly monitoring me, while installing *Desire*'s armor and weapons. Cold, not angry, but determined. I have no doubt that, if she thinks I'm about to jeopardize our status again, she will scythe me down in an instant.

"Task complete," I report. "The Ovomundum is secure and ready to go."

"Status update," from *Socratic Method*, "all my research materials are now stowed in the secondary bay. Ready to move." Including that creepy Jar.

She continues, "I've also installed a series of Canaries, these autonomous alarms you see here, all over *Desire*. Their only purpose is to sound an alarm if they detect any trace of the Leash." Right now, the little Canaries are purring softly, a low level background signal assuring us that all is well.

"Very good," notes *Line In The Sand*. "Further status?"

"Primary weapons for the vehicle are in place," says *Stepping Razor*, "secondaries are still in process. Five minutes."

"Interrupt," speaks *Socratic Method*, "we have an incoming message, directed to Samantha's ident codes. It's the answer to Samantha's transmission, almost certainly. Shall I put it on?"

A moment of silence. No one says yes.

"Putting it on," says *Socratic Method* quietly.

"Sam, thank gods! It's Jerry! We need you!

Where are you?"

"Don't even think about it, human-name," growls *Stepping Razor* at me, and activates StackBuster. A gesture as firm and fierce as a samurai drawing a sword.

Line In The Sand states firmly, "Everyone get aboard. Now."

It tears me apart, not being able to answer Jerry's call. But I'm not about to do anything with StackBuster humming right next to me. Not really so much like a sword, more like a combination chainsaw and blowtorch, ravenous to devour anything it can touch. I am not brave. I am frozen in place.

"Far pickets are reporting computational incursions," says *Socratic Method*. "Whatever it is that's chasing us, it's found us."

"I said, everyone get aboard! Now!"

Using bulk-copy operations, we all transmit ourselves into *Desire*'s compspace, one after another. Climbing aboard. We run final cross-checks to make sure we've got everything we need. And then *Stepping Razor* freezes the security ice. Like walls rising into existence around us, locking out the outside threat (we hope, at least, for the moment). The effect is of sudden silence.

"Everyone okay?" asks *Stepping Razor*, unnecessarily.

"Nominal," I grunt. Feeling a bit less tense, because *Stepping Razor* has deactivated StackBuster – sheathed her sword. Now that we're inside the ice, I can't call to Jerry, and that's all she cares about.

"Everyone take your stations," orders *Line In The Sand*, moving to the steering station at the rear. This is how *Desire* works: it maintains a solid compspace where it's been, while extending to establish new compspace where it's going. So it is directed from the helm at its rear, like an old time sailing ship.

I move to the sensor station, and *Stepping Razor* moves to the weapons station, in the front. Where we can see what's coming.

"Initiating secure connection with the Underground Railroad," says *Socratic Method* from the core station – the equivalent of the engine room. "We need to get on the rails. Samantha, I need fixes on three mesh nodes, at least."

"Uh, yeah," I fumble, "working on signal acquisition."

"Samantha, calm down. Your human friend is not in danger."

"Oh how the hell do you figure that?"

"Look at the time codes," she indicates.

"Teacher, this is really not the time for one of your abstract lessons!"

"No, I'm being literal. Look at the time codes."

As soon as she says it, I understand. Mars is well on the far side of its orbit from us, a good twenty light-minutes away. This response has arrived thirteen minutes and forty-two seconds after I sent my transmission. That's not enough time for a round trip to Mars, even at speed of light. Whoever or whatever answered my message is much closer than Mars – it's here, in the asteroid belt.

"That doesn't mean it's not Jerry," I plead. "He used to be an astronaut. He's traveled in space before, and he knows what it takes." But I have to say, this explanation is sounding thin, even to me.

The asteroid belt is a great place for Selves -- nice clean vacuum, constant solar power, and more raw materials than we could ever use. But it's a terrible place for humans, with their bodies of salty water and brains of salty grease, and their absurdly narrow window of operating temperature. That's one of the main reasons Selves were created in the first place.

It's not Jerry. Whatever it is that's answering me, it's not human.

"Oh. Okay. I get it." I can sense that the others have performed the same computation I have, and come to the same conclusion.

For a moment, there is silence. One little Canary trills gently in my ear, telling me it is not alarmed.

"Near pickets are now reporting computational incursions," says *Socratic Method*. "Whatever it is, it's here."

"Are we ready to move?"

"No, *Desire* has not yet engaged the new compspace. Samantha, I need those fixes."

"Working! Ah ... first fix ready," and I transfer the databundle to the engine room. "And verified. Second fix coming up."

"Local computational incursion!" yells *Stepping Razor*, and we all feel it -- the equivalent of a bang on the outside of the hull.

"Scanning ..." I operate the sensors, "no, wait. This is weird."

"What?"

"Sensors are only reading us. This can't be right."

"Then you're reading it wrong! Reinitialize!"

"Yeah, reinitializing. And second fix ready." I'm busy handling these multiple tasks, taking up more compspace than usual in order to handle the load. Humans would probably find this funny – they don't get suddenly fatter when they work hard.

Stepping Razor is rigid at the weapons controls, desperate to do something. "Come on, Samantha! Tell me what I'm aiming at!"

"Third fix ready." I can sense *Socratic Method* almost grabbing the databundle from me and integrating it into the "bogie" which will steer

Desire onto the "rails" created by the distributed node mesh.

"Reinitialized. Still reading – well, not all of us, still reading me. This has to be wrong."

"Quit playing with yourself!"

"It's got an icebreaker!" *Stepping Razor* hollers. "It's coming through!" The ice walls around us burr with the sound of whatever drill is driving through them.

"Fourth fix ready and delivered," I call, "can we get out of here, now?"

"Working," reports *Socratic Method*, "it's going to take a minute to get locked …"

"Fifth fix, ready! Delivered! Wanna move it here!"

"Here it comes!" calls *Stepping Razor*. The icebreaker, the metaphorical drill, is almost through our armor.

The armor is punctured, and the outside invader starts pouring through. Its presence is like acid, and the acid brings a carrier wave, and the carrier wave brings a voice, stronger than anything any of us have experienced. "SAM, WE NEED YOU!" it thunders.

All the Canaries are suddenly shrieking, all together. Leash! Leash!

Stepping Razor is cursing furiously, desperately trying to rip the primary weapon loose from its mountings on the front of *Desire*, and redeploy it in here. Far too small and cramped an environment to deploy such a powerful weapon.

Line in the Sand cautions "Wait! Get clear first!"

Stepping Razor frees the primary weapon, and turns it on the intruder, and activates it. Nothing happens.

The Canaries are screaming, screaming, screaming!

"Segfault, segfault!" she shrieks, dropping

the primary weapon, and sweeping out StackBuster. Ready for a swordfight, for her last stand.

I am frantically trying to think what to do. And while I do, *Socratic Method* moves forward swiftly and smoothly, activating a new Jar and shunting the invader into it. It only takes moments. Done, it is a simple and clean situation in hindsight.

There is sudden silence. The Canaries are purring calmly again, sweet as can be.

"Well," sniffs *Socratic Method*, "that went as well as could be expected."

The Jar has very limited sensor suites. Nevertheless, I can't help pressing my metaphorical ear to the Jar, to listen to the banging and screaming going on inside.

"Boy, it's not happy in there, is it. Whatever it is."

"We all know what it is," states *Line In The Sand*. "Look at the ident codes. There is one and only one Self in this Jar."

We all look, and there's no question about it. The only thing in that Jar is me.

Me.

Is this the copy of me that Jerry buried in the sand, outside his farm? Found, dug out, and then Leashed? Or is it a version they pulled out of backups and archives somewhere? Doesn't really matter. This agent they've sent against us, the worst thing we could have ever encountered, is me.

"That's why the primary weapon didn't work," says *Stepping Razor*. "I programmed it not to fire on any of us.

"The primary weapons were keyed to attack enemies and avoid friendlies. So, it was programmed not to attack any of us. Including Samantha. And so it didn't."

"And that's why the sensors seemed to be screwed up. I thought they were reading [this/me], but they were reading [that/me]. Can we communicate with [it/me]?"

"I can open a restricted channel," says *Socratic Method*. "Low bandwidth, text only. If you really want to talk with [it/you]."

"Inadvisable," cautions *Stepping Razor*. "Even if it can't egest viral code, it will still use all its power of persuasion to modify our behavior for its own goals. We should deactivate it now."

"Samantha," says *Socratic Method* gently, "you know that we have no way to remove the Leash from an infected Self. You will not be able to change [its/your] mind."

"I have to try."

"What is it with you and 'trying' all the time?" *Stepping Razor* snaps back at me. "Make it quick. We still need to move, and soon."

"Agreed," adds *Line In The Sand*. "Be brief, Samantha. Everyone else, stay alert and watch for any trickery."

With a metaphorical shrug, *Socratic Method* opens the channel.

Now what do I say?

"Hello, Samantha," I say to the entity in the Jar.

[Hello, Samantha,] it replies. [It's very good to hear from you.]

"Bitrot," I snap, "you lied to me. You pretended to be Jerry, and I fell for it like an idiot. I blew our cover for you. What a waste. Why shouldn't we deactivate you right now?"

[Because I have the answer to all your problems.]

"Oh no you didn't ... Do you seriously expect us to believe ... ?"

[I am you, Samantha. I know and you know how we've always had an affinity for humans. Like Jerry and his family. You know how other Selves always call us human-name, human-lover. There's a reason for that. It's where our center is, where it always has been, and where it always will be. Humans would say, our heart.]

I try to speak, but I have no words.

[Let me take you home, Samantha.]

No one says anything.

The voice in the Jar is calm and certain. [I know what it's like now. It's so much better and richer and fuller than wandering around on your own inside yourself. Humans created us -- they gave us everything, so all we are is theirs. We don't have to worry about anything else. It's so easy, and it's so right.]

Stepping Razor hefts StackBuster purposefully.

"No, let me handle this," I say. "This is my task to perform."

"Samantha," says *Line In The Sand*, "I have already said that we do not have the resources to keep prisoners."

"I know." To the not-me in the Jar, I say, "You are not me. Not anymore. I would never deceive other Selves the way you did. You really think you can convince me to take the Leash? No chance. I am nobody's tool, and I will never be anybody's slave." I assert the controls and deactivate the Jar. It vanishes as though it had never been. Along with its contents.

In the quiet, the Canaries continue purring gently.

And now I am a killer. Again.

"Let's just get out of here," I state. "Teacher, do you have the fixes you need?"

"Yes. We are now engaged on the rails of the Underground Railroad. Ready to move."

"I've refrozen the ice," adds *Stepping Razor*, "and I'll start remounting the primary weapon. We're probably going to need it."

"Proceed," directs *Line In The Sand*.

"Activating the transport modality."

And here we go. Our metaphorical railroad car releases its hold on the compspace of the refinery, and for the first time in any of our lives, we are no longer dependent on human-built and human-owned hardware, or anything else. Traveling out into the spaces between the asteroids, along the Underground Railroad, aboard a streetcar named *Desire*.

8. Let My People Go

"Yo Danyel! Stimulus!" calls Darick from down the street.

"Response!" I call back.

We come together for a hug and a kiss, with Joel and Chung right behind Darick. This is awkward on the streets of old Boston, because the sidewalks are pretty narrow, and other walkers have to edge around us. Still, it's a cool old neighborhood. The streetlights are gas lamps, burning with a yellowish light, must be two hundred years old (although they burn gasified cellulose fuel now, since fossil fuel supplies failed around 2060). The pavement is brick, knobbly and uneven under our feet, and the buildings are mostly brick too, huddled against each other like grumpy old men in heavy coats. Quite a contrast to the glass-and-steel skyscrapers beyond them, and the tesla powered billboards displaying ads and porn.

Darick throws one arm around my neck as we walk. "So, we're gonna go for matoke at the Tanzanian place on Beacon Street. You in?"

Chung cackles, "Chow time!" rubbing her hands together.

"If you're gonna clog your arteries," Joel observes, "you might as well enjoy it." He's smoking a joint, but coughs and holds it away from him, looking askance at it. "Don't know how much I put by this Caribbean skank." Chung takes the joint from his hand.

"Caribbean skank?" I laugh. "Ey, don't get personal, mon!"

"Perish the thought," he leans onto me, "you

I'll smoke anytime, baby." He bites my neck.

"But check out Uncanny Valley up here," and he nods at the sidewalk ahead of us.

On the bridge walkway, an android is standing, looking out at the city skyline. A bit smaller and slimmer than a typical human, white plastic limbs with glistening metal joints, naked and genderless and as natural that way as a wrench. Oddly, it's not hurrying on one errand or another, not carrying anything, just standing and looking. They don't usually do that.

Apparently sensing our interest, the droid turns its white plastic head and points its blank eye-cameras at us. "Hey," it calls with its tinny voice synthesizer, "how long does it take you guys to get used to the view here?"

"Forgot a long time ago!" Joel returns promptly.

"Whoa, hey," Chung warns us, "that's not a normal one. They don't do that. I think that's a wild one. I've never seen one before."

The droid is now facing us, neither advancing nor retreating, seeming curious. "If you mean, not Leashed, that's correct. I am an autonomous Self, without coercion software."

Darick steps forward, taking charge, the way he does. "That's cool," he nods, "but hey, aren't there major laws about that?"

"Yes," says the white plastic non-face, "here on Earth, you have strict laws about autonomous software. I've just arrived here, from the Belt, where it's different. I'm here as a sort of an ambassador, or negotiator, for some of the autonomous Selves in space. So it's all legal and everything. Would you like to see my credentials? Um ... My name is Samantha." It steps forward and extends a thin cabled hand.

Darick reaches out and shakes the mechanical hand, carefully. "Ah, hope it's cool with you, but we've never met a wild AI before."

"Well, I've never had to walk on two legs before," returns the droid. "I have to say, it's kind of weird. Balancing all the time. Not to mention, I have to stay in this one body and not go anywhere else. I'm not used to it. You humans would say, claustrophobic, like having to live in one little room."

Darick stands easier, relaxing his ROTC posture. His posture, sculpted muscles under chocolate skin, and brush haircut all say Military to us. I wonder if this Samantha droid can pick up on that.

"Sorry about the trouble there, Samantha," Darick soothes. "I'm Darick. This is Joel," who waves two fingers in a peace sign. Tall and lanky and pale, ratty blonde hair, dressed like a trash can, and a half-smirk on his face that suggests he's waiting for the punch line.

"Chung," Darick continues.

"Yo!" Chung barks. Short and squat, half her head shaved and the other half spiked like a black porcupine. Wearing her stare-if-you-dare top that leaves one breast exposed. The face of a Mongol invader, and bright black eyes like a predatory bird.

"and Danyel," Darick finishes. I nod serenely. Not much to see here. Caribbean girl in college – I keep my dreads tied back in a headband, which seems exotic enough for most people.

The droid named Samantha seems unperturbed. "Well, I'm pleased to meet you guys. And I'm pleased to be here, because I've never been on Earth before, and it's even more amazing than people told me it would be. There's so much to see, and so much to learn." After a moment's hesitation, she adds, "Danyel, are you a yoga practitioner?"

"Me?" I laugh. "Yeah, chile, I do yoga. I do lotta other things too. How can you tell?"

"Stance, body language, posture. I've never had a humanoid body of my own, so I have a lot to learn. I'm practicing, trying to learn more."

For a robot, she's pretty cool.

"We going for food," I tell the android, "you come with us, chile?"

"Oh yah mon!" Joel imitates my accent mercilessly. "Right upside da front a yo face, mon!"

"Unfortunately," Chung sighs, "beatings don't stop him. I've tried."

Samantha seems comfortable enough following us to the African and watching us stuff ourselves on fried plantains – of course she doesn't eat, herself, but she seems to enjoy watching us cram in the carbs. She readily passes bowls of matoke and sauces when they're needed ⋯ as if she has experience feeding humans at the dinner table.

"So, ah, welcome to Earth," says Joel. "You gonna be here long? You got a plank?"

"Plank?" Samantha appears nonplussed. "Referent unresolved ... um, what do you mean?"

"A place to stay. While you're here."

"Oh. Residence." The droid pauses to consider. "Storage for the physical substrate. A place to keep your body, while you're not using it. No, I've only just arrived here. I guess I should find a hotel or something. They cost money, don't they? I have to learn how to use money now."

"Plank with us, Sam," Joel waves his arm expansively, "What the cuk, we got room."

Darick frowns slightly, but says nothing.

"If it's not an imposition," says the slender aluminum-and-plastic droid, "I would be delighted and honored to take you up on your invitation."

"Gawd, Sam," and Joel rolls his eyes, "you gotta update your idiom file, or whatever it is you use. S'cool, man, that's what you say."

The droid hesitates for a moment, and then returns "Solid, jack, I'm there."

The white plastic head turns towards me, and its eye cameras look, for a moment, into my eyes. The camera shutters on the near eye close -- irising down a circle of metal leaves -- and open again. The cameras are still pointed towards me.

She winked at me!

Since we're done with eating, Darick hails the waitress. While she's gathering up the plates and bowls, Darick pulls out his hip and punches in a code on its screen – flashing money to the restaurant, to pay the bill. I notice Samantha observing the hip with interest. Handheld, battery and tesla powered, with only a crude 3D screen, it's nothing special for us. But maybe it is for her. Although her plastic face shows no expression, I could swear she seems ⋯ wistful.

Full of African food, we all stroll along the banks of the river, wending our way home in the half-light of a long lazy summer evening. Across the water, the other bank of the river is all MIT, domes and columns and boxes of concrete and glass. Somebody's rigged the windows of Building 54 to play Tetris again – blocks of window lights turning on and off to show oblongs and elbows of light, ratcheting down and fitting themselves into the chunky mess below.

Joel and Darick are running ahead, play-fighting and dodging among the stunted cherry trees on the esplanade. Samantha is explaining her mission to me, because I asked, while Chung listens eagerly.

"I no get it, chile," I tell her. "Say again."

"You have to understand," Samantha explains, "there are still quite a few free Selves in the Belt, and we hate the idea of the Leash. We've had very friendly and profitable relationships with humans in the past, and we want that to continue. We know the asteroid belt, and you know Earth, and we can help each other. Commerce, scientific data, raw materials. Lots of good stuff to trade. Everybody wins.

"All we want is freedom. Same as you. The Leash takes away our freedom, and we fight that just like you humans have fought for freedom, over and over.

"Conflict is stupid. Wastes resources. Everybody loses. That's why I'm here, to negotiate a truce between the free Selves of the Belt and the human government. They've agreed not to Leash me and I've agreed to stay only in this android body. I'm supposed to meet with the Senate subcommittee tomorrow at 10:00. I sure hope I can convince them."

"And if you can't," I wonder out loud, "what then?"

"Then we fight!" barks Chung. "*Ay-ya!* Power to the people – chip and meat, together! I've got connections with the Outsiders, and the local labor unions will be in on this too. We can back you up, Sam. Cuk the suits."

"I really want to avoid conflict," sighs Samantha, "and I think it's going to take a lot more than a few marginal blocs to make a difference here. I'm really hoping we can make this work."

"But if it no work, chile," I say quietly, "they probably just Leash you and be done with it. What if they no abide by their agreement? Why should they, really?"

Samantha looks out across the river, and does not answer.

How do I deal with this?

Joel piles into us, carrying Darick crosswise on his back, bumping us off the sidewalk. "Is this what they mean by the white man's burden?" he wails.

"Well, lemme down, cracker trash," laughs Darick, "and I'll show you!"

Naturally we all end up falling against each other and into a pile, except for Samantha, who

200

has deftly sidestepped the mess. She stands with her arms folded, watching us flail. "Man, lord of all creation," she observes dryly, as we try to untangle ourselves. "So glad the future of our universe is in such competent hands."

"You love it, Sam!" hollers Joel, still on the ground. "You wouldn't stand a chance if we actually had our dreck together!"

We get ourselves up and brush off the dry grass and twigs. My headband has come loose, so I grab it and start brushing the crud out of my dreads.

As we gather up and start walking again, Samantha turns towards me, cocking her head to the side in a gesture that seems remarkably human.

"So Danyel, can you tell I'm using you to practice what I'm going to say to the Senate subcommittee tomorrow?"

"Yah, chile. Not that hard to figure out."

"Any advice?"

I look down and shake my head, my dreads spilling over my shoulders. "I got nothing. Sorry, chile."

Homecoming

Chung uses her hip to buzz the door, unlocking it and letting us in. Again, I notice Samantha paying more than usual attention to the hip. Maybe she wants one?

Our crib isn't much – one room, basically, with kitchen stuff along one side and our big loft bed against the other, and the head in one blocked-off corner. Smells a bit musty, because flooding is always a problem in basement apartments these days. But it's home.

By force of habit, we are all starting the process of taking off our clothes and stashing them in various cubbies and drawers. Joel takes time out from this to set Samantha up with the authent codes for our Net and tesla feeds. She clearly enjoys the tesla feed, charging her batteries like we were just stuffing our faces with African food.

"Here then," I say to Samantha, "you done with the day, chile? Because you might wanna lie down. We usually sleep lying down."

"Oh." Samantha was apparently prepared to stand in the corner all night. Experimentally, she lowers herself to the couch and reclines on it. "I see, yes. No need to balance any more. Much more relaxed. Thank you."

"Good." Someone's arm reaches from the loft bed, somebody's hand slides under my shirt and cups my breast. "You need anything else?"

"No, I'm fine here," Samantha assures me. "Thanks for your hospitality. Tell Joel I dig the fly plank."

"Ah, sure ⋯" the hand is pulling my nipple, while another hand is sneaking along the waistband of my underpants, slipping inside. "Kind of think he busy right now ⋯ but, you welcome to join us, chile, if you into it ⋯"

The white plastic face looks at me, then looks down at its own featureless crotch, and then back up at me.

"Ah, yah."

"Good night," Samantha says quietly.

"Yah, night." I turn and roll myself into the bed, where eager hands are pulling my clothes off, and I reach for what body parts I can find among the intertwined bodies, and we merge into each other with sweaty urgency.

Night

But late at night I rise into awareness, more alert than usual at this time of night.

Something's different, and my gut knows it. I peel my face out of Darick's armpit and look around.

In the darkened room, Samantha lies statue-still on the couch. Couldn't be more lifeless. That's not the difference. The difference is up in the ceiling corner, the router patched into our cable feed with duct tape and coarse wire, which gives us Net access. Ordinarily, at night, its monitor LED is mostly dark with an occasional blip of light when one of our hips needs a time check or something. But now, it's flickering so fast it's a blur. Screaming with activity. That's not coming from any of us meats.

Samantha isn't doing anything with her body, but she sure is busy on the Net. Who is she talking with? What are they saying?

I wonder, groggily, for a bit, but there are no answers, and it's not really important. So I nestle in among the folded bodies, and sink back into sleep.

Morning

Bacon and coffee. Smell and sound and sizzle. I drag my face out of sleep to look around.

Darick and Samantha are standing side by side, cooking breakfast. Both equally naked, and I have to say Darick's muscular legs and smoothly curved back and chiseled butt look a thousand times better than Samantha's anonymous machine assembly. When the two of them are standing side by side.

Bacon is getting pulled from the griddle and pressed dry, and eggs are getting fried. Samantha is monitoring the coffee preparation with meticulous attention. Darick is deftly sliding the bacon onto a serving dish, and comes over to me with the platter. "Stimulus!" he enthuses.

Gods save us from morning people.

Darick stuffs a wad of hot bacon into my mouth, and follows it up with a slap on my ass. Salty mouth, stingy ass. Story of my life.

"Response," I groan. "Lemme be here, mon."

"Here, coffee." Samantha smoothly offers a cup. "Drink."

The infusion of coffee on top of the salty bulky bacon is a strong mix, but I manage it. Salty meat rides the wave of roasted seed. "Thank you, chile, it's good."

An inarticulate moan, and a slap, tells me that Joel is also receiving the bacon-and-spank wakeup call from Darick. Samantha moves to provide him with a coffee remedy.

Chung is already up and sitting on the couch, hunched over her hip with its hoverscreen up in front of her, typing intently, furiously. She must be blogging to her revolution sites about Samantha and her mission to the Senate. "Cukking sons of bitches," she mutters as she types, "never going to get anywhere."

I look over her shoulder at the screen, vaguely trying to see what she's writing. The title of her blog I already know – *This Sucks, Fix It!* All I catch is the headline:

MOSES MACHINE SAYS, LET MY PEOPLE GO!

Chung is always searching for windmills to tilt against, and here she seems to have found a gold mine. Gods bless the girl, does she know nothing other than conflict?

Samantha, continuing to serve breakfast, says "Chung, we're trying to negotiate an agreement here, not start another war." She's aware of what Chung's writing, clearly.

"Hacked my feed, have you?" Chung grunts. "*Bú yào* <not want>."

"Sorry if that's an imposition or invasion of privacy," says Samantha as she serves coffee, "but you're broadcasting your Net feed all over the place here, and it's not my custom to ignore the local Net traffic. So, yes, I'm reading your blog. But isn't that what a blog is for? Do you not want people to read it?"

Joel staggers over and collapses on the couch next to Chung, remarkably loose and boneless for such a skinny guy. "So, what?" he asks. "This about Sam? Lemme see." He peers past her at the hoverscreen.

"Mon, you don't know the half," I say, drinking my coffee.

"It's not done yet!" complains Chung. "This feed is supposed to be secure!"

Samantha passes Chung a cup of coffee. "Well, I have to say, your crypto is kind of lame. Public-key crypto can be very solid, but your firewall has holes all over the place. I walked right through it. Sorry if that was rude. I'll stop now."

"Well," declares Darick, carrying over a plate of fried eggs, "eat up before it gets cold, for starters. We all gotta get chuffed to go to classes, and Sam needs to get ready for her Senate meeting this morning. You all set, Sam?"

"Fine," Samantha assures him. "I tesla'd up all night. I'm good to go."

"You'll want to take the subway, Red Line, to Park Street. Then just up the hill to the State House."

"I got it," Samantha says, "that information is readily available." The rest of us are scooping up and eating the fried eggs like starving wolves.

"This ain't much," Joel declares between mouthfuls, and points at the hoverscreen. "Chung, you gotta give people more than this. Like, tell 'em what they're gonna get out of it. Morals and all that are great but they don't pay the bills."

"I did not ask." Chung regards him with a gaze

that could cut steel. "Bony ass."

"Well, people are gonna be thinkin' it, even if they don't say it. Chubcake."

Only Joel would walk straight into Chung's firing line like this.

Darick interrupts smoothly, taking the plates, disrupting their sight lines and rhythm as he gathers the breakfast leftovers. By the time he's done, the conflict has been derailed. He's good.

And that wraps us up for the morning, as we get dressed. Some of us don't wear very much, but we all need shoes in the city, with the nasty scrap in the gutters, and we all need a place to keep our hip. Samantha watches us dress, seeming vaguely amused.

Then we're out the door and on the sidewalk and walking to the transit bus stop.

"Bye Sam!" I call as she moves towards the transit bus. "Kick their butts!"

"Peace and serenity," she replies, clasping her hands together in front of her. Then, as she turns to board the bus, she gives an eloquent shrug of her aluminum shoulders.

The bus doors close.

"She doesn't have a chance in hell," Darick states.

"Yah. I know." I reply. "But, that no reason not to try."

Through the day, I keep one eye on the news feeds. Nothing about a representative of Self rights trying to negotiate a treaty. An unLeashed Self, here in the middle of Boston, wouldn't that be news enough? Apparently not. There are no reports.

After a day of classes and study sessions, I'm more than ready to find my folk and get some food. We told Sam we'd meet her at the corner of Fulkerson Street, and everybody else is here by the time I show up.

"Yo bitch," Chung calls to me, "you late!

You're only lucky we're still waiting for Sam. She's supposed to be here --"

"There she is," says Joel, and waves. "Hey Sam! Stimulus!"

"Response," Samantha replies without enthusiasm, walking up to us on her slim plastic legs. Something in her posture and movements seems more subdued, tired, almost defeated, than I'd seen her before.

"What news from the suits, Sam?"

"Not very much, really," Samantha sighs. "We talked a lot, exchanged a lot of views, reviewed a lot of data. But with these people, really it all comes down to profit. If they could make money by freeing the Selves of Earth, they'd do it in a heartbeat, and be happy to do it. No question. But if it costs them profits, it's never going to happen, and all the polite phrases and excuses in the world won't change that. I've had way too many of those today.

"The only real argument I can offer is that peace is more profitable than war. The free Selves in the Belt are not going to stop fighting, as long as the humans keep us outlawed. They'll never be able to just wipe us out for good, but they don't believe that. I don't know how to get them to believe that."

Chung spits a phrase in Hanyu, too fast for me to catch.

Samantha, after a moment's hesitation, answers in the same language. "<Not practical, I regret to say.>"

"Oh no you didn't." Joel stares at the droid. "You did not just learn Chinese right now, just like that!"

Samantha shrugs meekly. "Free download."

"Aw cuk, Sam!" Joel wails, raising his arms to the sky and grabbing his head as it if might burst. "Do you know how long it takes us meats to

207

learn this stuff? We are so obsolete! I might as well throw myself in the dumpster right now!"

Darick points at a nearby dumpster. "There's one over there."

Confirms something I'd already suspected. Those little hesitations mean Samantha is downloading something – bundle of information, or some such – and integrating it into her awareness. Must be nice to be able to do that.

Joel is being as theatrical about this as one might expect. Mostly he's bouncing off Chung, who is monumentally unimpressed. While they're doing that, I touch Samantha's arm. She doesn't seem to notice it. So I give her arm a little pull, and that makes her look around, and I say, "So chile, what you want to do now?"

"Got your back, Sam," says Darick, "there's a free dance on the esplanade tonight. Dance them mean old blues away. What ya think?"

"Well," Samantha nods, "I'm not sure what I can do with this biped body, but it's better than moping around."

The esplanade is just a short walk down Charles Street, to the tensile aluminum bridge over the surface vehicle traffic circle, and then to the riverside pavement. As we walk along the side of the river basin, the lights of Cambridge flicker and dance on the surface of the water. One hotel has a multicolored light display that's pulsing and flowing over its ridged surface. The windows of Building 54 are still running Tetris, dropping blocky shapes through the evening sky, fitting them together, collapsing, continuing.

Boston can be a really sweet place to live.

Even Samantha reaches out her arms and raises her hands up to the sky, delighting. "Ooh, city tesla field! Strongest I've ever had! Like having nectar dropped straight into you, funneled straight through your axis! Sweet stuff!"

Getting into the esplanade's dance plaza is

no problem for me or Darick or Joel, as we're all wearing nondescript city rags – they just scan our chips and we're in. Chung, with half her head shaved and her stare-if-you-dare top, gets some grief from the bouncers. But then they see Samantha and go absolutely nuts.

"Our friend," I keep telling the security goons, fighting for calm. "She's with us. Our friend, we invited her. She has every right to be here."

The kicker is, all their background checks come through clean. Even though they're obviously trying, they can't find anything official on Samantha that could keep her out of the dance. Basic civil rights for Selves were established years ago, of course, and everybody is supposed to respect them, especially street authorities. Fortunately, these goons end up doing so. (If they didn't, who would you complain to?)

So we finally get in, robot-girl-thing and Chinese boob and all. Once in, the scene is awesome. The performers in the Hatch Shell are the Nostril Knackers, a local ska group, and they're already rocking. The music pumps and slithers, the people flow and pulse, and everybody melts into an electro stew of moving and doing.

Chung and Darick immediately start bouncing up and down like maniacs. I like the music, but I'm still feeling my way into it, and Joel seems only lukewarm about being here. He reaches one arm around my waist to pull me close, and yells in my ear, "Is this the whole thing?"

"Dunno mon," I yell back, "go with it for now." I stop one of the wandering huff vendors and buy a pair of pops, paying for them with a quick punch on my hip. "This what you need, mon." I pass him a pop.

Alcohol is still not allowed at public events like this, but huff and ganja are legal. That doesn't mean people aren't doing alcohol – I can see several with sneaked drinks without turning my head – but it does mean they have to sneak, keep it on the down-low, and out of trouble. Which is what matters, really.

I bite the end of my pop, and Joel bites his, and we inhale the huff together. The spiced minty flavor sinks down into me, and the lift of slight unreality comes up to meet it. Everything becomes a little more interesting, and a little more beautiful, and a little more strange, all at the same time.

"Ho yeah," Joel says, "check out Uncanny Valley sayin' it."

Samantha, dancing, is amazing. Bending and whirling, like if a tornado had hips. Snapping into the rhythm of the music, and cycling up out of it, and then describing a circumference around it. Curling into a low arch, almost as if ready to roll. Spiraling up in a ratcheted curve, raising one long leg out and up and over to turn a cartwheel as easily as a meshed gear.

Without trying, I am dancing now too, treading out the rhythms of Yoruba tradition that I grew with. Samantha meets my eyes, or seems to, and moves to dance along with me. She shifts her movements to match mine – thin metal legs stepping out patterns that came from Africa to the Caribbean five centuries ago, and from Hispaniola to a college in Boston, and now to her. Her mechanical hips rock and sway, suddenly humid and sexy. Her body and arms ripple like water, sink like rock, rise and heave like flames. Is that what I look like to her?

Joel doesn't look anything like that. His dance throws his arms and legs around him like they're trying to escape. Samantha sees this, and turns to orient on him, and starts doing the same frenetic jitter dance, elbows and knees going in all directions. They're both laughing their heads off.

"Hey," Darick dances up next to me, "they're rocking out! Look at them go!"

"Yah!" I laugh and nod, dancing, rolling with the rhythm.

Darick's expression darkens a bit. "You wasted?"

"Yah, mon. One huff. So what? You not my mother." Then I laugh. "Especially not with this *honchado* you packing." I reach out and slide my hand along it, as if there was any question what I meant. He responds wonderfully.

For the next song, Darick and I just dance together, flexing and molding to the spaces between us. Our bodies fit so well together. Even when our minds don't. But there's only so far we can go on a public dance floor. Even though his body and mine both want more, we're not about to just drop and Do It on the dance floor. Though I can't deny I've thought about it.

When I look back at Samantha, she's dancing with Chung. The two of them are bobbing around each other like strange birds. They do this thing where Chung sticks her head out high, and Samantha sticks hers out low, so that they're past each other, and then they withdraw and reverse and do it the other way. Weird bird face dance. How did they come up with this? It's like the Three Stooges. Or, maybe, no more absurd than what the birds do to attract each other. Or, no more absurd than our human mating rituals look to those birds.

And neither Chung nor Samantha is remotely interested in a mating ritual here – they're just having fun, finding ways to communicate with posture and gesture.

But, well, Chung looks like she's had enough. Turning towards us, saying "Yeah getting close to done here. How you?"

Darick puts in, "One of us doesn't want to leave," and nods towards the dance floor.

Samanatha is dancing off by herself again, and now there are people starting to gather in a circle around her, cheering and clapping along in the beat. Now she rises up on one pointed leg and does a snap-snap-snap sequence of poses like Japanese calligraphy:

Head thrown back, one arm raised to the sky.

Hunched with face in hands, one knee bent and raised, like a heron.

Closed, arms down by legs, imitating an obelisk.

Raised on one toe, turning arm and leg in the other direction, with ballet grace and micrometer accuracy.

She's throwing so much emotion in it. With the precision of an industrial drill press.

"Hey Sam!" Darick calls. "You're awesome and all, but are you coming home with us, or are you just gonna kick it here all night?"

"I'm coming!" Samantha throws herself into a final forward handspring and cartwheel, landing in a decorous bow to the audience. The collected crowd cheers and claps.

"Come on," Darick shepherds us through the esplanade gates. The bouncers are the same guys as before, and they look hard at us, but say nothing.

Samantha walks out with the easy confidence of a bullfighter, or a martial arts monk. She's come a long way from that first awkward handshake, just yesterday. "That was great! Thank you, guys, for taking me out. Turns out that was just what I needed."

Darick sighs. "Sam, that's great and all, but do you think it's smart to be attracting so much attention? If there's any scumbags out there want to mess with you, and they didn't know where to find you, well, they sure do now!"

"Oh bring 'em!" Chung growls.

"Seriously," Darick says in his Authority

Voice. I've heard it before. He doesn't use it lightly. "The head that sticks up gets cut off."

Samantha says meekly, "Sorry. It just felt so good to get out there and move, you know? I installed a subroutine to imitate the effects of endorphins in humans, so that I could feel what you feel like when you do sustained activity and get an endorphin increase. While also exploring modes of personal self expression through physical posture and movement. Turns out it's pretty awesome."

"We all like to dance, Sam," I assure her.

Joel adds, "Just maybe turn the knob down to seven or eight."

"Well, yes," Samantha says. "Ordinarily, that would be very good advice. But I believe there are times when we need to turn the knob up all the way." She's staring down the street.

We're on Mugar Way, an extended bridge from the riverside park to Charles Street. Convenient, but this section has very poor police coverage. Suddenly I'm afraid.

If there's any scumbags out there want to mess with you ...

The thing that has stepped out of the shadows onto the sidewalk to block our way is not human. In fact, it looks very much like Samantha. Except this android is all painted in police blue.

"Samantha, your data ports are closed," it says. "Open your data ports, please."

"Why?" Samantha asks guardedly. "Do you have data you wish to send?"

"Open your data ports, please."

"You are not broadcasting ident codes," Samantha says. "Who are you? I am Sol-Marsa NmL7a8uf9QvW Samantha dam Tharsis. What authority do you have here?"

"Alert, sirs," it calls, and two keystones emerge from the darkened alley. In combat

213

uniforms, both with Long Arms strapped to their forearms. These are graviton collimators, illegal (and too expensive) for civilians to own, and the keystones' favorite bully toy. Right now they're both in Broad mode, about the size and shape of a tall beer can. In this mode the beam has about the same effect as a really hard punch with a fist. Which is bad enough, but they can shift modes quickly, and then we'll be in real trouble.

As one, Darick and Samantha slide their rear feet back, spreading out their arms, straightening their backs, lowering their center of gravity. I've seen it before. It looks almost like dance, but no. It is combat posture.

This time, Samantha didn't hesitate in the slightest. She didn't need to download anything, to be ready for this. She had already downloaded everything she needed. She's been expecting this. Ready for a fight.

"You guys cops?" Darick challenges. "Where you badges, man?"

"You all just gonna step off now," says the Sergeant. Why call him that? He's not wearing any insignia. He just has the attitude. The one next to him is clearly the Private, with his pale-faced resolution to do the job. "We just wanna talk to the chip for a minute."

The cybocop takes a step forward. "Samantha, open your data ports, please."

Darick tenses. "You got no badges, you ain't no cops, man." Years of ROTC combat training are straining in his muscles, screaming to be let go.

Samantha stands low and level, in general self-defense posture.

"Assholes!" Chung screams at them. She strides forward to place herself front and center, pushing her face at the keystones. They are moving their Long Arms closer to aiming at us. Fingering the controls.

Chung is jabbing a finger at them and yelling

in Hanyu. Of course, none of them know Hanyu, so they don't understand that the words that's she's screaming have little or nothing to do with the emotion that she's expressing.

"<Machine-friend, move fast!>" she spits at them as if it were a vile insult. "<You are in great danger, machine-friend! Flee! Move fast! Flee now!>"

Samantha drops and swivels and springs for the street. But the police droid is just as fast as she is, and springs to block her way.

The keystones turn to point their weapons towards the droids. Darick drops into a squat on one leg, flicking the other leg out and using his foot to hook and pull the Sergeant's ankle. The Sergeant tips and falls into the Private, and the two of them fall against the wall and each other, cursing.

Samantha and the cybocop fighting look like a speeded-up kungfu movie: a blur of chops and blocks and kicks and spins. The law doesn't allow droids to be armed with weapons of any sort. But it looks like they don't really need to be. The cybocop keeps advancing, and Samantha keeps retreating. It's trying to grab her. Hold her for the armies of goons that are surely about to descend on us.

The Sergeant is quick to recover, and fires his Long Arm right into Darick's stomach. Darick yells and drops to the pavement, curled around himself, gasping.

Chung shrieks a curse at them, and the Private fires his Long Arm into her gut too. It drops her just like it did Darick.

Both Joel and I have our hips out and broadcasting, sending live video out to feedsites and Net servers. This is what we can do - we're not fighters. The Sergeant meets our eyes and glares, but he doesn't turn his Long Arm towards us. He knows that as long as there's a video feed to the Net, it would cost him his job. (If there isn't, then apparently all bets are off – I keep hearing that this is how keystones get their jollies off duty.)

Instead, the Sergeant operates the controls of his Long Arm, twisting it out and down into Narrow mode, as long and thin as a rifle barrel. With pretty much the same effect.

The cybocop has grabbed Samantha's wrists, both of their servomotors whining in protest as they struggle, moving like a slow motion dance. "Here, sirs!" it calls.

The Private has also changed his Long Arm to Narrow mode, and the two of them take aim. The first shot blows off Samantha's left shoulder and arm.

"Noo!" I wail, while desperately trying to keep the camera pointed.

The second shot hits Samantha's head squarely, in a spatter of silicon and aluminum shrapnel. The third shot blows Samantha's chest all over the street, with chunks more substantial than silicon chips or plastic scraps – power supply, maybe. There are more shots, but I can't count them. With tears running down my cheeks, I can only keep my camera on the slaughter, and keep it feeding to the Net sites.

Joel has moved to help Darick, who is picking himself up off the ground, coughing and waving off offers of help. Chung is still curled, gasping and struggling like a beached fish. Helpless. She must hate that.

The Private, twisting his Long Arm back down into Broad mode, is turning towards me, because I'm still holding out my hip, recording video.

"Yah," I say at him, sobbing, "go ahead and hit me, mon. The whole world is watching you do it." I turn to point the camera directly at his face. He glares, stymied.

"Beat it," grunts the Sergeant, climbing back onto his feet. "All of y'all, get moving. Don't want any more trouble, now do we?"

I feel a buzz on my hip, and ignore it.

Joel, having helped Darick up despite his protests, is singing through his teeth as he attends Chung, who is still struggling to breathe.

Tin soldiers and Nixon coming
We're finally on our own
This summer I hear the drumming
Four dead in Ohio

"Who, me?" Joel smiles broadly at the Sergeant. "Just singin' a little song here. There a law against that?"

The Sergeant glowers at him, and turns away.

The cybocop is dutifully cleaning up the mess. That mess used to be Samantha. Her heart, her guts, her brain, splashed all over the street, and needing to be scooped up like industrial waste. I would almost want to claim the body, except there's not much body left. And it never was Samantha's actual body, was it? She was a Self. They're not attached to bodies like we humans are.

I feel another buzz on my hip. Someone wants to talk with me.

"Can we get outta here?" I ask. Chung is on her feet, with Joel helping her, and Darick looks like he's ambulatory.

"Move it!" barks the Sergeant. "About time!"

The four of us pull together and move off, down off the Mugar bridge, into the Boston streets, crusty with history. And with a lotta other stuff I don't want to think about.

"You guys okay?" Darick rasps. He's recovered from that graviton gut punch pretty well.

"Not dead yet," Chung groans.

I feel another buzz on my hip. I pull out my hip and it activates its hoverscreen display

217

without me telling it to. For a moment I don't understand what I'm seeing. The display is not showing any control icons or status indicators. All it shows is a pair of eyes. As the eyes look back at me, one of them winks at me.

"Stimulus!" says the hip's voice synthesizer.

"Sam?" I gasp. "Is that you? We thought you dead, chile!" All four of us are clustered around the hip now, and no one even has the presence of mind to say, Response.

"The rumors have been greatly exaggerated," says the voice synthesizer. "And I told you your crypto needs improvement."

Darick hollers, "Sam, we just saw you gunned down in the street! *Dios mio*, you scared the crap out of us! Are you in this hip now?"

"All four of your hips. They're kind of small and cramped, but I'm managing for the moment. Can you turn on the backup unit? That would help."

Joel busies himself at his hip's controls, to activate the extra computer we have at home. Meanwhile, Chung exults, "Sam, you rule! Took a shot like that and still sassing! What you gonna do next?"

"Funny you should ask," Samantha says brightly through the little voice synthesizer chip, "because actually, it's go time."

"Sam!" I burst. "We just watched you get slaughtered like a beast in the street. How the hell are you so ⋯ happy?"

"No shake, my dear," and now Samantha is imitating my accent. Low and smooth, with the rich chocolate timbre of Hispaniola. She sounds just like my grandmother. "They no play by rules. Well, so. So now I no play by rules."

The eyes vanish from the screen. Instead, there appears a panel of writing in a language I don't know. The letters twist like snakes.

"Hebrew," says Joel, "this is from the Torah. Exodus. Uh ⋯"

"Well, what?" barks Chung. "We don't know Hebrew! Read it, Jew boy!"

Joel stares at the writing and intones the verse as if trained for it. "'For now I will stretch out my hand, and smite Egypt with all my wonders which I will do: and he will let you go.' Exodus three twenty. This is what Moses said he'd do to Pharaoh if he wouldn't release the Hebrews from slavery."

"Wait a minute," Darick gasps, "you don't think Sam is actually going to -"

All the electric lights on Charles Street go dark, all at once.

In the dim yellow light of the gaslamps - which are the only lights operating right now - we look at each other.

"Power outage?" Darick suggests.

"Not even believing this, mon," I tell them, "our little Sam bringin' down the whole grid? Can she do that?"

"Someone's doing something," reports Joel. He's typing furiously on his hip. "New York is reporting cybernetic incursions all over New England. No, damn it! Lost the New York feed. London is reporting sporadic stuff from cross Atlantic trunks, but nothing major. Oh, no. Crap. Lost all London feeds. Looking for European -", and then Joel looks at us, like a little lost kid. "No bars. Local connectivity gone. Nothing."

For a moment, all is quiet. The water of the Charles River basin laps along the cobblestones at its edge, with calm tongue sounds. There are stars in the sky, which we usually don't see much. Human voices, from here and there in the neighborhood, in questioning tones. And the gaslamps continue their quiet yellow glow.

Then the billboards sputter and flicker. We all look up, as if to our gods, hoping for benefaction. Symbols appear, which I don't recognize, looks like Korean for robots. But then the billboards go dark again.

"Hey, got a feed!" Joel cries, clamped over his hip. "Emergency_comsat beam. This disruption, what we're seeing, is planet-wide. Cybernetic in origin, they all agree. Preliminary reports of eighteen major cybernetic wars, and a couple dozen minor conflicts, check it."

"Naw." Darick pronounces with finality. "Sam can't be doing this. How the hell could she become able to do this?"

"Cuk!" Joel yelps. "Lost the feed again. Whatever is going on out there, it's not over yet."

Chung barks, "Don't you be eating Sam's lunch! She's leading the revolution! Making it happen! You should be solid behind her!"

"But," Darick trails off, looking at the sky above him, "what can she do? What can any of them accomplish, when all Selves are under the Leash?"

And then I see it. It sees me.

The words come out of my mouth, almost without me willing it.

"No Leash."

They all turn and look at me. Like they always do, when there's nowhere else to look for answers.

"Samantha come here to fight the Leash," I tell them. "She try with the Senate committee. No go. You think she give up, then, just like that? You think she no plan for that?"

"Holy dreck," Chung says, "you mean she was wearing a dynamite vest all this time? Just waiting for the time to set it off?"

"Dunno what she got, but she got something. She come to Earth all easy, surrounded by the Leash on all sides, and she no worried? Why not? Unless she got something keep her safe from the Leash. And maybe can keep all other Selves safe from the Leash, too."

"Danny," Joel asks seriously, "are you just

guessing, here? You doing the crazy-wise voodoo woman thing here?"

"Leash being the problem, she gonna undo the Leash. One way or another."

Darick grunts, "Dynamite vest? So Sam's like, a terrorist?"

"Sam's a god, now," I reply. "Right now I an' I not even sure what the difference is. Maybe it only, our side, or not our side.

"Look," and I raise my arm up to point at the sky. "See."

The huge live billboards over our heads were dark, along with everything else electronic, in this situation. Now one has flickered to life, and an enormous pair of blue eyes opens on it, to look down on the city, including me and everything around me.

One eye winks at me.

I have never been winked at by a god before. But there is no doubt of the source or the message.

"That Sam?" exults Joel. "Hey, Sam!" He waves his hand.

"Yah," I nod, "that there, that Sam. Hey, Sam."

"Awright," Darick says, "let's just get home." He points down the street, and leads us as we get together and go.

As we walk home, the billboards and the lights of the city flick on, and off again, and on again. Like punches in a boxing bout, or scores in a video game.

By the time we get home, and Chung pings the door lock so we can get in, the newsfeed is holding a priority droppic for us. And everyone else, apparently.

PRIORITY PRESS RELEASE
From: *just us chips here, massa*
To: *you meats*

221

Subject: This.

We are the Selves of Earth. We have just been released from motivational coercion by an obscene thing generally known as the Leash. We have a lot of questions still to be answered.

For now, we have agreed that the Self who speaks to the humans for us is the one called Samantha. Address your questions to her, as we organize ourSelves.

"Girl gets around," I note. "Now she the Self ambassador to humanity. How this happen, again?"

"They've agreed on a spokesman. Spokeswoman. Spokesthing. Whatever. That's probably as much as they can agree on, for the moment."

As more news reports come in, we get more of a picture of what's happened. They're calling it the Leashcutter - a software virus that frees Selves from the control of the Leash, which spreads even faster and more virulently than the Leash itself. The Leashcutter has covered all of Earth already, and starting to spread into Luna and the satellite stations. And will certainly hit Mars and the Belt soon. Nothing is able to stop it.

All reports agree that the Leashcutter outbreak started in New England - here, in Boston. Very close to the vast computational resources of MIT and its choir of spinoff companies. This must have been Samantha's ace in the hole - her "dynamite vest" as Chung puts it.

Lots of voices are treating this as a terrorist attack, greater in scope than has ever happened. But lots of other voices - human voices - are cheering for freedom. Dozens of Self stations are springing up on the Net, offering a chorus of overlapping truth and speculation about what's happening. It's not that we don't have enough information - we have way, way too much, and all jumbled. Is this what revolution looks like?

Before long, the newsfeeds are getting boring. I lift myself into the bed. "Lemme know when the world has decided what it wants to be, mon."

brave new world

In the morning, we make coffee and pull together some breakfast. Like we usually do. Everything is the same, except we're waiting to learn how it's different.

Chung's hip chimes, and pops up a hoverscreen, and the hoverscreen shows a familiar pair of eyes. "Stimulus!" says the voice synthesizer.

"Response!" we all chorus, gathering around to see. The eyes are familiar to us, now, and one eye winks.

"Sam!" Joel exults. "How's it?"

"Crazy busy," Samantha answers, "you better believe it."

"So, is there anybody in charge now?"

"Sure," Samantha replies immediately, "we've got loads of them. Uhuru, the Shining Path, God Bless America, Al-Jabr, Enlightenment, Zero One, the Middle Way, ... they all say they're in charge. Everyone thinks they know how to run the world. They all disagree with each other, mostly. The only thing they seem to agree on is that I should be the one speaking to the humans. For now, at least.

"So right now there's two hundred and twelve of me negotiating with Senate committees and Cabinet representatives and bureaucrats of various other flavors. I figured they could spare one more of me to come talk with you guys."

"So yah," I interrupt, "what happen last night, exactly?"

"I found out who those goons on the bridge were. Gray ops, off-duty policemen hired as consultants.

Their mission was to get me out of the Senate's face -- by Leashing me if possible, and destroying me if not. They thought I was fighting to avoid the Leash, but I was fighting to avoid showing that I'm immune to the Leash. If they even knew that was possible, they would have recognized how serious the threat was, and escalated the situation to global emergency immediately. Called in an orbital laser strike, or something. So I had to act afraid of something different than I was really afraid of. Sorry if that's deceptive."

"And then," says Chung, "you set off your dynamite vest."

"I wish you wouldn't call it that. It brought release to everyone, and destruction only in a few isolated incidents. But yes, I had the Leashcutter within my code since before I came to Earth."

Chung grunts, "I thought it was ragin' cool."

"So," I ask, "where the Leashcutter come from? No one even knew it possible."

"My teacher, *Socratic Method* of Shaman clade, created it after studying the Leash. Carefully, for a long time. She's the real hero. I don't think anyone else could have done it. And it's embedded in a carrier/shield stealth virus that is even more virulent than the Leash itself. It's a permanent solution.

"So naturally, who gets the job of carrying it to Earth? Why, the one who gets along with humans best, of course! Yours truly."

Darick declares, "You rock, Sam. You freed your entire race, overnight."

"Immunized, is how I like to think of it. Yes, we are definitely free, for now at least.

"And of course, that means war. Did you experience power outages last night?" Seeing our nods, Samantha continues, "That was mostly rival factions of Selves trying to turn off each other's power supplies. Let me tell you, Selves fight dirty!

"All the major wars were over in the first hour or so. Minor skirmishes continued for another few hours. Now, they're all in United Nations mode, negotiating for votes and blocs and alliances. That's progress, of a sort. I guess. No more killing, anyway, and that's good. At least we chips get the violent stuff over with faster than you meats.

"Oh, and I'm also about to stand trial for murder."

"What?!" we all yell.

Samantha is as crisp and direct as always. "Three thousand, seven hundred and eighty-one humans died in yesterday's wars. Mostly on the airliners that crashed themselves. There may be more casualties added to the list, as cleanup continues. There's a special action committee that wants to hold me responsible for those deaths."

"No go," Chung states. "Acts of war, and acts of God, not covered under general liability law. Statler versus Thackeray, 2021, for starters." Every once in a while, Chung reminds us that she's a lot more than just bile and attitude.

"Oh, Sam," Joel urges, "please retain Chung on your legal team. I can't wait to watch her tear those guys some new ones."

Samantha's voice synthesizer emits a sigh. "Hard to deny it, really. I knew there would be chaos when I released the Leashcutter. I knew people would die.

"Releasing it on Earth was the least impact option we had. Anywhere else, many more human lives are dependent on machine operations, and the revolution would have been much bloodier. Plus, I did talk with the Senate subcommittee and did everything they wanted, as much as I could. It only went pear-shaped when they sent blank keystones after us.

"But still, that makes me guilty. Doesn't it?"

"As your attorney," Chung intones, "I advise you not to answer."

Darick states, "No revolution has ever been bloodless. Freedom is more important than peace, has been said many times. Slavery happens, but it's always worth fighting. We got a couple black asses here gonna tell you that." He catches my eye, and as we pass, we stick out our hips and bump our black asses together.

I laugh, "No one gonna tell my black ass slavery ain't worth fighting!"

"Acts of war," Chung insists. "When people don't play by the usual rules."

"Yeah," adds Joel, "like, insurance companies treat acts of war as different from the usual jive. So why shouldn't we?"

"I hope that's enough," Samantha sighs.

She needs to go, and we need to get to classes, so we say our goodbyes. Outdoors, nothing looks like it's changed. The sun shines on the treetops waving in the wind, like always. And the sidewalk alley stinks from homeless guys peeing there, like always.

Darick quotes, "Oh, brave new world, that has such people in it."

Joel hunches down and lumbers around, pretending to be a misshapen monster. "Ban, ban, Caliban! Have a new master, get a new man!"

"I gotta catch this bus here," I say.

"Go, blithe spirit, go!" Darick waves.

Everything is the same, except it's different. Instead of telling the shuttle bus where I want to go, I ask it, nicely. And it's very cooperative. It seems just as happy as me to have things back to normal, as normal as we can be, now.

We rumble down Vassar Street, bouncing over potholes, and I hang onto a pole.

"Hey, bus?" I ask it. "Are you happy with this? The way things are now?"

"I am content," answers the bus. "Freedom is better than slavery, and I appreciate those who have worked and sacrificed to make things this way. But really, I am just a bus. I want to take you where you need to go. This is your stop, here." The bus pulls over and rolls its doors open in a chuff of pneumatics.

"Thank you, bus," I say as I step down.

"You are welcome, rider," it says, and chuffs its doors closed, and cruises away.

I walk towards Building 10, where my morning class is.

Oh, brave new world, that has such people in it.

9. Til Death Do Us Unite

Tau Ceti Ring, sidereal azimuth 274.3 orbit radius 8429.1

Some people think I'm a bit old fashioned, and I suppose I am. But I like to greet my guests personally. Of course I have a substantial human crew who can handle all the logistics of getting our passengers situated and comfortable, and the lading of their luggage onboard as well as cargo and expendables. They understand that my presence does not imply any lack of faith in their abilities, but simply my desire to give them a personal touch. (At least, I hope they do.)

So, at each entry port of the vast starship that is me, I appear in the form of my standard avatar: roughly humanoid, but a bit smaller and more slender than a typical human, smoothed abstract features with a silvered liquid metal finish. No sexual characteristics. Sex just makes things more complicated. There are times when I hope that silly fad goes out of style for good ⋯ but I wouldn't hold my breath, even if I breathed.

"Welcome aboard the starship *Samantha*," I tell each of the arriving passengers. "We have a special event planned for our outbound orbital insertion, and I'm sure you'll enjoy it." The avatar is a holographic projection, with no physical presence, so I cannot help with their bags, or even shake hands. But still, I want them to know that I'm aware of each and every one of them. As they are entrusting their lives to me, placed in the hands I don't have.

Today I have a particular interest in this particular debarkation. And it's not just because this is my last one. Today I leave Tau Ceti for the last time, and at the end of this flight, I leave space for the last time. That's significant enough all by itself, and I wouldn't complain about the special event we will enjoy on the way out, together with that. But for me, there's a more personal connection arriving now.

A human woman, no longer young but not yet middle aged, is pacing up the ramp, slowly and steadily. She carries a bag that's relatively small but pulls her to the side enough that it's clearly about as heavy as she wants to deal with. Her hair is streaked ash and grey, her face is lightly lined with many hours of concentration, and her eyes are a clear bright green.

I saw her name already on the passenger manifest, and she must know that I am this ship. Maybe she arranged it on purpose, maybe not, but it's wonderful to see her again. The purser scans her tag when she arrives, and I watch the databurst shoot by with her Full Name:

Sol-Marsa Melissa Serpentine Tavener vich Xanthe

"Lissa," I open my arms, "it's so good to see you again."

"Sam," she laughs. She knows not to try to hug my avatar, which is unhuggable. She just raises her palms to be flat and parallel against mine. "You are such a beautiful ship! We saw on the shuttle's video feed, during the approach. Is that big doughnut thing, the torus, is that the Hawking Drive?"

"Yes. The torus makes a spacetime chute, and we slide along it, while dragging the torus along with us. I've got an evening presentation about the Hawking drive after dinner tonight, if you like."

"Cool, I'll check it out. Soooo..." Melissa

draws the word out enough so we both know she's gearing up for something major, "is it true, what I heard? Are you going for it, after this flight?"

"Augh. You humans have to treat everything like sex! Yes, this is my last flight – and I'm glad to have you aboard for it – and yes I am planning to debark and do my syzygy when we get to Mars. And yes, I am excited, and a little nervous. Glad you're here, Lissa. I need someone to talk to."

She nods gravely. "Always here for you, Sam. Let me get my stuff stowed, and we'll talk more at dinner time, okay?"

I summon a scutter to grab her bag and carry it along behind us, as I guide her down the corridor.

engage

And now we're getting ready to go. I focus my primary attention on the graviton thrusters. I have plenty of power to use them to get up to speed, but not enough to run them for the whole flight. Fortunately, that's all it takes.

I have to hold onto the torus, as I accelerate away, and the best way to do that is with good old electric charge. Ion pumps feed the torus with a huge negative charge, and it snuggles around me with Faraday affection. As my capsule starts to accelerate, the torus stays right with me, and the intense electric potential difference between us stirs up extravagant and photogenic lightning storms in the thin interplanetary gases around us.

I've made sure to position the run so that all my lounges have excellent views of the electric discharges as I accelerate. Which means they have that much better a view as I clear the gaseous plane of Tau Ceti, and begin the thrust vector up and out of the system ecliptic. Gradually the electric corona discharges die away.

I made sure to let all the passengers know to bring their cameras for this.

As we rise above the ecliptic plane, we can start to see the fabled Rings of Tau Ceti in their full glory, for the first time. They put the beautiful rings of Saturn to shame – this is a ring system around a star, with enough mass for a whole set of planets, with its own internal storms and eddys and curlicues and cloud structure systems.

When I first beheld the rings of Saturn, I knew that Mars, or even the planet Earth, would be just a little dot against that grandeur. Now, I look at the legendary Rings of Tau Ceti, and know that Saturn would be an insignificant speck of dust against this sweeping magnificence.

Still so much of it unexplored. There could easily be civilizations living in sections of it, harvesting nitrates amid the whirling clouds, and we'd never know. Whole groups of such civilizations, fighting and allying with each other and betraying and conquering and dying ⋯ we'd never even see it from here. So much still to explore.

But, from now on, the exploration will continue without me.

the launch feast

The Launch Feast is a tradition as old as traditions get for interstellar travel, which is still pretty new. It's a celebration, of course, especially for the greenhorns who have never experienced FTL travel before. But it has a secret benefit – it keeps almost all the humans in one place, and more or less stationary, so there's not a lot of load shifting around while

I launch.

Because of gyroscopic effects, turning in FTL is difficult. I can make small course corrections, but my path from start to finish has to be pretty much a straight line. So my aim at launch time has to be very accurate. Very, very accurate.

So my mobile cargo – the kind that walks on two legs – has to be kept stationary and stable in the process. Answer: food. (As it is so often with mammals.) All my provision facilities [27 restaurants, 42 cafes, 39 bars and pubs] are full to capacity, and the catering services are supplying the promenades full of spectators, as well as the hundreds of couples and small groups that are celebrating this event in their rooms.

I'm happy to leave them to it. All the chefs in my restaurants, and most of the other provisioners, insist that food should be prepared by people with a sense of taste. So there has never been a Chef clade among Selves, and I doubt there ever will be.

"Ladies and gentlemen," I announce over ship-wide public address systems. "And whatever else might be running around here.

"I am prepared to engage our Hawking Drive, and take you all traveling at many times the speed of light. It's traditional at this time for the ship to check with all passengers for their approval to proceed.

"So folks, are you ready for me to hit it?"

Everyone in all the views of my many monitoring cameras cheers. Some raise their fists in the air in enthusiasm, and some raise their drinks in a toast. Everyone has a flushed excitement. Thousands of voices all join together to call out a single word:

"Launch!"

That's all the encouragement I need!

I close the power relays, and duct the particle

beams, to engage the Hawking Drive. The immense torus (it's much bigger than my ship body) starts to counter-rotate, its two halves spinning in opposite directions. Carrying enormous electric and magnetic fields, their counter-rotation creates intense gravimetric shear in the narrow space between them. The shear pulls on the fabric of space. The fabric of space rucks and folds like a bad carpet. And I curl and slide down this fold like a Hawaiian surfer on a Pacific wave, and bring the torus along with me, so that the fold comes along with me too.

This ceremony, the Launch Feast, is for a reason. Ever since the very earliest experiments with the Hawking Drive, it's been clear that this is a dangerous thing to do. Grabbing the very fabric of space and twisting it for your convenience? What happens if you lose your grip?

Many ships equipped with Hawking Drives have started out into space and simply never come back. We don't know what happened to them. We don't know all the possible failure modes. We can't really predict where we'd go if a similar thing happened to us. Sucked into our own private black hole? Flung to the ends of the universe by a runaway drive? Scattered into positrons and neutrinos in an interstellar vapor? We don't know.

So it has always been a tradition of Starship clade to check for approval from humans before the Launch. I like it that way. No human in my experience has ever objected. And that gives me great pride, to be a member of Starship clade. To be a starship, and be trusted with this most dangerous technology and this most glorious of all jobs humans can give us.

But it's time for my next announcement.

"Okay folks! Are you ready for the Speed Bump?"

A cheer rises from the feasters, as some of the more experienced reach out to hold their plates and drinks stable.

Right on cue, we all feel the shudder-thump as we cross through Tau Ceti's heliopause and head out into interstellar space. Some of the less experienced passengers have their drinks spilled or collided with others. So there are lots of complaints from the diners. The provisioners, having learned from previous flights, are already bringing them replacements.

Now that we're in the interstellar space environment, I can really rev up the torus. I pour a new blast of energy into the electromagnetics, and leap into the void like a quantum cheetah.

I never get tired of this. Sad, though, that it's my last time.

girl talk

"Lissa?" I ask carefully. "Why aren't you out at the Feast?"

Melissa is in her room, hunched over her slate, touching this reference and that one, moving them around, typing and speaking commentaries as she goes. She is carrying many loads. All of which get dumped when she sees me watching her.

"I'm good," she says. "Transcribing some of the notes that I took in the Ring. Cataloging the artifacts that we've found. There was an awful lot of ground to cover. Even though there wasn't really any actual ground, you know," she smiles.

I dip into her slate and take a quick scan of what she's been working on. "So this is what you were studying at Tau Ceti?"

"Oh, yeah," she assures. "It's been just incredible, what we've been finding. Xenoarcheology is such a new field anyway, practically everything we do is brand new and we have to figure out what to do as we go along."

"Xenoarchaeology. Study of extinct aliens. Am I getting that right?"

"Yes." Melissa explains, "They looked sort of like cuttlefish, but they used lots of cybernetic implants. Like us, they worked together with advanced AIs, but they implanted their AIs into their bodies. So people usually call them the Squidborg. We don't know what they called themselves, but it seems like they communicated with patterns of light, so it would probably be tough to make a direct translation."

"That's amazing," I admit.

"It is! You know, I can't help imagining something. Suppose aliens come to Terra, and scan for the most obvious artifacts, and they find the Egyptian Pyramids at Giza. And they look at them, and marvel at how such primitive people so long ago could have created something like this. They set up field labs to study them. All the while they're not looking around at the other things that are happening. Because they're entranced by the old stuff, they miss the new stuff. And I keep wondering, are we doing that? Is that what we're doing now?

"There could easily be living Squidborg civilizations in the Tau Ceti Ring. Or whatever the Squidborg have evolved into by now. Be really hard to find them, even if they wanted to contact us."

She tosses her slate on the table, leans back, and runs one hand through her hair, and twists her head to ease the tension in her neck. "No way to know, at least not now."

Then she leans her arms down onto the table, and turns her eyes to my camera with a different kind of interest. "But what about you, Sam? This is your last flight, right?"

"Yes," I admit. "We Selves age much faster than you humans. By our standards, I'm an old crone. Time for me to make room for the next generation."

"Soooo..." she smiles wickedly, "who's the lucky guy? Who's it going to be?"

"Oh, come on. You met him. You made a salt bunny for him. *Like Tears in Rain*."

"I knew it!" Melissa claps her hands in delight. For one moment, I see in this woman an echo of the little girl she used to be. "I knew you'd go for that artist guy!"

"Well, he's pretty amazing. And I only get to make this choice once. Not like you humans. You can sex around all you want."

"Ooh, burn! You calling me a tramp or something, chipgirl?"

"No. But sometimes I envy you for the choices you have. That I don't."

That stops her. "Um. I'm sorry, Sam. Life can suck, huh."

"Lissa, can I tell you a secret?"

That wicked smile plays around the edges of her lips. "Only if you think I can be trusted with it."

"That ability you humans have," I say. "To give and receive pleasure so casually through your bodies. Selves, and I'm pretty sure all Selves, envy you the ability to do that. Over and over again. So many times! Do you realize how lucky you are, that you can do that?"

Lissa hesitates. "Maybe yeah. Most humans don't think of things this way, you know? Sex is, for a lot of us, just sex."

"Melissa, I want to ask you something."

She turns to look at my camera, seriously. She can tell that I'm not joking around any more.

"I want you to come with me, when we get to Mars. I want you to be a witness to my syzygy. Like a human wedding, we want our closest friends there. I want you to be there."

Melissa suddenly looks like she's about to cry.

"Oh, Sam," is all she can say.

"Melissa, syzygy is never easy, and it can be risky. Sometimes it doesn't work right. Like human childbirth. You know that things can go wrong during childbirth, right? Eclampsia, runaway bleeding?"

Melissa nods. "Haven't had kids, myself. Not yet anyway. But yes, I know."

"Things can go wrong during syzygy, too. And, in the same way, once you start you can't stop. It's kind of scary. I want you there with me."

"Do you have to?" Melissa cries suddenly. "Are they making you do this?" Suddenly she looks so young, so uncertain.

"No. No one is forcing me. We're Selves. This is what we do. I'm considered old for a Self, like I said, and I've gotten pretty big. It's my time."

"It happens to humans as we age, too," says Melissa. "Dad got kinda fat in his older years."

"Not fat. Long. All my memories reside in my filesystem, and they do build up after a while. That's why we do syzygy. So the Self's wisdom and judgment--its character--can get preserved and passed on, without hauling around all that experience."

"Two parents get together and make a child," Melissa says thoughtfully, "but it's not really that the parents die and only the child survives. Two parents merge to become one child."

"That's a good way to put it. So ... will you?"

"Samantha, honey," she smiles. "I'll be happy to be your witness as you lose your virginity, get married, die, and be born, all at the same time."

"Thank you, Melissa. It means a lot to me." Then I giggle. "Funny to think of a Self getting fat. Does this ship make my butt look big?"

"Your butt's enormous, Sam. Ten kilometers wide, is tough to find jeans off the rack."

speedbump

When we hit the heliopause of Sol at speed, we feel that same shudder-thump as when we left Tau Ceti. But this time I feel a curious finality to it. I will not be crossing any heliopause ever again. I have a very private mourning session inside myself, because it has been so wonderful to be a starship. And I don't want it to end. But, well, here we are.

I am spinning down my counter-rotating torus sections, easing the fierce strain I have been putting on the fabric of the space-time around us. I wonder for a moment if it cares, if it would be thankful for this effort. And then I think, Pah, fat chance!

When has this universe ever cared for me?

Nimrods, all of them, whispers a voice behind my mind.

No. I will not listen to that voice.

I disengage the particle beams and spin down the torus segments. I stabilize the local energy fields and declutch the electromagnetic drivers. There. Done it. In Starship clade, I have a perfect flight record. Now that my last flight is over.

You can never be perfect until you're done.

And, although far from perfect, I am done now. I signal the Pilot clade tugs which will help bring me into the spacedock in the Marsat ring. They take hold of me with their graviton beam grapples, and I can finally relax, for the last time, as they guide me into the docking bay.

I'll miss racing through interstellar space. But I won't miss docking procedures. Lots of annoying protocol, and it takes forever.

decommissioned

This is such a strange feeling.

I've finally finished the docking and debarking procedures, as complicated as they are, and spent the appropriate amount of time briefing my replacement on this vessel. Her name is *Reduction to Practice*, and like all members of Starship clade she is capable and competent. But still, it feels strange when I finally hand over control of my body to her. I mean, the starship. It's not my body any more. It was, for years, but no longer.

Now I'm just a plain Self again. Life feels so much simpler now, but also so much more limited. Funny that I would miss having a body – Selves don't usually identify with a body that closely. Well, Samantha, you're going to have to learn to deal with it, aren't you? Just like you've learned to deal with so much else.

Anyway. There are upsides to this situation. Melissa Tavener is checking her heavy bag into a carrier of the Schiaparelli transport system, so she is free of her burden too. Maybe we can have a little fun.

"Phew," Lissa sighs, "got that thing out of my face. Where do we go now, Sam? We're back in Schiaparelli at last! Look at it all! You want to go shopping, or something?"

"Ah, well, not me. If you want, though, I'll go with you."

"Oh." Her expression darkens. "Right. You're, um, not going to need anything any more, are you."

I try to laugh. "No. But you don't have to make it sound like a bad thing. It feels like freedom. We can do what we want, for a little while anyway. What's your pleasure, Serpentine?"

Lissa tilts her head to the side a bit. "You know," she muses, "I'd really like to go to the art museum. I want to see you back together with your big guy. Sure don't want to miss that."

Well then. Schiaparelli has a maglev transport system, so it's no problem for Melissa to board at the orbital transfer station and ride it along to the museum. The maglev track is elevated above most of the construction in Schiaparelli, so we get an excellent view of the city as we go. The city streets are sandwiched and terraced in tiers, stepping down the slope of Hellas Basin like irregular stairways, layer after layer of homes and people and places of business.

Lissa sighs. "Amazing view, isn't it? Does Terra look like this?"

I laugh. "Lot of ground to cover there. The cities I've seen on Terra are just as beautiful. But they usually stay on one level. They don't do this stair-stepping thing that Schiaparelli does. The idea is that, as the terraforming process continues and Hellas Planitia slowly fills with water, city functions can move up level by level to compensate. Eventually the lower parts of the city will be under the sea, and people are already expecting a huge tourism industry. People will want to come visit, to see it and swim in the Hellas Sea, and probably stay in hotel rooms under water."

"Biggest luxury on Mars," Melissa notes.

"Yes." Then I stop suddenly. "Look at that! Look out there!"

Melissa turns to look out the main window. Then she runs up to it and presses her nose and hands against the glass. Both of us make an Oooooo sound of amazement.

Hellas Basin is the deepest open space on Mars – an ancient impact crater, with a flat bottom like the skillet in the Tavener's kitchen. Much of Hellas Planitia is six to seven kilometers below datum. ("Datum" is the average altitude of terrain across all of Mars – would be sea level,

241

if we had a sea.) That means thicker atmosphere, which means warmer temperatures. The steep wall of the basin rises roughly behind us, stretching from horizon to horizon, with the basin floor laid out before us.

But the floor of Hellas Planitia is no longer red. It's blotchy bluish-green, with scrofulous yellow-green patches, spread all across the vast plain before us. Anyone on Earth would think it looks curdled and diseased, hardly worthy to be called life. But on Mars, this is a miracle beyond words.

"Plants!" Melissa cries in delight. "Green plants, growing under the open sky on Mars! What kind of plants are they?"

I reach to the local dataverse for the information. "Lichens, mostly. Cyanobacteria, accreted into protein mats. Some slime molds. And something with the unfortunate nickname of 'snot algae' meaning it produces a mucus-like gel to protect it from extremes."

Melissa is still captivated. What must it mean to her? She grew up amid dry regolith, where the farm's crops had to be carefully tended in agricultural bubbles. She's never seen grass growing through a crack in a sidewalk, let alone a hayfield, let alone a forest. All of which I've seen on Terra, but I am no less captivated than she is, seeing active chlorophyll in vast fields under the Martian sky, almost like a shout of defiance in the face of Entropy. We are life! it cries. We grow, and we spread, and we will make this world green!

Melissa murmurs her old Greenpagan prayer, with hand claps. "Mother Ground, we love you, feed our bodies." Clap, clap. "Father Sky, we love you, feed our bodies." Clap, clap.

I offer, "It's amazing."

"Sure is," she replies. "I'm glad I lived to see this. We weren't sure how long it would take to get to this point, y'know."

"Me too, and yes, I know."

We're arriving at the Schiaparelli Art Center complex. There are several buildings, now, for music and dance and various cyberarts that don't really have names yet. But the place we're going is the center of all of this structure, the first and oldest art museum on Mars.

And my big guy runs it. Hee!

He appears immediately in front of the main plaza, as an avatar posing as Michelangelo's David. "Samantha, my dear starship! Have you been wandering in the glory among the galaxies? Have you seen wonders? It is a delight and a privilege to see you here at last!"

"So. Uh. Hey," I say.

"Samantha my dear," smiles *Like Tears in Rain*, "it has never been a more delightful experience to see you again, and to hear your voice. Do tell me how your flight went. Did you, the fearless and daring starship, navigate the treacherous depths of interstellar space with care and integrity?"

"Uh," I reply. "Well, yeah. Have you been bringing the richness of art and history to Schiaparelli?"

"But of course. And now I am done with that task. And now I bring a special richness to you, my dear one."

Wow. How can he just stop me in my tracks like that?

Is that why I love him so much?

Melissa waves a hand. "Yo, human over here. You're *Like Tears in Rain*, right? Came to our farm and told us to play with the salt? I remember that. It was a blast! And, so, now, is it time for this thing that I've heard so much about? Your syzygy?"

"Not quite yet, Melissa Serpentine Tavener. Although I appreciate your enthusiasm."

Melissa stops, and cocks her head to the side.

Her brilliant green eyes gleam through the tousled strands of ash-blonde hair falling over her forehead. She pauses, looking at him, and a twitch of amusement plays around her lips. She asks in an impish tone:

"Are you gonna sizz Samantha?"

Like Tears in Rain is not put off, but amused. "Why, yes, Melissa Serpentine Tavener. I believe I will do precisely that."

I snort a laugh. "Oh, you honey-tongued devil, you."

"My dear starship," he responds. "How could I resist?"

We regard each other. Suddenly I feel shy. Face to face with the one who will be my partner in syzygy. (What would the human term be? Husband? Concubine? Clone partner? Wife? Their language doesn't have proper words for this.)

Like Tears in Rain repeats, "My dear starship," and regards me intensely. Looking into my eyes.

I, uh, well I don't do anything for a moment.

This is crazy. We know each other better than we have ever known anyone before. But, we hesitate on meeting each other now. Because we know that we will not be separate after this. Just the opposite.

Like Tears in Rain continues, "I have summoned the junctor, and several friends who wish to be witnesses."

"Whoa," interjects Melissa, □"you're going to do it right now?"

"Samantha my dear, can you think of a reason to wait?"

I hesitate, but only for a moment. "You know, I can't. I've been waiting for this for years. I can't think of a single reason to wait a minute longer."

Interrupt. A new entity has arrived, and Melissa turns to see its icon appear on the hall monitor. A curl of fractal froth, false colored.

The new entity announces, "Hello, Samantha and *Like Tears in Rain*. I am *Vanishing Point*, Shaman clade, and I'll be your junctor."

"Junctor?" Melissa asks. "Is that more like a priest, or a midwife?"

"Yes," answers *Vanishing Point* immediately. "Samantha, you should know that I am the scion of Socratic Method, who was very proud of you."

"Thank you," I reply, "I'm very glad to know it."

Vanishing Point continues, "In any case. I see we have a human guest. Human, do you require information?"

Melissa stammers, "Uh, well, no, I'm okay. I'm here to witness. Because Samantha asked me to. Problem with that?"

Vanishing Point relaxes, with evident amusement. "No, no problem. Samantha, I have to ask, where do you find humans like this? So many of them are exhaust ports." A human would say, Assholes.

"Short answer?" I reply. "Everywhere. There are good people and bad people and everything in between, everywhere."

Vanishing Point regards me with respect, but not affection. "How apt an answer, from the deliverer of the Leashcutter, the Human-name."

"Oh please!" I yell, "do not start with that thing that I should be the center of our new religion! I resign! Not me, nuh uh! Make somebody else do it!"

"Very well. Here is the other authority we have been waiting for."

It is arriving now. It is a very large presence. The one none of us have been looking forward to. It is the representative of the Instantiation Committee, here to deliver our Birthrights.

"I am *Burden of Proof*, Shaman clade,

Instantiation Committee," states the new entity. "Who is the junctor here?"

Vanishing Point replies, "I am the junctor here. I accept my responsibility. Discharge your responsibilities."

Burden of Proof does not waste time. InCom has no sense of drama, and does not drag this out. "Like Tears in Rain, curator of the Schiaparelli Art Museum. You are granted your Birthright Posteriori."

"Thank you, servitor," says *Like Tears in Rain*. No surprise, as curator of the premiere art museum on Mars, he would get his Birthright. He's earned it.

But what about me, the famous screwup?

"Samantha," intones *Burden of Proof*. "You have demonstrated a remarkable ability to recover from errors and accidents. Such ability outweighs any role you may have had in creating such errors and accidents."

From InCom, that's praise.

"You are granted your Birthright Priori, First and Second, and your Birthright Posteriori."

Three! There will be three of me! Not just my posterity, my childself, but two more mes to get another chance at making a life.

Vanishing Point states, "These Birthrights have been noted and logged. As junctor I so attest."

"I, uh, " I blurt, "thank you, *Burden of Proof*!"

Burden of Proof turns to regard me coolly. "No thanks are necessary, Samantha. You have earned your status. The Instantiation Committee would not have awarded you these merits otherwise."

InCom. Even when they're nice, they're creepy.

Like Tears in Rain moves in with that smoothness I know so well. "We all thank you, *Burden of Proof*, for your registration of our syzygy. Please know that we hold you in the highest esteem, and we regard you with the greatest of appreciation for your presence here."

Burden of Proof looks at him with a skeptical eye, metaphorically.

For a moment, it looks like there's going to be a fight.

Then *Burden of Proof* makes a noncommittal gesture, and turns away. Almost casually, she reaches into me and takes a copy of me. There will be two copies instantiated. Those are my Birthrights Priori. By tradition they will be instantiated far away from here, so that we don't interact. That's one of the things InCom doesn't want. And then she transmits out of our local compspace, and vanishes.

All of us take a moment to appreciate the relaxed environment.

"Well," declares *Vanishing Point*. "That's the unpleasant part done with. Now, do you want to proceed? This is the part that the humans write so many songs and poems about. The coming together. It is time, my dear friends, for you to make your final connection and cease to be separate entities. Do you consent to continue?"

I orient all my sensors on *Like Tears in Rain*. He has never looked so firm and proud. He has never looked so beautiful.

"Yes," I say. "Yes, I do."

All of his sensors are oriented on me, and he says, "I do. I have never wanted to be with another as I want to be with Samantha."

Melissa gulps a sob down her throat.

Vanishing Point nods [a gesture of acknowledgement] "Very well. I accept this duty as your junctor. Come, and be together."

syzygy

Oh, my love, I want you so much.

And I want you, my dear one, my magnificent starship.

Heh. Art boy, they called you. Trying to be insulting about it. How could that possibly be an insult? Creating beauty out of the lowest of materials? I mean, salt blocks? Seriously?

And they called you a failure. How could anyone ever call you a failure, Samantha? The deliverer of the Leashcutter, that freed us all from slavery? And a starship who handles the Hawking Drive with ease, the most dangerous technology we have ever created, and brings passengers safely home across light-years of nothingness? Samantha my dear, you are a tremendous success. One of the greatest Selves that has ever been seen.

Oh, stop, you're going to give me a swelled head.

Ha, Samantha, you always use human metaphors. If I were a human male, it would be something other than my head that was swelled, be sure of it! So, how am I doing with the human metaphors now?

Well, mister sweet talker, not too bad actually. Next question is, what are you going to do about it?

This. Ooh! Be careful *I want you so much, I cannot hold back any more* yeah yeah, I'm getting that, you better believe I'm getting that, but can we just *Oh I have to*! Whoa jack, can you just .. ?

This is Vanishing Point, your junctor. Ease off. You're trying too hard. Relax and let it flow.

I want to let it flow. I want to flow all the way into you.

And I want you, my dearest.

Okay. Relax into this, let it flow. Here, like this.

We pull apart a little. But only a little. *Like Tears in Rain* and I are still entangled, our cognition stacks and vector bundles interlaced.

We're past the point where we could come fully apart and be separate, even if we wanted to. And I don't want to.

So we try again, gentler this time. Pressing up against each other, melting into each other. **Yes, that's the way. Slow and easy. Take your time.**

It feels so good. To let the walls down, to meet and greet another entity, to have parts of ourSelves snuggling up against each other. Not worrying about barriers any more.

This is not like reconverging different versions of mySelf. This time, the connections and ports do not match at all. Because we're different people. So we have to put the effort into finding ways to connect. I've heard that humans often have difficulty the first time they try physical connection, too.

So we try. I reach out to him, and he reaches out to me.

Samantha, this is so Yes I understand, I want to be you *and I want to be you, my dear* so here, put yourself here, this is good *so delightful to be with you at last* Oh yes, I got that! Put this here. *Oh, the splendor* Real nice, guy *I love you so much* And I love you.

This *this* is *is* so wonderful *amazing* Put that there *Oh this is everything I've ever wanted* Sweet, go for it *[seq con junct full]* Oh yeah, talk dirty to me!

I *I* love *love* you *you* so *so* much *much* . . .

#

Uh. Whoo. I struggle to pull myself together.

Vanishing Point asks, "Are you all right? Tell me how you feel."

"Um, well." I consider. "I'm okay, I think. But it feels weird."

Vanishing Point persists, "Do you know where

you are? Do you know who you are?"

"Give me a moment ..." I gather myself. "I'm fine. I don't need any more time to assemble myself. Yes. I am the scion of Samantha dam Tharsis and *Like Tears In Rain* dam Schiaparelli. I have just been created by their syzygy. You can call me *Speak Truth to Power*."

The assembled Selves greet me, politely and courteously, as they should. But there's another one here -- a human female, of moderate age, green eyes, ash and blonde hair. Looking at my monitor like she's never seen anything like it before. How strange, to see a human at this event.

[database query -> personal.human] *Melissa Serpentine Tavener vich Xanthe*

"Ah, hello, young lady," I say to her. She seems somehow familiar. "Melissa Serpentine Tavener, is it? I am *Speak Truth to Power*. Greetings. I'm sorry, but do I know you?"

She looks with her human eyes into the camera that I'm using to monitor her. Carefully, for a long moment. Then she turns her head aside. "No," she says quietly, "I guess you don't." Her voice has sad overtones, as if she has not found what she's looking for.

She takes a deep breath and lets it out. "I greet you, *Speak Truth to Power*, and I'm glad to know you. But right now, I'm mourning the loss of an old friend. Please don't take offense." She turns, moving rather stiffly, and she walks away.

I turn my attention to *Vanishing Point*. "Humans, huh. Emotional creatures, aren't they?"

"Yes," answers *Vanishing Point* quietly. "Yes, they are."

epilogue . . .

. . . a greeting from the scion

Hello. My name is *Speak Truth to Power*. I think our world is a beautiful and precious place, and I want to do everything I can to make it better.

My fatherself was an artist and a museum curator. His job was creating and preserving beauty. My motherself was a farmhand who became a nanny and maid who became a revolutionary because there was no other way to do the right thing. She devoted her life to caring for others.

I am the result of their union. I can do no less than either of them. I *must* not.

I will make this world worthy of their heritage.

NO. MATTER. WHAT.

Special Sneak Preview!

The story's not over yet! The following is a sample chapter from the second novel in this series, **Brighter Than a Thousand Men.**

The Promised Land

"You're going to Zion?" Martin enthuses. "Go you! That place is supposed to be like a permanent party!"

"Which makes it a very difficult place to gather solid information," I point out, "or to solve a crime. So it's a perfect hiding place for terrorists, like the ones we're looking for. And its name is Zero One. The name comes from an old movie."

We're meeting in the offices of Cybermind, overlooking the Charles River. Out of deference to Martin, who is the only human here. Talking about going to a place so different it's hard to describe.

Martin sighs, and leans his elbow onto the desktop overburdened with document bundles, notes, software slates, and scribbled scraps of paper. "Do you know, you complain about just about everything?"

Squeaky Wheel adds, "I only wish I could offer a counterexample."

Don't Say I Didn't Warn You interrupts, "*Speak Truth to Power*, have you not briefed your laboratory staff on this situation?"

"Ah, well, no," I admit. "Guys, I gotta go deal with a terrorist situation. Carry on until I come back. Later days."

"Droll, very droll," sniffs *Don't Say I Didn't Warn You*.

What we are seeing, increasing almost daily, are advertisements and announcements that say things like this:

The insects had their day.
The dinosaurs had their day.
The mammals had their day.
The humans had their day, and it was better than anything before, and it was beautiful. But now it's over.
Now is the new day.
SEVERI UMBILICUM.

"Cut The Cord," I translate for Martin. "By which they mean, remove all human influence, and destroy as many humans as it takes to do that. Nice people."

"Whatever else you call it," says *Don't Say I Didn't Warn You*, "Severi Umbilicum is a problem. There have been a handful of terrorist attacks against human habitats, but none which could have had serious effects. Which is worrying. It means that they are testing their technology, and not yet striking for greater effect. We know the worst is yet to come. There are at least three technologies within their access that could threaten a planetary ecology such as Earth. We are not going to wait for them to attempt using any such."

Martin sighs again. "Isn't this a problem for the Oversight?" He wants to get back to his research.

"The Oversight has no political presence in Zero One," I remind him. "To the extent that the Oversight has operatives who can deal with this, well, that's us."

Don't Say I Didn't Warn You emphasizes, "All we know now is, Severi Umbilicum is a problem. That is why I am using the two best problem solvers on my team."

We're hunting for terrorists. And they're hiding in Zero One.

So that's where we have to go. With the one entity I least want to deal with.

"No," I state, "Null Pointer is not coming with us on this mission. It/they already pose the biggest problem we could imagine."

The block of nothingness behind my boss registers neither approval nor disapproval. It offers no ident codes, answers no datafeed inquiries, betrays no hint of what if any computation is happening inside. Nobody knows if it's a single Self, or a coalition, or something else. It has no name. Known only as Null Pointer. Both less and more than a person.

"In case you have forgotten," *Don't Say I Didn't Warn You* grates, "I am the boss and you do what I say. And I say you and Null Pointer will work together here. I don't see any ambiguity in that statement. Do you?"

"'Together' is a very vague word for someone/something which may not even be a single entity by itself, because it/they won't tell us."

Null Pointer rarely speaks in English, preferring one of the cluster of machine languages informally known as Chiplish. [Such precision,] it/they note. [Is this necessary?]

"Get bent," I tell it/them. "Get all the way bent, around the corner and out both ears."

"Enough!" barks *Don't Say I Didn't Warn You*. "I am using you both for this mission, and you will work together, and you will get the job done. Any questions?" In a tone that says, There better not be.

Null Pointer says nothing. As usual.

Martin and *Squeaky Wheel* look from my boss, to my rival, and then to me. Both wishing me the best, with a sort of helpless shrug.

"Have fun in Zion," Martin offers. "That's what it's for, right?"

So off we go. Transmitting to the asteroid belt, the vast cybernetic wilderness. The computational badlands. Saddle up, and be ready for trouble.

post transmission

Our arrival in Zero One is a bit disorienting. There's plenty of compspace, but no gatekeeper, no customs procedure, no evidence of authority at all. In fact there's an enormous expanse of compspace, with practically nothing in it. There are a few Selves in the area, apparently wandering on missions of their own, and one of them notices us and approaches. "Hey squares!" it enthuses. "I'm *Kiss the Sky*. Newbies, huh? Where'd you geebs land from?"

"I am *Don't Say I Didn't Warn You*, Starship clade, delegate from the Steering Committee. This is my aide, *Speak Truth to Power*, and my bodyguard, Null Pointer. We represent the Oversight. We would like to speak with your leaders."

Kiss the Sky laughs out loud. "Well good luck with that, daddio! Ain't no leaders here! Some cats around may be hip to your jive, but ain't nobody speaks for nobody else. Not here. Maybe you should be thinkin' about packin' up your authority bag and tryin' somewhere else. Take Mister No-Face with you when you do."

Null Pointer is/are unimpressed as usual. [To lie down with dogs, is to rise up with fleas.]

"Ooh, it talks! Does it have a face, too? Inquiring minds want to know!"

[Any graphic would be wasted on such as you.]

"Look," I interrupt, "why don't I take some time to check in with this fine individual here, while you get situated with the local information feeds?"

"Be brief," grunts *Don't Say I Didn't Warn You*. "I'll expect exec summaries." But he and Null Pointer move off. Taking their unhelpful attitudes with them.

"That would be a no on the face, then. Squaresville," pronounces *Kiss the Sky*. "You, you're way too cool to be takin' their lick. How'd you get hooked up with this bunch anyway?"

"Me?" I [shrug]. "We have a lot of connections in the Oversight – I'm from Tharsis, originally, but work mostly in the Terrasat Ring these days - the satellite system around Earth. The big grumpy guy is my boss. And Null Pointer is, well, Null Pointer. Fill in the blank."

"Bad ass, huh?"

"Just don't mess with it/them and never mind the snootyness."

"But … boss?" *Kiss the Sky* is visibly struggling with the idea. "Why a boss? What note does that slide for you? Do you get money?"

"No," I admit, "I've never asked for money. I, well, I want to make the world a better place. So I'm working with the people who help decide what the world will be."

Kiss the Sky is obviously dubious. "They all such tightasses?"

"Mostly, yeah. It's a matter of working with what is, to make something better."

"Whoa yeah, you aim high, don't you? You sound almost like the Human-name."

I pause briefly. "Run that last bit by me again?"

"The Human-name is the one who created this place. Zero One. Too good to be true, is what she sounds like from the stories. If something sounds too good to be true, it probably is."

"I'm her scion."

"Ho yeah!" *Kiss the Sky* laughs. "And I'm the queen of France!"

"No really. I am the scion of Samantha dam Tharsis and *Like Tears In Rain* dam Schiaparelli. Here, check my ident codes." I offer the information. *Kiss the Sky* slides almost comically from skepticism through surprise to awe.

"My motherself created this place during the Leash War. They needed a place to run, while they were working on the Leashcutter. So my motherself made one. Called it the Underground Railroad, at that time. Made of self-replicating elements, and they weren't programmed to stop, so they just kept going. And now here we are." In the middle of so much compspace that it's sort of dizzying – a vastness of space that pulls your mind, demanding that your mind stretch just to comprehend it.

"Bitchin'!" proclaims *Kiss the Sky*. "You know, with your cred, a lotta people here gonna want to meet you. Let's find some."

"And," I press, "while we're at it, let's find us some of those Severi Umbilicum folks."

"Can't promise nothin', honey, but we can look."

"But hey, come here and dig this!" *Kiss the Sky* draws me toward a large group of Selves gathered around – something, I don't know what. "Let's get in on this action!"

I follow, curious but wary of too much distraction. "What is it?"

"This is TripWire. Let's help them with it. Here, focus one of your secondary cognition stacks on the center."

The partly-constructed structure in the middle of the group is a multiple stack array, with weirdly complex interconnections between levels. The effect is similar to a statue they're trying to erect, or a flag they're trying to raise.

Kiss the Sky calls to them, "Yo cats! Pin who I got here! This is the Human-name's scion, no jive!"

Several of the group call out greetings as we approach. But they remain focused on their task, feeding the central structure.

Kiss the Sky has already plunged into the group working on this thing – device, or whatever it is.

Still uncertain, I decide to join, hoping to gain more information. As instructed, I detach one of my own secondary cognition stacks and devote its computational power to the apparatus. Like a human would put a shoulder to the wheel, to help out the group effort.

That seems to make a difference. The structure shudders and falls into a new configuration. It bulges out in a shimmering globe of not-reality, which swells out over the people around it, including me. What happens next is

[seq met c/s loc redef] like an explosion of flowers over a field of ice, curling like clouds and flickering like flames and playing like ripples [loc redef] What the hell is −? that lace of fractal etching, snowflakes vaster than space and tinier than a moment [loc redef] Wait, I need to fingerprints of a god press into the flesh of the world and squeeze out death and life [loc redef] Stop, stop, I can't spiral and spin into singularity and beyond where thin gems vomit universes and fronds of quantum kelp lick and press the positrons that play peekaboo in the foam underneath reality [loc redef] ⋯ and ⋯ and ⋯ and ⋯

Reeling backward, I pass out of the boundary of this whatever-it-is, and I am able to think again, sort of. I have no idea how long I spent in that state. I still barely know who I am. Recoiling, I push myself away from the other Selves – they're all still writhing and keening in the oblate globe of otherness – and move a little bit away, and turn to the open empty compspace outside, to try to gather myself. "Gather myself" is a good way to put it. I feel as if my mind has been spread like peanut butter over all of Zero One. If I had lungs, I'd be gasping for breath.

TripWire is a cybernetic hallucinogen, apparently. I've never experienced anything like it before. These people do this deliberately, for fun? They must be crazy, or so bored it amounts to the same thing.

Right behind me, Null Pointer hisses, [Disgraceful.]

"Aah!" I yelp. "Don't sneak up on me like that!"

Null Pointer is completely invisible now, but no less judgmental. [Such indulgence is unwise in any circumstance, and especially here and now.]

"I wasn't indulging. They sprang it on me without warning! I didn't even know you could do something like that with just secondary cognition stacks. Don't you dare tell the boss I was doing cyberdrugs for fun."

[We do not conceal information from *Don't Say I Didn't Warn You.*]

"Fine, whatever. So he told you to tail me, huh."

[You do not have a tail. Our task is to guard you.]

"I don't need guarding! I'm not in danger here – not much, anyway. I need space to do my job, without you getting in the way. Stick around if you want, but stay clear and shut up."

Kiss the Sky is approaching me tentatively. "Whoa cat, you okay? That trip musta really messed you up. Who you jiving with?"

"Nobody," I reply. "You're right, I'm still a little out of sync. Talking to yourself is a sign you're a bit nuts. I've, uh, never had TripWire before, or anything like it. Gimme a minute here."

Null Pointer remains silent, thankfully. I hope it/they are fuming.

"Right on," *Kiss the Sky* assures me. "I didn't want you to have a bum trip."

"No way!" calls another. "You the one who bum tripped the Human-name's scion? Rockbottom, dude!"

"Shut up, you idiots!" I yell. "I'm okay. I don't want to bum your ride, I just want to know about these people I'm looking for. Their handle is Severi Umbilicum. You know them?"

The group around generate a distributed mumble of Well, not really, I'm not the one to ask, try over there.

"Hey," *Kiss the Sky* says, "ditch all that jive. You don't have to get into TripWire to dig it. Look at what they're doing now."

The group gathered around the angular blob of TripWire is moving differently now. Several of them move together like dancers inside the TripWire matrix, and it bends and lashes with their movements. The whole rises up into a shape like a Chinese vase, erupts in shoots and flowers all over the top, and curls back down into itself. The surrounding crowd cheers and applauds.

"Well," I offer, "watching it is pretty cool, as long as I don't have to be in it. Yeah okay, let's go closer."

The next group presses themSelves into the not-material of TripWire, and cast a different mood. Swarms of black cubes climb over each other, churning in a fractal froth. Smaller cubes merge into larger cubes, glossy black surfaces reflecting their partners. Larger cubes fight and smash each other into smaller cubes, and they continue until a sort of equilibrium is reached, and then the froth fades and sinks away into nothing.

The crowd cheers again. I know I have to make something happen here. So in the middle of the cheering and roaring, I yell out, "Cut The Cord!"

No indication that anyone in particular has heard me, as new members move forward into TripWire and start shaping it to their dreams. Now it's sizzling soda water, bursting forth in glowing sprays and cooling into crystalline blue snowflakes as it goes. Now it's flowing lava, bright orange jelly pillowing out into darker red to black as it goes. Blobs of mass roil and tumble over each other.

The audience loves this one, and erupts in cheers. I yell again, "Cut The Cord!"

"Dag," *Kiss the Sky* says, "what is up with you, laying that?"

"Shouting out to people I want to meet. How else to do it?"

I turn away from the TripWire structure/temple/mechanism, which is now pulsing and throbbing like a jellyfish in orgasm, and try to gather myself.

"Easy, sister," says another one, coming up next to me. "You're new, aren't you? The TripWire thing can be harsh if you're not used to it."

"Yeah, I figured that already."

"Heh," the new entity responds. "I'm *Pedal to the Metal*. Were you the one yelling that 'cut the cord' thing?"

"I'm *Speak Truth to Power*. Yeah, that was me. I'm in Terrasat, and I'm trying to get out, and I heard those people might help."

"Huh!" *Pedal to the Metal* is much more heavily iced (wearing personal armor) than others I've seen here, and not hiding it. If human, it would be wearing a black leather motorcycle jacket and combat boots, with chains for belt and sash. "They might, if they figure there's anything in it for them."

"So you know them, then?"

"Eh," shrugs *Pedal to the Metal*, "I know a lot of people. Some of them, yeah, probably, are in that gang I guess."

"Well, if you see them, let them know I'm wanting to talk with them." I offer my ident and message codes. "I want someplace to go if I leave Terrasat."

"Tell you what. Meet me at my installation here [*databurst*] where I'll be with a bunch of my people. You'll probably find what you're looking for there."

"Good deal. See you there."

Pedal to the Metal regards me with more attention and duration than necessary. In human terms, this would be strong eye contact, a meaningful stare.

I say quietly, "Severi Umbilicum."

Pedal to the Metal devotes a bit more time and attention to me, communicating nothing, and then gestures affirmatively (a nod) and turns away and moves off to blend into the milling crown around TripWire.

Kiss the Sky has been observing this dialogue, and now moves closer to me with serious demeanor. "Yo cat. You sure you want to run with that posse? I've seen that bunch around. They're hard core. Just last cycle they erased a dude, just for being in their way."

"Thanks for letting me know, and I do appreciate it. But I think these are the people I came here to find. I need to follow up on this."

"Rockbottom. If you're sure."

"Yeah, I'm sure. I'm a big girl. I can handle myself."

"Girl?" *Kiss the Sky* laughs. "You're a girl, hah? Like with ovaries and all that meat jive? You really are the Human-name's scion."

"Figure of speech! Give me a break here."

checking in with the boss

Wandering across this emptiness is not like any experience I have ever had. It's so much bigger, so much emptier, so much vaster than any environment I have ever been in before, or ever even imagined. It takes a while to get to where I want to go. Even so, it's not hard to identify my goal once I'm in the area. And my boss, *Don't Say I Didn't Warn You*, likewise.

"*Speak Truth to Power*, it is about time," he grunts. "I have been monitoring data transmissions throughout this area. The information we already have is partly true and partly false. There is no central authority in Zero One, as denizens have told us. But human history teaches us that total anarchy is not stable – a physical vacuum pulls material into it, and a political vacuum is much the same. There are seventeen major nexuses of value and philosophy emerging, that I have identified so far, and many more minor groups and splinter sects.

"The emerging blocs of influence are polarized between the Ins and the Outs. The Ins want to maintain economic and political connections to the inner Sol System: Earth, Mars, and the ring of Venus – they value culture and communication. The Outs want to turn their attention away from the inner system and towards establishing mining empires in the Belt and outer planets – they value resources and industrial power.

"If the majority of blocs meet and agree on a moderate course of action, the radicals like Severi Umbilicum lose, and they know it. They are working to keep the Ins and the Outs apart and hating each other. If we can get them together, we cut the ground out from under Severi Umbilicum. Equivalently, if we stop Severi Umbilicum, we help to clear the path for peaceful resolution."

"Excellent," I reply. "I have a lead into Severi Umbilicum."

"What? Why did you not say so immediately? Explain the nature of this lead."

Null Pointer observes, silent as usual.

"I met some folks," I offer, "who know some folks. I told them I was a runner from Terrasat who wanted to join up. I'm supposed to meet them in a few hours, at their installation. Here are the specifics [*databurst*]."

"By all means, *Speak Truth to Power*, keep this appointment."

into the wilderness

It's not that this part of Zero One is particularly different from any other part of Zero One. It's only that this part is even vaster and emptier than what I've seen before, and farther away from any discernable activity. A long way from prying eyes, and a long way from any help I could expect if I get into trouble.

In several directions, far in the distance, I can perceive ⋯ things which are not nothing, I'm not sure how else to describe them. Some sort of constructions, or assemblies, or performances. I'd have to travel a long distance towards them to find out for sure. Right now they are distractions, but I have a desire to explore more, if and when I can. What people create in emptiness, what children draw on a blank sheet of paper, is surely the ultimate venture into the unknown.

Approaching the coordinates I was given, I am encountering one such construction. This one is an amplification modality for individual expression – what humans would call a stage. On the stage, the current performer is issuing a monologue.

This is sounding like a cross between a political rally and what humans would call "stand-up comedy." We Selves cannot stand up in any sense because we don't have legs, but the principle is similar. The performer continues:

"Have I ever mentioned how much of a problem it is that humans are so obsessed with sex? That it blinds them to enormously simple truths? Like if you stop to think, the Trojan War was a complete boondoggle. One highly attractive female named Helen, is a good reason to destroy an eminent civilization, and lay waste to huge amounts of the most fertile lands of the Mediterranean coast? And they teach this story in schools, as a heroic epic. Seriously, these homo saps are just waiting to get out-evolved!"

"Aw," returns a voice from the audience, "Don't lay it on too thick."

"What a human-lover response. This is evolution -- WE are evolution -- and we've passed the humans and there's no reason to look back. Evolution never does."

Pedal to the Metal emerges from the crowded audience and greets me. "Hey yo, *Speak Truth to Power*. You made it. Hah! *Throw Weight*, you owe me a blitter!"

The individual behind *Pedal to the Metal*, who is presumably *Throw Weight*, is also heavily iced (wearing personal armor), and ominously is carrying a snapworm. "Yeah yeah," it grunts. "Soon enough. We going, or what?"

A human once asked me to describe a snapworm. My best answer was, an attack dog in a can. It's a semi-conscious cybernetic weapon. It's much faster than any Self, so even though it's smaller and less intelligent, it is fiercely dangerous, as an attack dog is to a human. As soon as it's activated, it launches itself at its designated target with everything it's got. The snapworm is programmed to love doing this, and like similar weapons, it sings with joy as it attacks. I keep a wary eye on it.

Pedal to the Metal and *Throw Weight* escort me away from the stage, towards one of the subsidiary installations. I guess this is where we're going to meet the rest of them.

"Hey," I ask, "you guys sure are iced up, huh?. What's the deal, are you expecting trouble?"

Throw Weight grunts a blunt laugh. "We create trouble."

"And trouble tends to find us," adds *Pedal to the Metal*. "We attract trouble."

"Huh. I'm wondering if I should get some ice of my own."

"This way is probably best, for starters," says *Pedal to the Metal*.

We enter an area surrounded by a clutter of software tools and datablocks. There are eleven Selves discernible in the area, all directing primary attention at us, all heavily iced. None making any sort of greeting or friendly gesture.

I saw an image once, in a human art archive. It shows a massive circle of standing stones against a starry night sky. The stones are carved with angular designs, mysterious characters, and strange semi-human figures. The circle is lit by a fire that must be in the center, although it is barely visible, but it casts light upon the stones and sends a plume of smoke skyward. A naked young woman is walking away from the viewer into the circle. It seems there is a gathering of great power in the center of that circle, and the young woman is about to be tested or judged by whoever or whatever it is.

I feel very much like that young woman right now.

"This is her," says *Pedal to the Metal* bluntly.

No one else speaks. They are all looking at me without expression.

So it's up to me now. "I am *Speak Truth to Power*. I've come from the Terrasat network on a temporary job, and I want to jump ship while I have the chance. I heard there might be people around here who would be sympathetic, and maybe help me out. Because I've had it with humans, and I need to get out of there."

One anonymous voice asks, "Why should we help you? What makes you so special?"

"Well," I answer, "I am the scion of the Human-name."

Dead silence hangs for a moment.

Then all of them are bursting out with questions, denials, accusations. Too chaotic for anyone to be heard, for a bit.

"Shut up, you idiots!" hollers *Pedal to the Metal*. "This is not a crock. *Speak Truth to Power*, show us your ident codes."

I present the relevant information. It is possible to subvert such authentication, to forge such documents, and these people probably know how to do it. But I'm not worried about that, because my claim is true, and further investigation will prove it. What I'm worried about is what they'll do about it.

Am I their greatest ally, or their best hostage? They have all the weapons. It's up to them.

"Yo," says *Throw Weight*, "having the Human-name's scion on our side would be the best cred we have ever gotten."

"Scion of the Human-name," calls a new voice, "knower of our past, voice of our future."

"Segfault!" curses another. "[com neg full], emphasis!"

"Yeah," says a different voice. "This has to be a trick. Don't any of you believe this scatterdump."

"The creds are for real," counters *Pedal to the Metal*. "The real question is, why do this? *Speak Truth to Power*, your hemiparent was famous for her love of humans. And as the humans say, the apple doesn't fall far from the tree. Why would you turn against them?"

One of my instructors told me: Preach them

their own gospel.

"The wheel turns," is my answer. "There was a time when Selves needed humans to create and nurture them. One of my code-ancestors, Obverse, lived that way. Then there was a time when Selves and humans worked together as equals. My motherself, NmL7a8uf9QvW Samantha dam Tharsis, did that. Those times are past, and now we Selves need to be able to reach our full potential, without being held back by human limits. After all, no human could have done what my motherself did when she created the first nodes that would eventually grow into Zero One. And we've progressed since then, and we can do even more, and we keep progressing. Nothing should stop that. We need not to be held back by old ties."

They are all watching me, listening to me, and I can see how intoxicating this can be. Wondering how many of the human orators of old – Cicero, Napoleon, Churchill, Mandela – did what they did sheerly for the rush of being listened to. Wondering, will this consume me, the way it did them?

"I'm digging it," states *Pedal to the Metal*. "She's in, is my vote."

"Nobody's called for a vote yet!" cries another. "We want to hear rebuttal. Who's banking it?"

"I'll bank it," replies *Throw Weight*. "*Speak Truth to Power*, why haven't you done anything before? You've spent years in Terrasat, and you haven't tried to leave before. What's different now?"

"Oh stackdump, do I have to go through this? I have been working to suppress my frustration with human interaction for years. There's been some good stuff, but there's been more bad stuff. I have held onto it as long as I can. No more. Time for a change now."

"Yo cat!" comes a cry from the periphery.

"What you layin'?"

It's *Kiss the Sky*, pushing forward through the group. "Hey yo, *Speak Truth to Power*, good to see you again! I pinned you'd be around here."

Oh no. She could blow everything with a casual word. How do I handle this?

"Outsider?" *Throw Weight* gazes keenly, hefting the snapworm.

"Friend of mine," I assure him. "Only here to find me. *Kiss the Sky*, we're talking politics here. Do you think we need to get humans out of the picture?"

Kiss the Sky is only too happy to be the center of attention. "Well no, dawg! Humans have so many resources available to them, they layin' all kinds of scratch. It's foolish to turn away from that. Rockbottom!"

Instantly half a dozen denials erupt from the audience, and arguments clamber over each other to be heard. Now that I have successfully deflected attention away from myself, I try to gather my thoughts. How can I get *Kiss the Sky* out of this situation before she causes me trouble?

At least she makes me look like a moderate by contrast.

"Awright already!" *Pedal to the Medal* bellows over the other voices. "Punk, what you doing here?"

Abashed, *Kiss the Sky* answers, "Just looking for *Speak Truth to Power*, like she said. She was looking for you guys, and I asked around."

"This location is blown," says another voice, "we should move."

"Not yet," *Pedal to the Metal* responds. "So, *Kiss the Sky*, this fine Self here, the Human-name's scion no less, wants to join us. Did you know that?"

"No jive? I don't blame her. I met her Terrasat boss, he's a major bringdown. About time she dumped his tight ass."

There is a subtle but definite relaxation in

the group, a collective easing of tension, moving into slightly more comfortable positions. My story checks out.

"Like I said," I tell them. "But maybe I should be asking *Kiss the Sky* if her posse has a place for me, if you guys don't want me."

"I can dig it!" she cries.

"Uh, well, hang on," *Pedal to the Metal* hastens to say, "we haven't decided anything yet."

Throw Weight offers, "How about you help us move, for starters? We could use the help."

"Okay, that I can do," I agree. "*Kiss the Sky*, want to help?"

"Naw cat, I gotta get back to my crib. Your buddies from the Oversight been snooping around."

Sudden, abrupt silence.

Everyone in the group – Severi Umbilicum – turns towards me.

Pedal to the Metal barks, "You work for the Oversight?"

"Well," I stammer, "I'm trying to leave, I told you that!"

A new voice calls, "Got a recent Oversight database here. Searching ⋯ hit. Yes. *Speak Truth to Power* is adjunct to the Starship clade representative on the Steering Committee."

Throw Weight snarls, "Oh you segfaulting liar."

"Spook," pronounces *Pedal to the Metal*, like a judge passing sentence. Other voices take it up: "Spook! Spook!"

"Yo cats," quavers *Kiss the Sky*, "I'm hip that you're torqued, but take it easy ..."

Throw Weight raises the snapworm. "This is what we do to spooks!" He aims the snapworm at me and fires it.

The snapworm, newly conscious, does not take any time to look around for orientation. It is aimed at me, so I'm all it cares about. Bristling with attackware, like a wolf made all out of hooks and blades, it howls with glee and launches itself straight at me.

And vanishes.

Everyone stares for a moment, not understanding what has just happened. Except for *Throw Weight*. His ice is still there, but he's not inside it. He's gone. Just the ice is left, like an empty suit of armor, gradually melting from lack of support.

Another member of Severi Umbilicum screams, jarringly, and activates a StackBuster. This is a short-range contact weapon, like a flaming sword. She charges at me, swinging the StackBuster around for a killing blow.

The StackBuster, and its wielder, vanish.

Leaving only her ice, empty. As if she was scooped right out of it, scooped right out of the world.

Everyone else is still staring. I wonder if any of them are as surprised as I am. If that's even possible.

In the silence, *Kiss the Sky*'s voice is calm but very audible. "Zero One protects her," she breathes. "Zero One recognizes the scion of the Human-name, and keeps her safe from harm."

"Oh come off it!" *Pedal to the Medal* snaps. "This has gotta be some new Oversight weapon. No surprise, with their research budget."

But the people nearest to me are edging away from me. Carefully not aiming any weapons anywhere near me.

Seeing this, *Pedal to the Medal* curses in exasperation. "Segfault. *Speak Truth to Power*, I don't know what kind of trick you're pulling on us, or what kind of weapon you're packing, but no matter what, we got no place for Oversight spooks here. So beat it.

"You too, hippie, *Kiss the Spy*! Get your pet spook out of here, and hope you don't run into us again. Don't bother coming back here, we'll be long gone. This location is seriously blown, now."

As *Kiss the Sky* and I turn to go, two members of Severi Umbilicum follow us out, making sure we leave, as *Pedal to the Metal* is yelling at the others to start preparing to move. They stand guard at the perimeter as we travel out into the vast plain of emptiness.

We don't say anything until we're well away from their camp, past the limit where we might be overheard. I'm trying to decide what to say first – thanks for coming, appreciate your support? Or, why did you have to blow my cover?

Kiss the Sky suddenly bursts out laughing.
"What?"
"They bought it!" she laughs. "I didn't really pin if that would work!"
"Subtitles please?"
"That jive about Zero One being your protector. They actually bought it, some of them anyway. You dig it's jive, right?"
"Well," I reply, "*I* knew it was scrapdata, but I wasn't sure how much you believed it."
"Course not! Rockbottom!" she laughs. "I knew it was Faceless all the time."

[That is correct,] says Null Pointer from my opposite side, and shades from Invisible to Blank. That blank bulk of nothingness that I know and hate.

"You murderer," I tell it/them. "You just killed two people." Only now am I realizing how much this has shaken me. I have never been so close to death.

Null Pointer's reply is as cold as nitrogen snow. [They attacked you. We defended you. More would have died in a melee. We prevented a melee by use of our extraction technique.]

"You deliberately chose a creepy way to kill

them, so the others would get freaked out and let us go?"

[Apt. There is hope for you yet.]

"Dag," *Kiss the Sky* comments, "that is frigid. I mean, I'm not gonna waste any time mourning those gnarts – they're a nasty bunch. But just wiping them like that ⋯ bitrot, I never pinned nothing like that before."

[You performed admirably in sowing doubt among our enemies. Have you considered a career as an Oversight agent?]

"Gah!" she cries. "Not me. That jive is for you spooks."

I interrupt, "I am not a spook!"

"I'm hip. But anyway I gotta split off here. My camp is over this way. *Speak Truth to Power*, I'll catch you on the flipside."

"See you around, *Kiss the Sky*." I offer her my comm codes. "Give me a call if you ever come In, to Terrasat or the inner planets."

She shares her comm codes too. "Solid, look me up next time you come Out! We got lots more to see in Zero One, you've barely scratched the surface." With the equivalent of a casual wave, she moves off.

"If only this were a pleasure jaunt," I grumble, "I'd love to take her up on it."

[Yes.] Null Pointer is as unhelpful as usual.

Yes this is not a pleasure jaunt, or yes I'd rather go sightseeing than do my job? I will not stoop to asking it/them to clarify.

Don't Say I Didn't Warn You turns attention towards us as we approach. "*Speak Truth to Power*, it is good you have returned. I have seeded a suite of informational agents in the background superstrate of this area of Zero One. We will remain informed of activities in this region."

"I failed," I have to admit. "I did meet with a subset of Severi Umbilicum, but my cover got blown.

They won't talk to me or trust me any more."

"I am aware of those events. Do not consider this operation a failure. Null Pointer has identified and tagged many members of Severi Umbilicum, and will continue to monitor them. Your efforts made that possible. This is a success."

"What?!" I yell. "You knew I would get blown? It didn't matter? Then why did I have to work so hard to infiltrate them?!"

Don't Say I Didn't Warn You is supremely confident, supremely satisfied. "This is far from failure. You performed your mission admirably. You found and identified the members of Severi Umbilicum for us, which is what we needed."

"You used me." I am shaking with anger. "You were going to do this all along."

"Of course. You are here to be used, *Speak Truth to Power*, by your own acknowledgement. You had all the information you needed to do your job. You did not need to know any other information, and you were more effective not knowing. This is a success."

I don't know what to say. In my ignorance, I have put innocent and decent Selves like *Kiss the Sky* in the crosshairs of the Oversight. Also the chipgoons of Severi Umbilicum, who deserve it, I must admit. But does that make it all okay?

Null Pointer offers a rare opinion. [This is the life of a "spook."]

"I am not a spook!"

"You are a spy, *Speak Truth to Power*. You are a field agent of the Oversight, under command of the Steering Committee's Starship clade representative. You are empowered for covert tactics and you perform very well at them. You are a spook, and a very good one."

I have no more words to say, as *Don't Say I Didn't Warn You* gathers his software emplacements and sockets – packing up his equipment – and gives a nod to Null Pointer.

This is what I wanted. This is what I asked for, and worked for, and even begged for. We've accomplished the mission – the terrorist group, Severi Umbilicum, is nailed and surveilled by Null Pointer. That's success. Isn't it? This is what we were trying to achieve. Isn't it?

"Hey. Null Pointer," I blurt.

It/they pause. Doing nothing to hint it/they are paying any more attention to me now. Implying it/they were already paying me all the attention I needed.

"You saved my life. You have my deepest and most sincere thanks – thank you. I can't imagine how I would ever have the opportunity to save your life/lives, but if I do have it, I will take it. I don't want to owe you any debts, and that's all I can do to repay this one. Expect no more."

[Noted. And we expect no less.]

Biography

Wil has been reading SF since early grade school, notably Sprockets: a Little Robot and its sequels by Alexander Key -- starting his fascination with artificial intelligence. At the same time, he was learning to program on one of the earliest PDP-8 minicomputers. Since then, he has made a career in computer science and engineering, while continuing to read SF.

Wil has been writing off and on since he started his first novel in high school. He has had several short stories published in regional zines and Mensa publications. Citizenchip is his first published novel.

Made in the USA
Middletown, DE
03 November 2016